If I Touched
the Earth

Also by Cynthia Rogerson

I LOVE YOU, GOODBYE
STEPPING OUT

If I Touched
the Earth

Cynthia Rogerson

BLACK & WHITE PUBLISHING

First published 2012
by Black & White Publishing Ltd
29 Ocean Drive, Edinburgh EH6 6JL

1 3 5 7 9 10 8 6 4 2   12 13 14 15

ISBN: 978 1 84502 442 0

ALBA | CHRUTHACHAIL

Typeset by RefineCatch Limited, Bungay, Suffolk
Printed and bound by Nørhaven, Denmark

Dedicated to the fictional memory of
Calum Ross (1971–1996)

and all A9 casualties

and all the casualties of casualties.

Acknowledgements

For insight into grief, I would like to thank my aunt Florence Nelson, who likes happy endings. I am also grateful to Janne Moller and Kristen Susienka for nagging me to keep tweaking. And to Peter Whiteley for proofreading, for being patient and encouraging. I again take my hat off to Creative Scotland, whose generous bursary gave me the time to finish this novel.

Finally, I am grateful to all the publishers who rejected a much earlier version of this novel – thank you! You were right, it was a terrible novel.

Clown in the Moon

My tears are like the quiet drift
Of petals from some magic rose;
And all my grief flows from the rift
Of unremembered skies and snows.

I think, that if I touched the earth,
        It would crumble;
It is so sad and beautiful,
So tremulously like a dream.

Dylan Thomas

In 1963, when Prime Minister Harold Wilson talked about the upcoming 'white heat of technical revolution altering the UK beyond recognition', he was accurately describing the fate of small Highland villages like Alness. In the early Seventies the North Sea oil industry at Nigg and the Invergordon Aluminium Smelter created thousands of well-paid jobs, and by 1973 eight times the original population swallowed sleepy little Alness. It disappeared! Completely smothered and gasping for air, so quickly no one even heard it gasp for air. There was a time folk complained about mysterious farting noises, which may have been dying gasps, but that was conjecture.

The facts are these: One day Alness was quiet and clean, the next day Alness was a mess.

Excerpt from *History of a Small Place
that Got Big* by Janet MacInnes

Part One

1:32pm 5th January to
4:12am 12th January 1996

After

Something strange happens seconds after Calum's car crashes. A sudden change in the atmosphere of the material world. In nearby Evanton the light flattens so anything unbeautiful becomes almost sinister, and the things that are pretty seem slightly surreal. A breeze arises, a chillier breeze than even this winter day warrants. It eddies in the cul de sacs of Camden Street and Livera Street and creates small whirlpools of icy dust that sting the eyes of cats and runny-nosed toddlers in their pushchairs.

A middle-aged woman shopping in the Spar, who has never met Calum and now never will, suddenly sighs and slumps inside. She drops a bottle of salad cream into her basket, though it is over-priced and not her favourite brand. She simply lacks the heart to do anything else.

Outside the paper shop, a recently retired man, likewise unknown to Calum, shivers and zips up his jacket and suddenly thinks of people who are dead. His old workmate, Jam Jimmy, who always ate ham and jam pieces. His niece with bifocals, who used to sing 'Hey Nannie Noo Noo'.

Across the road at Marty Dunn's garage, a small sticky-faced girl bursts into tears and is inconsolable for ten minutes, though her mother holds and strokes her, and in the end slaps her bottom impatiently. The child hiccups and can't say why she's crying, only sobs as if her heart is broken.

Eighteen miles away, Calum's mother Alison Ross sits and laughs with her call centre colleagues in the Market Bar in Inverness, riding the tail wind of a late lunch. She has just marginally missed her own mouth and is laughing and wiping lager off her face and shirt with a cloth the barmaid sweetly offers.

'Hey, don't worry,' says the barmaid. 'A mouth's a small thing to aim for, I'm always missing mine, and look at the size of my gob – it's huge, compared to yours.'

'Ach, you're always bragging about the size of body parts, you,' says Alison, and returns the cloth. 'Anyway, I was aiming for my chin and shirt.' She has a fake tan face and slightly more orange neck.

'So, is it time to head back to work, ladies?' asks a young woman, who also sports an orange neck.

'Aye, 'spose it's time,' says a plump woman, flushed-face, slightly hectic.

'You look awfy hot there, Shirley. Getting the hot flushes?'

'No! Me? No! Not old enough.'

'Ah, come on, look at you. Like a radiator, you.'

'It's not that,' she whispers. 'It's my socks. Compression socks. My veins, you see.'

Alison and the others laugh cruelly in a burst that involves at least one of them spraying more lager onto the table. It's been a one-and-a-half-pint lunch, and no food except crisps, to save on calories. They do this once a week, their girly lunch, a lunch which will leave no memory. Shirley's face is not smiling.

'You're young, but you'll see. You'll get the veins. And you'll get the hot flushes and all, too, you all will.'

'Hot flashbacks, more like,' says Alison defiantly. Raising her glass, swallowing the last of the lager, she feels nothing of the atmospheric shift that chilled Evanton. Perhaps it dissipated somewhere over the Cromarty Firth, leaving a trail of sighs and sobs and snappiness behind. Perhaps it never existed at all.

Alison is told by a policeman and policewoman early that evening. Both of them are young and have unconvincing facial expressions.

'Where?'

'About three miles away. Between the two Evanton slip roads on the A9.'

They tell her there were no other vehicles, no witnesses. Possibly black ice? Nothing certain. No obvious cause. They are very sorry.

'Aye, alright, please just go now, please,' she says, and after an awkward moment, they do.

She sucks in air fast, fast, and makes strange whimpering noises. Races out to her car, then races back to the house for her car keys, which she then drops twice. One of her shoes slips off as she hurtles into her seat, and she has to lean out to retrieve it, but does not bother replacing it on her foot. She flings it to the back seat and drives out of Alness, down the A9 to Raigmore Hospital. Wants to look for evidence of her son's car crash, but finds she cannot. Cannot look. In her head, a quiet but shrill whistling noise begins. She shakes her head slightly and the noise sloshes around. She closes her car window, and it grows louder. Just before she reaches the hospital, a huge drowsiness engulfs her, and she widens her eyes against it.

Later she finds herself back home, though she cannot recall the journey. Alison walks around her house. She checks her reflection in the bathroom mirror every so often, as if she expects something from it. Calum left his bedroom light on again, and she switches it off and closes the door hard. Then opens it and closes it softly. She picks up the phone three times to call her sister Chrissie, but she does not dial. Occasionally, she makes little mewing sounds and sighs asthmatically, but is otherwise silent. She opens the refrigerator, retrieves all the ingredients for an omelette, cooks the omelette and does not eat it. Opens a bottle of whisky, drinks a mugful and vomits into the kitchen sink.

At ten o'clock she turns on the news, stares at the wall, and at ten thirty-five she brushes her teeth and gets into bed with her clothes on but her shoes off. She lays under her quilt, cold and clammy, unable to get warm, and she keeps breathing and listening to her own breathing with disbelief. She falls asleep but is woken by her own shuddering jagged breath ten minutes later, as if she's stopped breathing and has woken seconds before dying. Or as if she has dreamt of weeping. Her throat aches and her chest and stomach ache. She pictures her son lying in the hospital morgue, alone and cold. This is, of course, unbearable, but she cannot stop herself. All his life, she has worried about him being lonely.

Neal is Alone

The next day is bright. Luminous low winter light that excites everyone, but the day ends anti-climactically without sunset, in drizzle. Like the over-long Christmas afternoon two weeks ago, when Neal and Sally's tree suddenly looked tawdry and the air bereft of anticipation, only a sense of flatness. Dingwall can be beautiful, with its church steeples and the hills swaddling it right down to the firth, but there is nothing beautiful now. Not a thing, and nobody either. Just a few unhealthy-looking thirteen-year-olds loitering around the war memorial, and a woman, drunk and singing as she makes her way to the train station.

Neal, who like Alison had felt nothing at the moment of Calum's death, can't hear the woman. But he can hear the boys hooting and hawking, as boys do around war memorials at dusk. He guesses they'll be smoking and discussing sex as if they know what they're talking about, and maybe they do. Neal sighs and goes back to work.

His head bows over an old newspaper, gleaning old facts to feed into the computer humming in front of him. This week it's Thirty-Two Years Ago Today. Last week it was Sixty-Four Years Ago Today. The newspaper is one hundred and thirteen years old, so some weeks he does 113 Years Ago Today. Is it a boring task? Not for Neal. He likes dreamy occupations, like walking and reading history books. He notices patterns that mean nothing to anyone else, like the fact all the babies born to his neighbours last year were given one-syllable names, and yesterday the women in his queue at Tesco were all wearing their hair in ponytails. Patterns please him. Predictability pleases him. He's had a few problems with his car lately, and his cat had to be put down at the vets, this is about as much commotion as his life can take.

He's become very like his granddad. Perhaps through childlessness he's skipped the stage of becoming his father, who recently eloped with a waitress called Myrtle and lives in a caravan in Skegness. *Life's a beach, and also short. Lighten up, son,* his father wrote on a postcard. The photo was of a naked bottom with a smoking cigarette sticking out from the crack. But Neal had not smiled, had not lightened up in the least. He is more like his ginger-haired granddad, a gentle pottering soul, given to beginning and not finishing sentences.

Neal's own ginger hair flops over his forehead right now, and he frowns a little as he types. In concentration, not irritation. He loves his job. The column is never boring, and besides it's not only the column he does, he also organises adverts. Though he prefers the columns, of course. They have fewer numbers. He sets his research aside for a minute to sip his coffee and switch on the radio, the local station – Moray Firth. The news, and he almost switches it off again – current news never has the same appeal – when a name jumps out at him, punches him in the ear drums, also somewhere in his stomach. He flinches. Sits up, sets his coffee down too fast and it splashes on his old jeans. Neal

6

often talks to himself when he's alone in the office, and now he says, 'Damn. *Damn it.*'

First the car, then the cat, now Calum. It seems all the C things are in great danger.

Funeral Prelude

Calum has been dead four days. He's in Chisholm's Funeral Home on Huntly Street in Inverness. No one except his mother has been to see him. But then, not many folk came to see him alive, either. Calum led a solipsistic, contradictory existence as a long-distance runner and a smoker of fat joints, a watcher of violent videos and a fan of Blind Melon. He was also an active member of the local long-term unemployed.

Neal sits alone at home, looks out the window at nothing. Poor Calum, he thinks. Another A9 fatality, it's enough to make you want to close the road down. In the last twelve months, fourteen people have died on it, and dozens injured. In his mind, he constructs an A9 victim memorial alongside the war memorial. Instead of an armed soldier, a metallic sculpture of a scrunched car, some personal items in unlikely places. A toy on the bonnet, a shoe through the windscreen. Red gloss paint splashed on the dashboard. A plaque with names. A long plaque, with space to add names.

He puts his head in his hands, and presses his fingers into his tear ducts. How has the span of his own seemingly short life overlapped the beginning and end of this other life? For a minute, to calm himself, he reminds himself that his body is sitting on a piece of furniture in his house, which is anchored to the earth's surface, which is rotating around the sun at the very same time it is spinning on its axis through dark space. *Right now.* And every creature breathing on this illusory stable surface is transient. Himself and Sally and Alison included. A hundred years from now – same stage, different cast. *Whooosh*, all gone. Nothing matters. Imagining this, reminding himself of the big picture, is oddly like praying. And like praying, it delivers relief. Relief and gratitude.

The front door opens and shuts with Sally's quietly decisive click. Neal sits up straighter, clears his throat and grabs the newspaper off the coffee table, though why he should need props for the woman he's been married to for seventeen years is a mystery.

And Alison Ross, mother of the dead Calum? She's being pulled away from him, the currents are too strong to resist, and by some fluke he's been trapped and remains exactly the age he was when he crashed. Nothing is recognisable now. Time itself has splintered. When one day passes Alison tells herself *this time yesterday Calum was alive*, but already that seems unlikely. By the time she tells herself *this time four days ago Calum was alive*, it is almost not credible. Waking up and acknowledging another day without him in it feels a betrayal, and worse. A lie.

She is alone but she is not. She is surrounded by her sister, her nieces, her friends from the old days, her friends from all the days since, her neighbours (some of whom she does not recognise), and is in sporadic contact with the strangers who deal with the formalities and consequences of death. The registrar. The bank officials. The police. The coroner. The funeral home. The minister. The benefits office. The DVLA. Calum's exit seems to require a lot of signatures and phone calls. In a way, it is more exhausting than the labour leading to his birth. The contractions of grief are unimaginable, even to her, and so they ride way down deep. Subterranean grief she subconsciously alters her breathing to accommodate. Her coherent thoughts wouldn't fill a thimble. She moves through these days on tip-toe. Steps gingerly around lethal black clouds, bottomless pools of howling.

It takes immense energy, this tip-toeing around and talking politely, yet she is not tired. She does not sleep, and doesn't take the pills her sister offered. She bathes daily, yet her body has a peculiar smell. Unpleasant. Sour. Her breath is sour too, and has a metallic taste as if she is pregnant. Despite this offensive odour, she can't recall ever having been embraced so much, even at her parents' funerals. She feels invaded, sore, bruised by this physical attention, but she senses a responsibility to accept all the wet kisses and tight squeezes. All the intimacy. She's never been an especially polite person, or even an especially kind person, but now she can't say please stop touching me. She shrinks further and further inside herself. She is the size of a dot. A hard, black dot. There's not much room inside a hard black dot, which suits her fine.

Yet there are interludes of silliness, of weird distractions. Such intensity is simply unsustainable. Once on the way to the post office, feeling so odd the town itself looks like a foreign city, she stops by a shoe shop window in the High Street. Stares, because there is the perfect pair of shoes – she's been wishing someone would make a pair of shoes like this forever, and there they are. Red tartan patent leather, with three black suede buttons running down the side. Chunky, almost flat-soled, but flirty too. They are absolutely adorable, and she cannot stop herself entering the shop to see if they have her size. They do and she buys them without looking at the price, then continues on her way to post letters ceasing Calum's car insurance and his Run UK subscription. The whole shoe episode feels surreal, inappropriate, yet she cannot resist putting the new shoes on the minute she is home.

One morning she notices light shining through a window. It slices through the air and falls on the chair Calum used to consider his. A great cold shaft of light. A visitation of light. It occurs to her she has never properly noticed light before. She sits, her shiny new tartan shoes on, and watches this light. Concentrates on it, as if it's a compelling television programme. As if it's personal and has something to say.

Tears in a Cold Place

The day cruelly decides to be summer, with diffused summer light. A confusing blue sky. A disturbingly pleasant crisp breeze, which also seems blue. Neal enters the church, takes one look at Alison and the whole place keels. He stares. Her eyes are still milky blue, with deep grey smudges under. Her hair has become blond and her face fake-tanned since he last noticed her, but she still has the same deep groove of worry between her eyebrows. He remembers her abundance of freckles, but can't see them from this distance. Arms and back, especially. She is not beautiful or sexy or looking-good-for-her-age. He doesn't know what she is, except she is herself in all her flawed glory, and no one else has ever made him feel exactly this way. And no, if you asked him, he would not have a word for this feeling. He might say it felt a little wheezy, though he is not asthmatic.

Aside from his briefly manic expression, he looks like a billion other forty-three-year-old men – slightly paunchy, very slightly slope-shouldered, a wee bit crinkly about the eyes, a few white amongst the ginger hairs, and a receding hairline that reveals a rather tender-looking scalp. He looks conventional – nothing to say he'd once had a ponytail, worn a sheepskin coat, worn an earring. He's marginally still in the handsome stage that finally arrived when he was twenty-six, but in a blurred temporary way. Handsomeness is on its way out, is saying goodbye to Neal.

Luckily, after five heart-hammering minutes (his heart, not hers), Alison recedes and the church re-asserts itself. Neal is beached on his old island of normality, and remembers a funeral is about to begin. He has a glance round. The place is packed. He recognises a few faces from the old days. Half-blind Eddie, and Jen and Mick (Christ, he's looking old!) and is that Mandy in a full-length fur coat?

An organ grinds down to its last echoing notes, and the northeast wind replaces it. This is the wind that's responsible for the cloudless sky, but right now it seems too high a price to pay for blue. Too lonely a sound. Calum was not a churchgoer, but the minister lives in Calum's estate and knew him as well as most. Knew that he hadn't won big prizes at school or begun a fascinating career, or been known for his bag-piping prowess or any artistic gifts whatsoever. Nor had he been hilariously funny or heartbreakingly handsome. But a nice kid, everyone said. A really nice young man.

The minister is an old man, a very thin tall old man. Eyes hollowed out of his head, and dark, sad. He stands at the lectern and lets the congregation settle. Lets the coughs be coughed, the coats re-arranged, the bottoms and feet find comfy positions. Then he begins. His voice is low and deliberately gentle, as if he's using it to actually touch them. First the ritual words, the incantations he doesn't have to think to say, and he feels calm exude from these words that no one listens to. Necks un-crick. Heartbeats slow. Eyes look attentive, even cynical eyes, willing today to accept whatever version of existence he can give them. Hope is the thing.

He cannot remember how many funerals he's taken, but death still takes him by surprise. He just can't get used it. Every funeral like a first funeral. Lately, especially early in the day, he's felt as if his edges are blurring a bit, his mind and heart not quite solid, so this funeral is more of a challenge. And already it is bleaker somehow than any funeral he can remember. Perhaps it's simply the accumulation of these kinds of funerals. So many young men.

Neal sees Alison's shoulders quiver. Is she cold? Crying?

After the biblical balm, the minister is quiet. Tilts his head to one side and considers the congregation. Generally, they look hung-over, winter-pale, and there's an air of unease about them. He sees that mainly they're not churchgoers and they're afraid. That the younger ones have little experience of death, and the older ones too much. The mother looks distracted, tense, brittle. He's a fatherly man, this minister, so he scoops them all up in his mind, gathers them in like frightened children and holds them. He sighs, decides to scrap his prepared sermon. He almost always scraps his sermons these days.

'Calum left us too soon, and there is no mending this,' in slow deadpan voice. He feels the church heat up. Indeed, the temperature rises by five degrees. Two men take off their coats, a few women loosen their scarves. 'There can be no possibility of seeing his face again, hearing his laugh, touching his hand. Sadly.'

Pause.

'Calum loved to run and he will never run again. We will never see him run down the road again, or roll a cigarette

14

again, or buy chips again.' The church becomes even less chilly, almost humid with human dampness. Salty tears and sweat, warmed-up perfume and cheap teen deodorant. The minister, pacing himself like a conductor, senses all this and is glad. No use pretending there is anything to celebrate. A young person's funeral is hellish, but once the ball is rolling, it can be cathartic.

'But Calum will be loved and remembered, yes loved and remembered. That is what we can do now. Open our hearts and reach out to him, silently tell him. Say, "Calum, I love you." Not loved, but *love*. Say it as many times as you like. There is no such thing as . . .' He struggles here for a second. Excessive love? No, that isn't true at all. 'As wasted love,' he says finally, on an exhalation.

He smiles at them. Not in a happy way, but inviting them to acknowledge mortality with grace. Like a host who is tired at the end of an evening, but who says goodnight wistfully, recognising there is still something sad about the end of anything.

The air in the church quivers, updrafts and downdrafts spin round each other. Dust motes dance. On an old stone relief of St Boniface, some particles of dust suddenly slide off and several dozen of these land on Alison's shoulders and hair. She doesn't shake them off because she doesn't notice them. She doesn't notice much of anything. She's the only one the minister's words do not reach. She sits like a statue and watches and waits for when she can leave the church. *This is wrong.* It is ridiculous to be here. It's Wednesday. She's meant to be doing the easy shift at work, she has a load of ironing on her bed, Calum has a dentist appointment she has to remember to hassle him about. Above the pews to her left is a stained-glass window, and it draws her attention now. Not because of the biblical scene, but because there is a piece of glass in it that's more recent than the rest, and the light shines through it in a different way. As she watches, it grows in intensity till the rest of the picture is almost obliterated. It hurts to stare at, and this pain is a relief. Then the light dims and releases her. *Must be a cloud*, she thinks.

In the congregation there are many people who hardly knew Calum, though they'd known him all his life, and many who hardly know Alison. But there is a hard core of people who have dipped deeply into both their lives at some point. Near the front sit Alison's sister and nieces, and her workmates, entirely in black. Further back are almost all of Alison's former lovers. These men, if seated together, would fill three pews. There's the one she'd dumped three months ago, Joe from Ardross, looking like he's just crawled out of bed. He'd said he was gutted but forgave her within hours. Relieved, actually.

There's a young blond woman in a red coat who Alison has never met. Zara has more right than most to weep and wail. She weeps and wails with convincing gestures and noise, before finally blowing her nose and running from the church. Her red high heels clatter loudly all the way to the door. Some turn to watch her go and can't help but notice how attractive she is. How she manages to remain so, despite the tears. The door bangs shut, and some men's hearts lurch after her.

Sitting shyly at the back of the church there is a couple who have not met Calum. In their sixties, plump in identical places, proof of a long shared life eating too much of the same fattening things. There is about a foot of space between them, and their faces are slightly turned away from each other.

On their way to his chiropodist appointment, they'd come upon the accident exactly six seconds after it happened. They'd been bickering again. The way he'd spoken to her earlier, so patronising, and she'd held her anger in till she felt articulate enough to attack him. The air had been thick with the usual hatred. Then suddenly there was the car crumpled up, steam rising from the engine and the sound of metal screaming still reverberating. They'd pulled over. They'd done what they could, which wasn't much. Called 999. He swore and she prayed, both out loud and simultaneously, so it sounded like an obscene Gregorian chant. A Green Day tape was still playing, there was a hissing sound from the engine, but from the boy a terrible stillness. His body squeezed between the steering wheel and the seatback, a space not big enough for a body. As they'd stared at him, blood began to seep from various places, as if he was a sack that had punctured.

That was over a week ago, and not a single cross word since. Nothing seems important enough to argue about anymore. Now he reaches for her hand without looking at her, and she takes it. Both look straight ahead, and her eyes fill. Not for Calum this time, but because she'd thought she'd never feel this way about her husband again.

'. . . drench us with despair, that's what death can do. Just exactly as if it's a liquid, a thick bitter . . . syrup. A molasses of melancholy. But life will continue, times goes on and I promise you,' pausing to look directly at as many eyes as he can, to make this consolation personal, 'the despair will be diluted. The darkness will waver and fade, and light will return. Let us kneel and pray for light. Our Father, who art in heaven, hallowed be Thy name . . .'

The organ accompanies the final hymn, and the coffin begins its slow departure. The faces of the six pallbearers seem naked, though their features are composed. For many of the congregation, the coffin is a surprise. They'd not focussed on it before. But here it is, and incredibly it purports to contain the very same person they are all missing. It almost seems an unrelated coincidence that Calum is physically present, as well as in their hearts and thoughts. Between twenty and thirty people who are not habitual weepers burst into tears.

Neal is one.

While he's been staring at Alison's profile, half listening to the minister, he's not thought of Calum. But now, unbidden, comes Calum's smell – unwashed boy, Ribena, sweaty feet. Neal remembers the freckles on Calum's nose, his gap-toothed smile, the way he used to laugh when tickled. Almost silently, with a girly squeak. On top of these images comes the scent of hash, the damp walls, the coal fires of Brae Cottage, in fact a whole un-edited chunk of Neal's past. And yes, there is even a soundtrack. Pink Floyd, *Wish You Were Here*. He'd always liked that whole album, Calum. When he was a wee kid. *We're just two lost fish swimming in a fish bowl, year after year*. And that very same Calum, that sunburned giggling kid, is now inside this dark box, with no air to breathe, not a single second left of life to live. Neal's facial muscles spasm and he shudders, long quaking shudders that travel over his entire body but are worst in his chest and throat.

This is the first time Neal has cried since childhood. He's ... well, he's ugly to look at. Embarrassing. He emits choking, whimpering noises. He tells himself, *Jesus Christ, get a grip*. It's an ambush, like being wrenched out of a comfy armchair, but a very small part of him is grateful. Now he knows what it feels like to lose control, and he's always wondered. Ah! To slip like this, now and then, into just being.

What People Need

The coffin is gone. Alison is nudged by her sister till she understands she is to leave first. As if it's a wedding, she thinks. Not that she's ever been a bride, or even been to many weddings. Weddings are not fashionable in her group. She stands and walks stiffly and carefully. She feels a long way from her feet. She nods to friends and relatives, and squints at faces that are not familiar, of which there are a lot. They are all noisy, yet subdued. She wonders if the noise is not actual, but atmospheric. Maybe their thoughts, their grief, their anxieties about death, are tumbling into the air. Maybe the air is a soup of emotional exhalations. Alison holds her breath. Feels faint, nauseous, numb, and is aware she's out of synch on a day when it's important she be in synch. She is, was, his mother, after all. She is the star, no matter how reluctant.

Outside, the pallbearers ease the coffin into the hearse, shake hands with the undertaker, and silently retreat to the east wall of the church. Avoid eye contact. They huddle as one holds a lighter for all their cigarettes. One of the boys, Finn, has never smoked before, but it seems bad form to not join in.

'Totally and utterly sucks,' says the one called William. A tall, stocky lad, more manly than the others.

'Aye,' says Finn, a pale skinny five foot four. Acne scars across his forehead. He holds the smoke in his mouth, then lets it out. The taste makes him want to be sick.

'In fact, I'm kind of pissed off with Calum. Big time.' William inhales expertly, blows the smoke out forcefully.

'Me too. Big time.' Finn is the shyest of the boys. Always repeats what the others say.

'Yeah. It's got to be the biggest rude thing ever, right?' says one of the others, blowing a smoke ring. It rises impressively, then the wind whips it away.

'Bastard,' says William, and spits.

'I know. I mean, what the fuck?'

'Yeah. What the *fuck*,' says Finn, leaning against the wall because he suddenly feels dizzy.

The old minister is watching them from the path. Knows he mustn't go over, though with every atom he wants to. He watches till they throw clumsy arms around each other. Good. People need to cry. People should cry. Then he sighs and turns his attention back to the woman in front of him who claims to know what kind of flowers he should grow in his borders. He rocks gently on the balls of his feet.

'Alison!' says Neal. 'Ali! Ali!' he says when she doesn't respond and continues on her tentative walk down the steps outside. She turns at last, sees him.

'Is that you, Neal?'

'Yeah. It's me.'

'Christ. Neal Munro.' Blushing under the fake tan. Orange-pink.

'Aye, well.' He flaps his hands upward briefly.

21

She leans forward, grabs his arm. 'What are you doing here?' she whispers as if they're alone, back in the past, and there's something clandestine they have to discuss. One of her abortions? A drug deal? Neal used to fetch dope for her sometimes. He never minded. Quite liked feeling useful. And unlike her fellow stoners, Neal could always be counted on to bring it all home.

'I'm here because, well, you know.' *Calum*, he mouths. Something passes between his sore eyes and her dry eyes. A pulse.

'Oh. Yes. Of course.' She pulls him to one side, and people make space for them.

'Do you still live in Strathpeffer? I can't believe I never see you.' She looks at him hard, though her eyes are glazed. He stops himself from correcting her. From saying that they have, actually, bumped into each other occasionally. At Tesco, at parties, on the High Street. Of course they have.

'It's so strange,' she continues, vaguely.

'Yes. It is strange.' Strange indeed, this sudden sense of intimacy. Strange, the way the church had keeled an hour ago, when he first set eyes on her.

'Just never give each other a second's thought, do we. And here you are.' She reaches out to him, but stops just short of touching his face, her palm open. His skin tingles where she might have touched it. 'You look the same, Neal.'

'Do I really?'

'No, not really. The same! What are you like?' She giggles, in an unstable, pre-tears way.

'Look, Alison, I . . .'

'What?'

'Look, is, is, is there some kind of . . . tea later?' he stammers. Flaps his hands again.

22

'Yes.'

'Where?'

'Chrissie's house. She's doing the tea.'

'Chrissie?'

'My sister. Her house.'

He looks around, as if for clues. He can barely remember Chrissie, has no idea where she lives. It feels intrusive to ask. Everyone seems to be walking away or getting in cars.

'Will you come?'

'No. No, I don't really know, I mean I think I'd better be going now. What about the . . . you know. The burial.'

'It's a cremation, Neal. No need to be there. What's there to see? To do?'

'Oh.'

'I know, let's go for a drink.'

'A drink?'

He's picturing Calum's coffin entering the flames, witnessed by no one but strangers. Again, he looks around for people, her sister, her friends, maybe even a boyfriend. Surely the chief mourner will not be allowed to drift off. Sure enough, a posse of middle-aged women draws near. Alison hisses:

'A drink, yes! Quick now! Where's your car?'

As they push through the crowd to the car park, at first they leave a wake, then the crowd turns towards them, begins to plunge after them. Sixty-four people, including the minister and the pallbearers, watch Neal unlock the passenger door of his old Fiat and let Alison in. Only thirty recognise Neal, but when his car turns north, all sixty-four record this event for later dispersal.

Neal gets on the A9, shifts up to fifth. This is Calum's funeral day, you should be at your sister's, he keeps trying to say, but Alison is having none of it. She's a fount of questions.

'What do you do now? Still at the paper? Still married to Sally? Did you never have kids? Why on earth not? What do you think of these shoes? Do you remember the day we stole those Doc Martens? Remember how we used to always steal loo rolls from pubs? Hey, remember that day we hitched to Rosemarkie and got stuck at Munlochy till dark? Remember when we used to take the ferry to Inverness? I kind of miss that ferry, bridges are boring. Did you know I'm working at a call centre? Mad. But everyone's working at call centres now, aren't they. Call centres are the new Nigg. Hey, did you hear that Nigg might open up again? At least that was decent money, call centres are crap money. You hated working at Nigg, didn't you? But imagine if Nigg hadn't happened – you'd still be down in Glasgow, and I'd be this whole other person, probably be married to a farmer and entering jams into WI competitions. And Calum ... well shit, Calum wouldn't have been born.'

Neal tenses. It seems almost sacrilegious to say Calum's name like that, out loud and matter-of-fact. She is the only person with the right to say his name just that way. Then a short silence.

'Neal, this is a little weird, isn't it?'

Yeah, he wants to say. Like an out-of-body experience. Isn't there a reason we've lost touch? *Who are you?* But he just laughs instead, heart pounding.

'I mean you and me,' she continues, looking out the side window at the saturated winter fields. 'But it's great to see you, Neal. I think I must have been missing you for years and years, and not even known it.' Pause. 'Actually, what's weird is not you and me in this car, but the fact it doesn't

24

feel weird at all and it should. It feels, well, it feels weirdly normal. To me, anyway,' she concedes, a shade hesitantly.

And it is this note of uncertainty that ends the spell. He arrives back in his body with a jolt, followed by deep calm. Suddenly, nothing feels more natural than to be driving north for the sake of driving north, with an old friend who is grieving. He glances at her face, and it's dear to him; it is, for this moment anyway, *the right face.* The rest of the world, all those people and things, his wife Sally – well, they can just bugger off. At least for the next few hours. He fully expects they'll turn around soon, he'll drop her at her sister's house, and by eight he'll be home playing Scrabble, drinking cups of tea and eating Sally's banana bread. Alison just needs a breather before dealing with people. She'd often used him like that in the old days. Someone to be silent with. Or to chatter to, till the nonsense drained away.

It's dark by the time they stop, though only five o'clock. A candle snuffed without ceremony. They end up in a hotel bar, and then a hotel bedroom where Neal takes off his clothes because if he doesn't, Alison will tear them. Nothing about this day astounds him more than her appetite for his body. She has never so much as kissed him on the mouth before. This is sex, solid wet sex with no bits of tenderness attached to it, and he's never had it without bits on. It's hot, it hurts, it feels sad, lonely, heady, feverish, and it thoroughly dismantles his twenty-year-old crush. And what rushes in to replace it? Love, it seems. His heart is scalded with love, and alarmed at the work it now has to do. The business of love, after all, is a serious one and Neal is a serious individual. He frowns. His new protectiveness dilates his pupils as he thinks about all he must do now. Love is already making him pay closer attention.

Alison, on the other hand, is swooning gratefully in a temporary faint – the business of sex, at times like these, being obliteration. Besides, she has no heart for love. To keep breathing is her main challenge, and one that she meets only half-heartedly. They lie silent a while, stunned for different reasons. Then, as if to hasten the end of breathing, she says, 'I'm going to start smoking again.'

'Aye?'

'Have you got any smokes?'

'No. Sorry.'

'Starting in the morning, then. Mind all those times in the cottage?'

Into Neal's mind comes the first glimpse he had of Alison. He's not thought of this in a long time, but up it pops, pristine and poignant. She'd answered the door, Calum clinging to her leg, glared at Neal a second, stood back and shouted for her father. 'Da! It's the Glasgie mannie come to look at the cottage! Da!'

She'd worn faded bell-bottoms and a white short-sleeved peasant blouse with a red rose embroidered between her robust breasts. Her breasts turned out to be the friendliest part of her. Like downy gorgeous pillows, they were. (Still are, actually, he notices now. Very white, on the tide line where the fake tan ends.) But the way she'd studied him, unimpressed. He'd been smitten by her because it seemed so very unlikely she was asking for smitten-ness.

'Aye. I mind the crowd of boys waiting to snog you.'

'Ach, there were never that many.'

'There was a queue of at least six at any given time. Fergus? Johnny? Burt? Not to mention all the Ians.'

'Six. Well, right enough, six maybe. But that's never a crowd. And they weren't in love with me, I can tell you that.'

26

'They were all in love with you.'

'Never. Not one of them ever said it, any road. None of them ever acted it either. Free love. Ha! Those were the days of free feels, not love.'

'Shush. Lots were in love with you.'

'Well I think you're just saying that, you're feeling sorry for me.'

'Of course I'm sorry for you,' he whispers.

'Are you? I can't feel anything.' Even to herself, her voice doesn't sound like her own. Too high-pitched, quick, tight.

'No?' He wraps his arms around her again, trying to absorb this pain lying in wait. This is some of the work his love must do. Alison accepts the embrace, but looks away. Face hard.

'I had a crush on you, Ali,' he mumbles.

'No way. You never said anything.'

'I did.'

'When?'

'That time, mind that time? In the hall, Guy Fawkes Night.' He's only just now remembering it, himself. Oh! Desperately humiliating moment, mercifully buried under the dross of years. She'd laughed. Laughed! And in a particularly cold way.

'Oh aye, that time.'

Is there a shadow of a smirk on her face even now? No, that's only the way gravity is pulling down the fold of one cheek to the pillow.

'But you never meant it, Neal. Surely. It was just something to say. And then you went all posh. Married and moved to Strathpeffer.'

Neal says nothing. Posh, in her mouth, is a swear word. Should he apologise for marrying and living in a nice house? In fact, his love has humbled him to the extent he almost does apologise, but then she says, 'I saw him. Twice. First in hospital, then in the mortuary. I wasn't going to the second time, but then I did.'

'Did you?'

'You know, Calum always thought of you as his dad.'

'But . . . why?'

'I don't know. I never contradicted him.'

Neal wants to ask who the father really was. That old question. Takes a quick gulp of air, holds it, lets it go. He looks at the ceiling, at the pink lightshade, which looks grey. He's lying on his back while she curls on her side, facing away from him.

She's mentally reviewing the possible fathers of Calum. It had been a busy, blurry, party month, full of handsome Nigg workers buying her screwdrivers and rolling her joints. What a year to be sixteen and finally growing proper breasts! It's an old habit, this reviewing, and is over within seconds, with the usual no-conclusion drawn.

Alison and Neal are both naked and covered to their chests with a heavy duvet. It smells unpleasantly floral. Sweetness over something less sweet. The only light is from the bathroom. The room is small, full of oddly assorted furniture, including a huge wardrobe from the fifties. Like a spare room minutes from being a storage room. They haven't noticed any of this. Each, separately, notices the ugliness now and minds. It seems an unnecessary extra blow.

'I let him think you were his dad because I wished you were,' she whispers hoarsely. 'You were the nicest man I knew.'

'Oh god! Wow. Thanks. Thank you.' Suddenly he remembers Calum at age . . . nine? Scabby knees and a Cookie Monster t-shirt, asking would he come play footie with him. It was drizzling outside, he remembers that. And Alison was sitting at the kitchen table smoking, drinking coffee, laughing at the fact he never used the last drops of milk in the pint. Always threw it down the sink. Did he play footie that time? Did he brave the drizzle, sacrifice time with Alison, go outside with Calum?

'I'm going to sleep. I'm going to sleep, and when I get up I'm buying a pack of cigarettes.'

'Okay, goodnight, I'm going to sleep too.' Then after a minute, he adds, 'You were a good mum, Alison.'

She says nothing, which is what he feels he deserves for such a glib statement. He kisses her in a brotherly way, lust a distant memory, but he does not sleep. He lays there and in his over-wrought state, suffers a moment of lucidity. A sudden sickening sense of wasted time. As if he is one hundred years old and his own mortality is just sinking in. It seems quite clear. All the important events of his life happened by age twenty-six, then he'd gone into a high-speed forgettable loop till being deposited, on this bed with Alison snoring beside him. He blames every unpleasantness of his past on the absence of Alison. Right now, he can hardly recall his wife's face. Who was she anyway, and why did he marry her? Was it simply because she'd asked him, and getting girls to just sleep with him had been so excruciatingly confusing? Were his life's major choices as random as that? If only he and Alison had done this all those years ago.

He creeps out of bed to phone his wife from the pay phone in the hall. He tells her a lie. When he returns, he spoons into Alison's back. Close but gently, to not wake her. He is only slightly taller, curls easily around her. And he thinks, in his quirky way, about gloves, because he imagines that no glove in the entire history of glove-making has ever fitted so perfectly as their two bodies. And after a minute, their chests rise and fall in unison. But Neal is not asleep, and neither is Alison. Words, softened, half dreaming, 'You're beautiful.' To the back of her neck.

'Stop. I know what I am. I am not beautiful,' she says.

He stops himself agreeing. The words travelling from his brain to his tongue are going just slow enough to do a brake skid. Finally, she falls asleep, and he does too, around dawn. His last thought is that his life has finally begun. They will always be together now, and he has been waiting twenty years for this.

An hour later, Alison is riding south in the back seat of a taxi, with sticky thighs and something quite jagged stuck in her chest. Another instrument, more like a serrated paring knife, has gone to work on her abdomen. Her insides are slowly tearing. And her eyelids are swelling, her tear ducts are hot, her throat is closing up. It's hard to breathe, to swallow, to see, to hear. Good, she thinks. I've heard something like this is supposed to happen. Let it begin.

'Look at that sun,' says the driver. 'Going to be a cracking day.'

'Aye,' she says, sucking the word back in through her teeth like an old woman.

Meanwhile the pallbearers have all fallen asleep, except William and Finn. They sit bleary-eyed and still drunk in a room littered with beer tins and ashtrays, as well as the snoring bodies of their friends. No one wanted to go home last night, so here they all are.

William and Finn stopped talking a while ago. Finn turns the lamps off and opens the curtains. They both flinch. Not another sunny day! It's too cruel. Where is the rain when you need it? As if complying, the room dims and hail suddenly pelts the windows like pebbles.

They catch each other's eyes, glance away, then back. Up till yesterday, they'd hardly seen each other since school. Right this minute, the world has shrunk to this room and each other. The hail turns to rain, and they turn to look out the window, standing at opposite sides of the small room. Finn with a yawn and a stretch, William with a tired half-smile, head tilted. Smoke curling from the cigarette in his mouth. They glance at each other again.

'Another thing,' William's croaky voice says into the silence as his eyes slide away back to the window. 'He never returned my Green Day tape.'

'Bastard,' slurs Finn.

'Still. By fuck, I'd buy him a pint right now.'

'Two pints.'

'Hey, are you okay?'

'Fuck off,' says Finn.

'Hey, hey. Nothing wrong with crying. I was only asking, like.'

Finn can't speak for a minute. His eyes are streaming, his mouth clamped shut angrily. Then he says:

'It's sad, man. I mean, it just fucking is.'

William crosses the room, stepping over bodies, and it seems he is about to hug Finn, to comfort him, but then they start play-punching each other. First the shoulders and jaws, and they even giggle a little because they are so tired and this is so bad. To be playing like this, when Calum is dead. Then without warning, William delivers a sharp punch to Finn's stomach. He doubles over, moaning.

'Sorry, Finn. Got carried away, like. You okay?' He whispers, because the other friends are still asleep.

'What'd you do that for?' Also whispering.

31

'Don't know.'

'Fuck. You're off your head.'

'I said I'm sorry.'

Finn stands up suddenly, swings for William's face. Not easy. William is about six inches taller. Lands one hard on his nose, which instantly spouts blood.

'Screw you to hell,' says William nasally, holding his nose.

Finn looks at the blood, makes a strange sound. A girlish wail, followed immediately by a short uncontrolled roar. If helplessness had to just be a noise, this would be it. The friends have roused now, and Finn rushes out of the house. Walks down the dawn road in the pouring rain, fast, breathing hard. Needing to pee, needing to vomit, needing to . . . oh he doesn't know all the things he needs to do. He is exploding with them.

William follows with deliberate strides. Catches up with him, holding a tea towel to his nose. And without saying a word, they enter Finn's empty house together. After a minute, Finn draws the curtains and bolts the door. Moves with jerky motions, pulls off his wet clothes. Everything but his underpants. Face like a five-year-old, energised by his own tantrum. William just watches him, like he'd watch a slug without its shell. Some compassion, but also cold curiosity. And then he stops thinking altogether, both of them do. Desire, dark and heated and heedless, is curling into the room like smoke.

The old minister is drinking tea in bed. He doesn't normally drink tea in bed, but he couldn't sleep last night, and his wife is slightly alarmed by his pale exhaustion. But he's alright.

'I'm alright, you know,' he tells her in his tired, kind voice. 'People die.'

'But a young person, Henry. Calum was so young.'

'Sometimes young people.'

Then she passes him a hankie, but she doesn't tell him not to cry. He's told her often enough: People should cry. People need to cry.

In the Golspie hotel, Neal finally wakes up. She's left no message, no souvenir, not even a sock, a tissue. She is gone and he is glad and drives home as quickly as possible. As if his house is in great danger, on fire, or about to crumble in some unpredicted landslide.

A9

If the A9 was a person, it would be named Morag and be about sixty-two. A modest, well-maintained, post-menopausal woman, with occasional flashes of real beauty. Wholesome, trustworthy. A road to be proud to call your own. She snakes over the Kessock Bridge from Inverness, winding over the Black Isle, shrinking into two lanes at Tore; over the Cromarty Firth causeway, scooting by Evanton, Alness, Invergordon, Barbaraville, Saltburn, Tain and further. Up the east coast she goes, past oil rigs, up and down long braes, in and out of wind-warped woods, past fairy tale castles and sandy beaches with singing seals. Sensible, graceful, calm Morag, all the way to Scrabster, that scoured-out place at the very top. Though in certain places, like the ten-mile straight stretch leading to the Nigg turn-off, the A9 is more like a maddening seventeen-year-old called Josh, daring you to open it up; overtake that Volvo estate, that combine harvester, that rental car driven by elderly Japanese. Go on, shift down and floor it!

Most people here use the A9 every day. And like most daily routines, like getting dressed and brushing teeth, like breathing, A9 journeys are rarely recorded in people's memories. They don't notice the way it can gleam, shush, murk, slide, light up, depending on that day's mood. If they are lucky, they will live an entire life without a single clear memory of it.

The place on the A9 where Calum crashed his car has not reverted to innocence yet. There are still tyre marks in the mud, deep grooves where his wheels spun, and in the long grass there are various items which flew from his car when the windscreen disappeared. An Oasis cassette case, a Golden Virginia tin lid, some Jelly Babies, half-melted now. There are also some tribute bouquets, a half dozen, mostly wrapped in Tesco plastic, and weighed down with stones. Roses, daisies, hyacinths, some daffodil buds which will never bud now. Rain-smeared messages: *Keep on running, Cal. Miss ya, pal. Luv u 4eva.*

There are some roadworks planned about half a mile north, and a Highland Council truck pulls onto the verge not far from where Calum crashed. Two men in yellow jackets hop out and debate whether they should place the plastic cones here or further down the road. Then they spot the tribute flowers.

'Must be where that boy went off the road, few weeks back. Mind?'

'Oh aye. Mable's brother-in-law knows the auntie. Chrissie somebody. Alness.'

'Terrible shame, that.'

'Oh aye, a terrible waste.'

Then a short silence, because small talk now seems almost rude, but there's not a lot else to say about a dead boy they never met. They sit in their cab, and to cheer themselves they have an early tea break. Open flasks and eat ham sandwiches and Mr Kipling cakes. Listen to the football scores on the radio. Fart and burp pleasurably. No hurry, is there?

A young woman with blond hair, wrapped up in a warm red coat, walks towards them on the verge. She's carrying a bouquet of roses in a cellophane wrapper. Pedestrians are rare on the A9, and the men stare at her a minute. Zara avoids their eyes and, head down, walks quicker.

'Must be one of them. One of them flower-leavers.'

'Aye. Looks frozen, poor lass, so she does.'

Five minutes later, they decide to set out the cones up the road, away from the flowers. Seems only right. They toss their crusts out the window and pull out on the road again. Less than a minute later, some crows discover the crusts, and squawk the good news to their friends.

Part Two

20th January to 23rd January 1996

Post-Coital Life with the Wife

Neal married Sally only three months after losing his virginity. To Sally, though he never told her that. And here he is: after seventeen years of fidelity, he's lost a kind of virginity all over again, and it's every bit as upsetting as the first time. As if he's been in a car crash too. He wanders slowly through his house with a vacant look, is distracted, stunned. *Horny.* His thoughts are slow and his body is slow too. The hours seem too long somehow, the days interminable, and his body has a too-clear memory of hers.

He thinks about Calum now and then, and feels uneasy, deficient in some essential way because he feels numb. What is wrong with him? What could be more straightforward than grief for a young person's death? But Neal feels like an amateur, emotionally. He knows the loss is terrible, but since his tears in the church, the actual feeling of sadness has faded. Besides, Calum's absence makes no difference to his day to day life, so is easy to forget.

Instead, he thinks about Alison. When he thinks about her, he feels a curious hollow pulling down, and there is a darkness, a heaviness about this desire he's never felt for his wife. He wonders a dozen times if he should've worn a condom. He might have grave cause to regret it one day, but looking back, he can't remember a moment when he might have brought the subject up. Besides, he didn't have any condoms, and probably would've made a cock-up of using one if he had because he's never worn one.

He's had several good looks at himself in the mirror after showers, looked to see if there were any give-away signs, and could find none, bar a faint pink mark on his lower back, perhaps the imprint of Alison's hand. Has Sally noticed? After a week, which includes one sexual episode which is strange (Sally's body feels too long, her breasts too small, her lips too thin) but surprisingly better than usual, it doesn't look like she's noticed anything. She's swallowed Neal's lie about the late drunken funeral reception and overnight stay at a friend's house. In fact, his domestic life is so normal and cosy, he feels in danger of losing his sanity. He wishes he'd never gone to the funeral at all. He is exhausted and nauseous. This is not who he is – a man who lies and cheats on his wife. It's all very upsetting.

'Tea's ready!' calls Sally from the dining room.

It's his favourite – toad in the hole, with mash and peas. Ironically for a childless couple, they have childish tastes in food. Or perhaps not ironically. Neal begins to eat but can hardly swallow. Must be a tummy bug going around, he thinks. Didn't Harold at the office mention a funny tummy? He makes himself eat – after all, he feels so empty, so gnawingly empty, but he can only manage a few bites.

'Alright, dear?' Sally asks.

'Delicious,' says Neal, and smiles. 'Just not feeling that great.'

'You don't look that great either. Pale as a ghost.'

Desire is so counter-productive. It makes Neal look thoroughly undesirable. After dinner, he waits till Sally is

40

busy with laundry and he looks in the phonebook for Alison's number. Finds it – incredibly, it was there all along – eleven pages from his own name. Scribbles it on a piece of paper, shoves it in his pocket. He tries to recall what it felt like to be a man who had no curiosity about Alison. Phones her, heart pounding. It rings and rings and he pictures the dark empty room it rings in. It rings hopelessly, though his heart beats fast. He is both relieved and agitated when at last he puts the phone down.

Sally sails down the hall with a plastic basket piled high with ironed clothes. Wholesomeness wafts in her wake. Neal stands in the kitchen and closes his eyes. Summons Alison's face, the feel of her lips, the small moans she'd moaned. Her sighs. Her face in that blessed moment of forgetfulness, that brief escape from consciousness. Ah! He can almost see her, smell her, stroke her soft belly again, run his fingers further and further down, where things get a bit damp and heated.

'Put the kettle on, will you, Neal?' Sally calls from upstairs. 'Nearly done here.'

'In a minute, dear.'

He tries the number one more time, and here comes Sally again, humming as she heads to the utility room. He hangs up the phone.

Later, Neal and Sally have sex for the second time this week. An aberration, but one Neal hopes will cancel out his recent peccadillo. It is just a peccadillo, isn't it? He is still a good man, isn't he? He's angry at himself for letting this fluke, this accident, affect him. He's heard that holidays are good for marriages. He sold an ad just the other day at work, for Thomas Cook. It implied foreign beaches brought older husbands and wives closer. He'd studied the photo some time. The man seemed to be looking at his wife as if he'd just met her. Maybe they should book one of those cheap flights to Majorca. It's probably the kind of thing other couples do all the time, but Neal and Sally have never gone abroad. In Majorca Sally would tan, but he'd have to hide his redhead skin from the sun, like a shrivelled, pale grotesqueness under a rock. Maybe they could go in winter? Hmm, he thinks. A chilly deserted seaside resort sounds even more depressing. They usually stay home, and take day trips to Ullapool, Gairloch, Durness and Smoo Cave. By far, the wisest course of action.

It's cool in the bedroom and they've left their bedclothes on. She wears a full-length pink cotton nightgown, and he wears the navy blue pyjamas she bought him last Christmas. The bed is the same one they've always had. It creaks and rocks and digs grooves into the wooden floor. One day, when the bed is finally moved, someone might be amazed at those four dents in the floor – testimony to Neal's virility and Sally's allure.

Aside from the fact it occurs at all, tonight doesn't *appear* remarkable in any way. In fact, it's curiously un-erotic, the childish, sweet sex of routine. Yet Neal is extraordinarily soothed by slipping inside his wife. It sanctions their marriage somehow. And the mediocrity, especially the mediocrity, draws attention away from the scenes in his head. Yes, shockingly, mere millimetres from Sally's innocent head, are scenes of lurid sex. Breasts far larger and squishier than hers are pummelling Neal's thighs, while a mouth wide with hunger is sucking on her husband's cock (about two inches longer than his actual one), before the entire assemblage of edible womanly parts moves up and rolls over, her lush backside inviting him to finish off.

No, no, none of this actually happened with Alison, of

course not! She was way too sad and he was too conventional and shy. Neal feels a little guilty for fabricating without Alison's consent, for transgressing a love copyright. But these images come unbidden and what's more, they can't be shifted. Sally doesn't know about the real Alison or his fantasy Alison. He can have a secret life – well, doesn't everybody?

Though now, as he climaxes on several planes at once and Sally topples over into her own version, Neal has conflicting feelings. For instance – how can he truly love Alison, yet make love with his wife? How can he truly love Alison, yet have her star in pornographic scenarios? How can he love his wife and cheat on her, both literally and imaginatively? There are, of course, no flattering answers.

But tiredness wells up regardless and Neal and Sally curl up together, very husband-and-wife-ish. Snuffle their goodnights, draw apart and fall asleep the same second. They snore gently in unison, achieving a harmony in sleep that eluded them in sex.

Alison is Alone

A week after the funeral, Alison has an eighteen-hour sleep. When she gets up in the early afternoon, she feels groggy. The sleep has been too deep, following too little sleep for too long. Her eyes feel heavy, her muscles slack. She's lost weight according to her jeans, but she feels a stone heavier. She has a shower, feels marginally better, and notices for the first time how clean the bathroom is. Even the walls look shiny and clean. She frowns, looks closer at the room, as if she's been away for a long time and needs to reacquaint herself with things like the position of towels and purpose of toothpaste.

Her sister Chrissie has been cleaning every inch of Alison's house (aside from Calum's room), and baking and cooking when not cleaning. She's downstairs now, tormenting the linoleum. She's abandoned her own family, her two daughters and their four female offspring, all of whom temporarily live with her. Aside from the post-funeral night, she's been by Alison's side since the dawn she got the call. Ali's voice, hollowed out and low.

'Look, Chrissie, could you come over? Please. Now.'

'What is it, Ali? Only I'm late for work as it is.'

'Shit, Chrissie, will you just come? Something really bad happened to Calum yesterday.'

Now she squeezes the mop into the sink, feels numb and angry. Boys and their cars. She wants to shake her nephew hard. Kids put you through it, that was a fact. And what had Ali been thinking, having just one kid? Helluva lot of eggs for one basket.

She shouts up the stairs, 'Thinking of heading back to my own house later today, Ali. They'll be tearing the place apart, it'll be chaos.' Then more to herself, 'Unless they've killed each other by now, in which case it'll be dead quiet, but still a right bourach. Blood everywhere.'

'Yes, fine. You should, they'll be missing you, Chrissie,' says Alison, walking down the stairs.

'Are you sure, now? Sure you'll be alright, Ali?'

'Yeah.' Alison brushes her hair as she speaks, but doesn't look in a mirror, just tugs it through. Her hair parting is wonky.

'Ready to tell me where you went off to with that Neal Munro yet?'

'Nope,' snaps Alison. 'And you can stop asking me.'

'You'll tell me one day, you know you will, Ali. You'll have a few too many and out it'll come. Might as well tell me now.'

'Oh, will you please shut the fuck up?'

Unoffended, Chrissie takes clothes out of the washing machine one by one, folding them as she does even though they're wet. 'Listen,' she finally says. 'I think you should come and stay with us.' She leaves the damp clothes, goes to Alison, puts her arms around her. Alison stiffens, allows her sister's embrace for one minute, then moves out of it.

'No, I'm fine here, Chrissie. Thanks anyway.'

45

'If you're sure, then. I'll be round in the evening. I'll bring you some soup, will I? You'll not be in the mood to cook for a while yet.'

'No, no, Chrissie.' She wants her to go. She wants to be alone. 'There's plenty food here still, Chrissie. Leave it a bit, hey?'

'Aye, but Ali pet, I don't think you should be alone.'

'Well, I'll hardly be alone. This place is never empty these days, is it? It's driving me a bit crazy. In fact, I think I might go away. I've got some time off work.'

'Away? Where?'

'Maybe to see Kate over in Gairloch. She's always saying I should come and stay. She's got that wee spare room.'

'Good idea, why don't you go visit her, get away for a while, you could do with that.'

'Aye,' says Alison, fighting a yawn. 'Think I'll do that. I like Gairloch.' In her new, stretched-over-the-abyss voice. Anything to get rid of Chrissie, her watchful eyes. Go! she wills her.

'I'm having a bath now, Chrissie. Okay?'

'I thought you just had a shower.'

'Aye, well.'

She locks the door and stays in the bath an hour, and finally Chrissie, who's been waiting for her to come out, has to shout through the door, 'I'm off then, Ali. I'll phone later. Tell me if there's anything you're needing, right?'

'Of course, Chrissie. Thanks for everything.'

The front door closes, the car engine drifts away, and Alison lays in her tepid bath with empty eyes in an empty house. There is a static-y sound in her head, which might have been there all along.

All the rest of the day, she is nervous. She keeps expecting the tidal wave of folk to resurge, but no one comes. Perhaps they intuit she needs solitude now. Perhaps their interest recedes because the melodrama has become mere tragedy, and their own lives are reclaiming them. Perhaps Calum's death is beginning to be a tiny bit boring. Alison is stranded in a surreal place, very like the place she used to live in. She wanted this. To be alone.

It is unbearable. Nothing is bearable.

When the phone rings, she unplugs it. When someone finally knocks on the door, she waits till they go away then locks the door.

In her own house, a ramshackle farmhouse at the back of the estate, Chrissie opens a bottle of red wine and pours a glass. Her sister no longer needing her has dropped her back into her old world, which used to feel full but suddenly does not. Calum's exit has left an ugly gouge in the shape of her . . . well, her life. Used to be a kind of round life, she considers, sipping her wine. Well, not perfectly round of course. There'd been lumps and dimples, but basically it used to be like an overripe peach. Squishy in places, a bit soggy, but basically pink and round. Now: round and pink on one side, horrible dark gouge on the other. Nothing is right. It's all gone squint.

Her daughters and granddaughters are in their rooms sleeping or watching television or playing video games. She pours another glass and thinks, what tears they've all shed for Calum! And all those memories of him bubbling to the surface. She imagines how they must seem from the outside, her family. They must seem close, a small army of women. Comrades! But her daughters rarely confide in her, rarely ask her how she is. How she *really* is. Even now, they're all wrapped up in their own lives. Staying here is mainly a financially expedient arrangement till they move out again.

That is the bare truth. And now that her sister has shut her out, now that Calum has gouged out part of her life, she feels her solitude keenly. *No one really knows me, how I'm feeling right now*. Her throat swells with self-pity. *Does anyone even really love me? Nobody loves me.* Then she imagines being Alison. Imagines losing one of her children suddenly, and instantly slams that door shut. It is too terrifying. And now, it also seems too possible. If it happened to her sister, it could happen to her. In fact, it's a miracle it hasn't happened a few times already!

She slips out of her clothes, puts on her old green striped housecoat and old hiking socks on her feet. Opens the bag of posh crisps she's been saving. Finishes the bag, then gets the cheese and bread out. And the olives, salami and ham. Pours a third glass. Thinks, with relief, *It cannot happen to me*, because *it happened to Alison. Statistically, the odds are now in my favour, and my girls will die of old age. Hopefully, in their sleep. Hopefully in the middle of a happy dream.* What more could any parent hope for their child?

Chrissie sighs and chews and sips herself into a soporific trance. Falls asleep on the sofa again, while Alison is entering Calum's room for the first time since it happened. No one has been in it. The room smells as it always does. What is it? It's familiar, but what is it? It smells of the outside. The wet hillside earth he ran on, still caked on his trainers and boots. The winter air, the wind. His perspiration, his unique masculine pungency – eau de Calum. A whiff of dope and Golden Virginia, both of which sit on his desk. Videos and tapes and CDs are stacked on shelves. Books on running, magazines too. His old grey Gameboy, batteries flat, on the window ledge, covered in cobwebs. Oh, the fierce arguments they'd had about that. Probably the last item she'd felt strongly enough to object to. After that, she just let it go. If his pals had it, Calum had it too.

Maybe she'll ring his friends, see if they want some of these things. She'd talked to Finn yesterday, on the High Street. A very brief chat.

'Hi, Finn.'

'Hi, Alison.'

'How are you?'

'Not bad, ta.'

Then another one of Calum's pals walked by. That tall one. William. Same stilted conversation.

'Hello, William.'

'Hello, Alison.'

'Right cold today, eh?'

'Aye.'

She hadn't noticed, but now she thinks of it, how odd the two boys did not speak to each other, did not even look each other in the eyes. No smile, no anything. What is happening? Nothing is right.

She picks one of the t-shirts off the floor and sits on his unmade bed, then collapses sideways, her head on his pillow (more of that same smell), and she keens. There is no other word for this sound – this high, dry, drawn-out cry. It scratches the air and her throat. After a while, she stumbles from the room, dragging his duvet with her. His shirt is grasped in her other hand. Wraps herself in the duvet, collapses on the sofa downstairs. Wonders without concern if she is having a heart attack. Perhaps a seizure or an aneurism.

Sally is Concerned about Alison

Neal opens a new document on his computer. Types:

20th January 1894: 102 YEARS AGO TODAY

Then he scans an old paper that cost 1d, for items of interest. Keys them in.

- The Royal Hotel in Dingwall now boasts a ladies' tearoom.
- For Sale: Melodians – no home should be without one!
- Ladies and Gents can get their visiting cards printed at the Ross-shire Journal now at a bargain price.
- Wanted: Housekeeper, one cow kept. £5 a year.
- Lost: A lady's grey fur necklet, lost on evening of Oddfellows concert.
- Found: Four black-faced sheep, Invergordon beach.
- Cures for ills: Balsamic Elixir – a drug to cure everything, especially bilious and nervous disorders.
- This week in Avoch, the main pigpen flooded when the local burn overflowed.

- In Alness, a farmer was taken to court for defaming the reputation of his housekeeper. He denied doing so and was unrepentant.

Then Neal stops and just sits. He often enters a dreamy state, writing this column. It is a soporific occupation, and lowers his already low blood pressure. One hundred and two years ago today. Same day, same place, different year. Some days Neal feels like he is slicing down to another level, excavating to another time, and things that occurred here, back then, are still here. That he is living not just on the skin of the surface of the earth as it spins in space, but also on top of everything that has ever happened. A sedimentary layer of compressed experience. Dense with sorrow, streaked with joy, soggy with humour and ugliness and love of all kinds. Everything always changing, always nebulous, yet not a single new atom ever thrown into the equation. Nope – no such thing as a clean slate here on Earth! One way or another, all lives are written over other lives.

These dead people, these past events, are entirely vivid to Neal. Reassuringly distant, but real. This unrepentant farmer has a red face and a large stomach, and his boots are filthy. He stinks. His housekeeper has a bulging belly under her pinafore, and in a cold church she kneels and prays to Mary for help, because she can't think of a single person to ask. And Jesus and God, well, they're just more bastard men.

Then, while considering the farmer's snigger, Neal picks up the phone and dials the number he knows by heart now. The ringing – the knowledge that an action of his is altering an object in Alison's house – thrills him, but suddenly it is not enough. He puts the phone down. Finishes his column methodically, spell-checking, word-counting, cutting and pasting it onto the next day's issue, Page 5 as usual, bottom right column, where he is quite sure no one will notice it. He tucks the old newspaper and his mental picture of all those ladies in long black crinolines and men with whiskers back into the filing cabinet and leaves the building. He gets into his little Fiat and drives up the A9 to Alness. It's a hard cold day, a day with small flecks of ice in the wind. The fields are flattened to their frozen unadorned base, and the Cromarty Firth glints like metal. He drives by the overpass where Calum crashed, and notices the floral tributes are still there. A sad soggy heap of cellophane and petals and flapping notes.

He passes Brae Farm Cottage, where he used to live with Alison and Calum. A stone house on the outskirts, now renovated with box dormers and a tidy lawn. He has no idea when this transformation took place. Neal is curiously unobservant about the present world, but he clearly remembers the day he rented Brae Farm Cottage from Alison's father. And the day a month later when Alison and Calum moved in. Calum had been about five. Nose permanently running, knees always scabbed. Must have been four years, all living together. At least four, maybe five. Neal pauses, as he does the calculations. Could it have been only three years? Three years in those days is equivalent to three decades now.

And a few minutes later, he's on the High Street thinking, Wow! When did Alness get pretty? How has he failed to notice? Seems the whole town has finally shaken off that discordant feel from the seventies. Several signs announce the Alness in Bloom competition – it's in the *Ross-shire Journal* too, but he hasn't really taken it in. Planter boxes line the high street, no doubt full of sleeping bulbs. Empty flower baskets hang from shiny new antique lampposts. Pedestrians look wholesome and washed, with purposeful strides. The street looks like a stage, all set and waiting for the show to begin. Some of those babies in prams might be the grandchildren of those original oil workers. It's possible Alnessians and the incomers have already meshed into a new hybrid tribe, perhaps with a lingo all their own. Highland, with a dash of Weegie. Heegie? *Pure dead brilliant, so you are Gudgie. Got any Carlsberg?*

Neal remembers his first few weeks in Alness. The way the A9 used to run right down the High Street, a constant flow of traffic, noise and exhaust fumes. And the way the pavements had been solid with gum and cigarette butts. The sense of claustrophobia at first, then liking the lack of anonymity. So what if he couldn't even go to the shop for a bag of milk (yes, pints in plastic bags!) without seeing a dozen people he recognised. A chaotic, rowdy town in some ways, but he remembers a cosiness too. A homeliness to the mess.

And the locals? They were friendly, but he hadn't mistaken that for acceptance. He knew as far as they were concerned, he was from Mars. Just lucky he had some money to spend. And lucky that some of them, like Alison, opened their doors a bit to incomers. So to speak. By the time he met her, she'd opened her door to quite a few Martians. He doesn't like to think about that. Anyway, she'd opened the one door to him that really counted. They'd been friends, which on her terms was far more intimate than lovers.

Now the quiet High Street shines in the winter light and disorients Neal while he replaces his memory of Alness with the reality. Enough time has passed for the big picture to emerge, and he wonders how many of the Nigg workers

(Nigg-ers, riggers, Sassenachs) had simply been like economic migrants everywhere. Mostly misfits, risk takers, people with little to lose.

For himself, he blames his hair. Not just ordinary ginger like his grandfather, but neon orange – thick and luminous. That in itself, set against his anaemic skin and blue-green eyes, was enough to brand him an untouchable from the day he left his adoring mother's side and entered the school gates. Ginga, he'd been called. Sometimes Ginga girl. Perhaps there's an evolutionary purpose for the outcasting of redheaded men. Neal's theory is that, historically, redheaded men had terrible tempers and were always to blame when the tribe was decimated by the herd of raptors. Redheaded women don't suffer quite the same stigma, strangely, so perhaps breeding with redheads is not the issue. In any case, his hair and his unhappiness were linked, and somehow liberating. He'd punched the air, reading about Nigg and the Invergordon smelter in the *Evening Times*. No skills needed! North Sea oil adventures! Helter-skelter in the smelter! Goodbye, Mother; goodbye, Father; goodbye childhood bedroom with depressing odour. He was never going to fit in at home, so why not stick out somewhere else?

Oh sure, he'd been optimistic, he'd even been heroic in a sentimental way. But mainly he'd been desperate. And the incomers like himself who remained here despite the smelter and Nigg closing, were they akin to ... rhododendrons taking root in foreign soil and thriving? Or eucalyptus trees? Neal has a brief image of himself as a eucalyptus tree. What's worse, a eucalyptus or a ginger-haired loser living with his parents? His glorious stint at Nigg had only lasted a year. He'd felt clumsy, sissy, disillusioned, and when the *Ross-shire Journal* job came up, he'd grabbed his chances. Half the salary, but so what? Nigg had only been the excuse.

Now he gives himself a serious shake, and focuses. It takes him eleven minutes to crack the coded maze of winding streets in Alison's estate. Number 129 hides, but he finds it at last. He steps up to a mid-terraced, two-storey house and rings the bell. No answer, but he's there, where she lives, where Calum used to live. She could appear at any moment. These steps have been trodden by her shoes. Her hand has rested right where his rests now – this iron railing. Surely it would feel different from all the other identical iron railings along the terrace. He looks at the two front windows of her house, one downstairs, one up, but the curtains are drawn. She is not here, not here, not a bit of her is here. But she's been here, and for one minute this is sufficient.

After sitting in his car for a further five minutes, watching her house, Neal drives slowly home. His face drooping, his eyes vacant. If this is love, there is nothing joyous in it.

When he gets home, Sally says, 'So why are you so late, Neal? Are you alright? You look shattered.'

'I'm fine,' he says. Takes his time removing his jacket, hanging it up. 'Thought I was coming down with flu, but no. I'm fine. Stopped for petrol on the way home.'

Amazing, how he can lie now without his heart racing. Is this what unpremeditated sex can do, corrupt an individual's very nature? It worries him. Maybe this is the way everyone lives, editing their own lives for public consumption. Maybe he'll need to look at people differently now. After he makes a cup of tea for them both, he sneaks a hard look at Sally and asks, 'How was your day?'

'Oh, fine. The same. Insane.'

But what does she really mean? Sally always refers to her job this way. She works at Marks & Spencer, in the customer service department. Elite, this team. She's explained they are not like the stockers or till girls, the cleaners or the security staff. Not the tired ladies who measure breasts for bras. Customer service ladies like Sally wield power. People suck up to them all day. Maybe she has sex with disgruntled customers on her coffee break, trades kisses for receipt-less refunds. If illicit sex can happen to him, it can happen to anyone, right? If he can keep it secret, then anyone can. Neal feels tired. It's a tiring way to look at things.

She's been watching the news, and now she turns her attention to it again. Neal focuses on the screen and wonders for the first time what it would feel like to have a son and then lose him. But he can't imagine it. He can only know how it feels to want to imagine it. A kind of guilty hunger, that's it.

The next day he phones again before he goes to work, while Sally is brushing her teeth. She takes exactly three minutes to do this. She is a serious tooth brusher, and what's more, she is a flosser. He lets it ring ten times. No answer. Tries again that night, after Sally is in bed. He crouches in the dim kitchen, prepared to whisper, should Alison answer. This does not become necessary.

The pattern of phoning repeats itself all week. He varies times of calls. Once, he returns to her house, but her curtains are still drawn. He stands on her doorstep long enough to draw the curious glance of a neighbour, and he thinks this thought: *Life has become stranger than I ever imagined it could be.* He tells himself that he loves her. It's the only explanation for this compulsive behaviour. It has physical symptoms – there is frequently a congestion of blood in his groin and upper chest, causing lack of concentration further up. Love at his age, with his serious and detached personality, is no fun at all, but he doesn't will it away. He watches it with curiosity. It explains things to him, like why people do foolish dangerous things. Why they humiliate themselves. Like his dad running off to Skegness with a waitress called Myrtle, for god's sake, who is younger than his father by eight years and wears turquoise leggings. And oh! The things a broken heart can lead to. Like his deserted cardigan-knitting mother taking up gin fizzes in her despair, then salsa dancing and Spanish classes, and finally Buddhism. He watches his own emotional transformation as if it's a lunar eclipse.

And then, with just as much interest, he watches as it begins to fade. He can eat again. His sexual fantasies wilt. His libido slinks furtively back into its dank cave. He begins to doubt Alison wishes to be contacted. His name is in the book too, surely she would phone if she wanted to speak to him, to see him again. He begins to feel petulant, rejected. Humiliated, even. Probably she deeply regrets her behaviour on the funeral day. Probably she never wants to see him again, thinks him a fool. She hates herself. She hates him. He hates himself. Stupid woman – he hates her too! Anyway, he is tired of not feeling like himself. It's been a huge strain, hardly worth the titillating hours in Golspie, and he will try to forget it happened.

But Sally inadvertently fans the embers one evening, over steak and kidney pie, 'That poor woman, that old friend of yours – Alison Ross. I worry about her, just thinking about it.'

'Yes,' replies Neal, swallowing his steak hard.

'That A9! Worst road in Europe for accidents. Read it in *The Herald* last week. Mostly young men.'

'Aye? Terrible.'

Pause, while Sally has a quick look at Neal. Something about his tone. In fact, there's been something a bit odd about him for weeks.

'Are you in touch with her? With Alison Ross? Do you know how she's coping?'

'No. I don't really know her anymore,' he says, looking away. 'Not for years. I don't know how she is.' *Shut up about Alison*, he thinks as loud as possible.

'But didn't you share a house in the old days? You and her and her boy? When you came up to work at Nigg?'

'Yeah. You know I did.'

'Oh. I'm exhausted, Neal. Of course I knew. Sorry.' Her eyes widen, bewildered.

'That's okay, Sally. Hey, I'm sorry too, okay?'

Neal and Sally are always polite to each other. Always.

'So anyway, you and Alison lived together back then. That's a long time ago. Twenty years?'

'Aye.' He pours a glass of wine, having given up on the pie. He doesn't even like wine. And his stomach bug seems to be attempting a return.

'When did you stop being friends?' she asks, pouring a glass for herself.

'We're still friends.'

'Well, when did you stop seeing each other?'

'I don't know. When I met you, I guess.'

'But you were just friends, right? Not boyfriend-girlfriend.'

'Aye. Just pals.' He remembers his finger inside her. Takes his plate to the sink.

'So why . . . oh never mind. I remember her a bit, I think. Your hippie days, eh?'

Sally has a way of saying hippie that makes Neal feel defensive. Hippies are a joke now. He feels defensive; they

58

were a good bunch. Better than the footie fanatics or the hunting-fishing-shooting lot or the alkies or worse, the golf-playing Thatcher lovers. Anyway, what had Sally been? A pretend hippie? She'd worn those clothes, had those records too. Traitor! Then suddenly he's reminded of the way Alison referred to his marital status and Strathpeffer; she'd attached the word posh to them, like something tainting. Christ, women and the way they spoiled things with tones of voices.

'Poor woman,' she says. 'I can't stop thinking of her.'

'Yes.' Why, even at the beginning, has he never had this, this *heated yearning* for Sally? People might live entire lives without experiencing this visceral kind of love; well, he almost did. He scrapes the remnants of his pie into the bin and thinks of Alison's kiss, pressing his lips together as he does. Strange that Sally has not noticed this other kiss on his lips. But then, he has trouble remembering the last time he's properly kissed his wife at all. They've skirted round each other's mouths these last five or six years, as if properly kissing is a stage they can skip now. Like the way they've begun to skip hoovering the inside of the car, or inviting folk round for dinner. Things are slipping on many fronts. When did it start?

He remembers the very first time they fell out. There'd been no angry words, just her scary sulk followed by her lecture on his anti-social behaviour. Afterwards, their marriage was never quite the same. As if their relationship had been chemically altered, diluted with a bitter alkaloid. He'd try kissing her properly right now, but she might be suspicious. Anyway, what's so bad about the way they are? Quite relaxing, most of the time, this friendly distance.

'Still, I expect she has lots of good friends to look after her. And family. People generally rally round, times like these.'

'No doubt. No doubt, no doubt, no doubt,' he repeats stupidly, clearing the rest of the dishes away and nibbling on a hard crust of French bread left on the cutting board. He never mattered to her a bit. The more he imagines Alison surrounded by her friends, her relatives, people he doesn't know, the more she recedes, till she vanishes. She makes a little muffled pop as she exits, or that might be the noise of his jaws as he chews the bread, despite the fact he should stop eating now, really – all this talk is playing havoc with his digestion. He thinks of Golspie, again, and automatically swells down there, and this ache weirdly becomes a little smear in the air above the refrigerator. Sally seems to notice the smear, and rubs her eyes. It's been such a long day, even her eyes are tired.

'Nice pie tonight, Sally. Was it from Cockburns?'

'Aye. They do a nice pie, alright.' She yawns. 'Though you didn't finish yours.'

'No. Well, this bug, it keeps ruining my appetite. But the pie was good, I could tell,' he says inanely. Anything to change the subject. 'Any pudding?'

'Ice cream. Was Calum's father at the funeral?'

'No. What flavour?'

'Vanilla. Who's Calum's father?'

'Calum's father? He didn't have a father,' he snaps.

'Of course he did.' She frowns, squints thoughtfully. Neal never snaps.

The kitchen is dense with unspoken words (his), and unwanted words (hers). Not to mention the sexual charge (his) that has crept in. Perhaps there is increased electrical energy with all the tension, because the refrigerator becomes audible. Also, the lights have flickered twice since Sally first mentioned Alison. This was unnoticed.

Then suddenly, it's over. Neal slumps against the kitchen

counter, and Sally remembers *EastEnders* is about to begin. The refrigerator lowers its volume, the lights steady. Neal decides to have a walk and leaves the house.

It's a clear night with a full moon so white it's blue. Frost sparkles on car windscreens. The grass under his feet crunches in a satisfying way. He wishes it would crunch louder. He wishes there was a big icy puddle he could go smash up. He wishes he could throw huge stones onto a frozen loch, let the noise of splintered ice and disturbed water wash over him. He wishes, he wishes, he wants . . . what? Only to hurtle himself, once more, into Alison Ross. Only that.

But when he is walking home again and sees the lit windows of his house, his steps quicken. Because isn't that what marriage is, after all? A lit house on a dark street. And although it's exciting for a little while, alone in the lovely dark, who wouldn't prefer the cosy house?

A9

Roads are compared to arteries for a reason. A road map looks exactly like a drawing of a multi-hearted circulatory system. And like platelets afloat in blood, we flow along roads to our various hearts (homes), lungs (holiday destinations), fingers and toes (work, shopping, dental appointments). All of us in our different moods, our various states of decay, our hangovers and daydreams, get in our cars and head out every morning. And though young men have more chance of dying in a car accident than from anything else, none of them feel fear as they release the handbrake. None of them anticipate sudden death. Not a single one anticipates causing a shrine.

The quarter moon is low to the earth tonight, lopsided and yellow, and altogether not very helpful. Zara moves carefully. Opens the boot and takes out three saplings, three rose shrubs, a bag of bulbs, a rubbish bag, a spade, puts them all on the ground. Opens the rubbish bag and gathers all the dead tribute flowers into it, puts the bag in the boot. All the time, thinking, *Sorrysorrysorry Calum. Sorry, I didn't mean to say that. I do love you, I was off my head when I said that. So fucking sorry darling.*

Sighs, begins to dig. After five minutes stops. Sits. A car engine begins to be audible from a mile away, and she tenses and lowers her body to the ground, waits till the taillights disappear before she breathes easier. Not much traffic after midnight. Zara is an absentminded girl, and after a while she forgets to chant *sorry* and begins to chat to Calum. Just inconsequential things. The price of her new jeans. She lights a joint, and rambles on about the fact she saw his auntie in Boots. She mentions that his mum is much younger-looking than he'd made out she was, though she's only seen her the once, at the funeral. She complains, but not in a dramatic way, that the avocados she bought yesterday were all mushy and bruised inside, and her own head and throat and guts still ache all the time. As she talks, she weeps quietly, and she plants things that can be planted in winter. Two silver birches, a pine tree, some rose shrubs, some daffodil bulbs. The cold snap is over and the ground is not hard. Around her are the winter skeletons of whins, thistles, broom, as well as old beer tins, a few bottles, crisp packets. And what is that under that blackened whin? A shattered wing mirror. She needs a tissue, can't find one, and in the end uses her sleeve.

Pictures Calum.

He's driving down the A9 in that icy mid-day, and he's thinking, *No traffic, brilliant.* And the low winter sun makes it one of those in and out days, light-dark-light-dark, driving by trees and buildings. Maybe he's trying to find his sunglasses in the glove compartment, but no. His fingers can't feel them, and he can't look, going too fast now. Fifty-five, sixty, sixty-five, seventy. Bloody fine cars, Vauxhalls. No matter what anyone says, and Calum always defends his car.

Probably he's not thinking of anything but this: The low glaring sun. The empty road. Herself, of course. And what she said the night before. Still hurts. To hell with her!

His mobile phone rings, he reaches over to answer it because it must be her – none of his pals have mobiles yet. Himself and Zara, trendsetters with their matching blue Nokia phones. What a laugh they had in the shop, choosing ring tones and styles! He'll be thinking she's ringing to admit she was wrong. His hands turn the wheel ever so slightly, so he can reach the phone and her apology, and when he tries to correct the angle, keep on the road, it's too late. He's over the verge lip. Again and again, close where she is sitting right now in the dark. It's possible Calum notices there are some empty bottles in the grass, and for a second scans the labels – Carlsberg Special – and suddenly the bottles sparkle like torpedo-shaped stars. A dozen crows fly off the telegraph wire. No, there's fourteen crows. They pause, frozen in mid-wing beat, and maybe Calum notices each of their wings, their hard sharp feathers, their hard shiny eyes.

Once he explained to her: *Sometimes when I run, it's like the world has . . . stopped, and everything I see is really amazing and weird and . . . completely still. Like I'm the only thing alive in a frozen world. Running is like stopping time.*

His car slides over the verge lip and he hears his own voice say *Zara!* He notices he sounds quite urgent. No, not enough time to notice that. Just time to say the two syllables of her name.

Zara blows her nose hard and gets back in her car and drives home. Thinks briefly of her mobile phone. It sits uncharged in her sock drawer. Been there since her last unanswered call to him. *I'll bin it*, she decides again. *Just bin it*.

Approaching Evanton this time of night and in this state of mind, the yellow streetlamps make her think of her mum, of Christmas trees, guardian angels, soft duvets. Some days there really is, she thinks, no place like home. And later, as her head hits the pillow, she thinks about Calum running, about how he'd seen so many strange and beautiful things in his life already. This helps, and she falls asleep trying to imagine all the things Calum has seen. A lullaby of movie stills.

Part Three

Last Days of January to Valentine's Day 1996

Alison is a Wee Trout in a Big Loch

She's in Glasgow. A little scrap of Alness adrift in the big city. No matter that she doesn't know anyone here and she doesn't even like big cities. No matter that it was mainly Glaswegians who'd colonised Alness. Who seduced young country girls like herself, and didn't bother with condoms (yes, she is feeling a little sorry for herself). That before they came, the sight of a woman walking down the High Street with a cigarette hanging out of her mouth was proof of the devil. That doors were unlocked, car keys left in ignitions, house prices were low, police were decorative, accents undiluted, neighbours were people you knew the whole history of, drugs were a thing you read about in *News of the World*.

Alison sits in one of the last non-cappuccino cafés, The Swan, just off West Regent Street. Unpretentious, certainly, but also terrible coffee. She can't get warm, and she feels Glasgow all around her. The room itself is padded with their quick, gravelly voices, their sudden barks of laughter and phlegm-coughs.

She's not thinking about Calum. She's giving that a wee break, because otherwise she will disintegrate. She's thinking mean things about Glaswegians instead. Oh yes, Glaswegians had ruined her life. Corrupted all of Alness . . . or had they? In any case, the incomers were also from the Western Isles, from Livingston and Clydebank and Lothian and Manchester. They were from lots of places, and they didn't corrupt everyone. Alison's sister hadn't been corrupted. Her parents hadn't. Some of her school pals hadn't – in fact, they'd sneered at the urban incomers, thought them above themselves, loud, garish. Tacky. They'd snubbed the incomers because they believed they were being snubbed. A pre-emptive snub. *Let's face it*, she thinks, *it was me. I was drawn to their city ways, their hippie ways, because I was bored, and it was fun flirting with the boys, and it felt like I was joining the big world when I listened to Woodstock for the first time, smoking some Moroccan.* She was not in Kansas anymore, but to be honest, hadn't she wanted to leave Alness with all her heart anyway? Moving in with Neal and making friends with all those non-Highlanders had felt like joining another tribe, the tribe having more fun, but she hadn't anticipated abandoning her own. And she was not forgiven, not really. Chrissie was the only one who never let go of her. In the end, Alison didn't really belong to either tribe. She had become too unlike her fellow Alnessians, but banned in some essential way from the incomers too. Though she was rewarded for her loyalty, included in their incomer parties, their friendships and confidences, she never felt one of them. She knew there was an inner circle, and she knew she would never see it. No, she was on the outside, no mistake about that. She was neither one thing nor the other, and the only people like her were other outsiders. She hated this, still does. Hates it! So avoids other outsiders like the plague. Mocks them. What about Neal, then? Where does he come into this?

She swallows the last of her coffee quickly. She can't think about Neal right now. A young waitress catches her eye, and Alison signals by lifting her cup. The waitress nods, brings her another coffee.

'And can I have a toastie, please? Cheese and ham.'

'Yep, no problem. Five minutes.'

Imagine being a waitress, she thinks. *Quite alright, I bet.*

Then she looks backwards again. Thinks. Quite easy to do, this far from home.

She sees her life split in two by Nigg wickedness. *Don't forget Nigg is an actual place too*, her mum used to scold her. *Nay just about them oil workers and their money and their drugs.* She used to take Alison and her sister there for beach picnics, before North Sea oil, before she was dead. So, there was pre-Nigg and post-Nigg. Time weirdness: Alness in the early seventies was stuck in the fifties, then suddenly catapulted into the swinging sixties. From thinking The Beatles had shockingly long hair, to overnight fancying boys with hair down to their shoulders. It was like having dual nationality, belonging to two different pasts. A weird place and time to grow up, alright. Though she hadn't thought about it much at the time.

'You alright, hen?' asks a bald man dressed like the chef.

'Aye, fine.'

'More coffee?'

'Better not. Oh, go on then. Ta.'

It's not that strong anyway. And it's good and hot. She has trouble getting warm. No matter what she does, she is cold. Her fake tan has faded and her freckles stand out, accentuating her pallor. She has a jumper on, but she's chilled and dizzy. She glances around and notices that no one is taking notice of her. *Good*, she thinks. She must still look normal. This is amazing to her. It makes her wonder

71

how many other people feel as hollow and frightened as herself. If everybody is just faking it, and if everyone is so equally desperate, what's the point? Who are they fooling? *I should just go and ask someone*, she thinks. *Ask that old geezer over there, sitting with his* Daily Mail *and ham roll. 'Excuse me,' I'll say, 'but are you really reading that paper? Are you sure you're not just pretending to be curious about the state of the world? We could both just howl together, instead. Want to?'*

But Alison is not that daft yet. She finishes her coffee. Charade or not, the day has to be lived through, and she can only sit so long without the chill reclaiming her. A brisk walk down Buchanan Street among strangers, that's what she needs. No familiar eyes to meet, no polite conversation to make. No sympathy, just the bracing effect of all those posh shops. The newness of this place is a tonic, or as much a tonic as she is able to absorb. Maybe a liquid tonic is what she needs, a real drink somewhere, but where? She's not up to any of the places she walked by earlier, full of laughing attractive people. She pays for her coffee and pulls her good coat on, long black wool. Wraps a red tartan scarf, which matches her shoes, around her head and neck. The only flesh that's exposed is the middle part of her face. Even her hands are inside thermal gloves.

She drinks in the air. She swallows exhaust fumes, cigarette smoke and the wintry exhalations of thousands of Glaswegians. She's tried smoking, but hasn't been able to get through a whole pack, they made her nauseous. But this polluted city air is perfect. She breathes deeply. She walks and keeps breathing. But after a few minutes her walk is less brisk. She's heavy again, sluggish, as if her heart is reluctant to pump. It thuds and does the minimum it must. The weight of Calum's absence seems to travel in her blood. And nowhere in her blood or mind or heart is Neal, not even one little wisp of him. Only the shadowy memory of sitting sticky-thighed in the back seat of a dawn taxi. The way Alness had looked in that early light, as if it too needed a good wash.

Alison shivers and walks on. She walks slowly down Buchanan Street, then along Argyle Street. She lets the Calum thoughts in again, in a controlled way. Like a vaccine, small doses to prevent the landslide. Repeats to herself, *Nope! Calum is not here, he is not anywhere now.* The trouble is, she cannot turn off her radar for him, it keeps forgetting and reaching out. It has a mind of its own. She sees running shoes on sale in the window of a sports shop, thinks without thinking – *Calum!* – just a little careless thought of him, and it goes nowhere, it runs into a wall, it's sucked into the ether. When he was here and she thought – *Calum!* – the thought had somewhere to go, some conversation waiting to be resumed, some argument, their evening meal in front of the telly. He could be ticked off the list. The whole thing used to take three seconds, about a half dozen times a day. Back in the old days, when life did not feel like an emergency every minute. Now the unspoken Calum thoughts are damming up in her chest.

Where are his ashes? The wee box of him, the collecting of which was her last act in the Highlands, is in the B&B she parked herself in for tonight. On top of the telly, which only has two channels. She'll take a train back to Inverness tomorrow, and carry the box in the same carrier bag she brought it down in, a Tesco carrier bag. She can't stay long, she's brought nothing but the box with her. She's no idea what she'll eventually do with the box. It isn't really a box, it's a dark brown plastic container, the shape of a catering-size Nescafé. Body-shaped, in fact. Alison has no interest in ashes. And yet, she felt too passive to refuse them, she's paid for them, and now she seems to be stuck with them. In the train earlier today, she tried to leave them on the seat, but a young man picked up the bag and came running after her.

'You forgot your bag!' he said, puffing.

'Did I?'

'This *is* your bag, isn't it?'

'Aye, so it is.'

The ashes are a nuisance, and worse, they bear no relation to Calum. Calum is gone, gone, gone, and she's not told him so many things. Can she tell him now? As if he can hear? And forgive? Comforting thought, lovely image. A forgiving angel, a warm sad glow. But Alison is not a believer and so Calum cannot be an angel; he cannot hear. He isn't anywhere, and there are things she's not told him.

26th January 1916: EIGHTY YEARS AGO TODAY

- For a good wash, use Coal Tar soap, 3d at Fraser's.
- Wanted: Smart messenger boy for grocers, £35 per annum.
- Rationing notice – Register with your butcher by 30th Jan.
- Lost: Would the party who accidentally took the pair of fur gloves from the Conon Public Hall on New Year's eve, please return them to Miss McKenzie, Killen.
- Needed: Volunteers to do the teas at Dingwall Station for the floods of thirsty servicemen.
- Men, are you feeling old at forty? New Oysterix tonic tablets contain general invigorators and raw oyster stimulants. 1s/9d a bottle. Instant results!
- The Canadians arrive! After lustily singing 'Tipperary' and 'Roll Out the Barrel', the Canadian soldiers marched ashore at the west coast port, the second battalion of Canadians to arrive. Note: All ranks on leave may wear civvies.

- Missing in Action: Joseph Munro, of Jamestown, aged 18 Theo McPhee, of Dingwall, aged 18
- Killed in Action in France: Tommy Henderson, of Delny, aged 19

While Alison negotiates the big city, Neal types names no one will ever read, and this makes him sad in a pleasant, familiar way. It is 11:55am. His life, incredibly, has swallowed the Calum tragedy. He's cheated on his wife for the first and possibly last time. Guilt has been denied, accepted, analysed, digested, rationalised and finally expelled. The momentum of normality, lumbering indifferent beast that it is, has stream-rolled over everything, and he's preoccupied with trivial things again, with the addition of constant but quite manageable Alison thoughts murmuring under everything. That night-time walk a week ago, when he felt he might expire if he couldn't see, no, not just see her, but make passionate love to her for at least four and a half hours – well, he's relegated that longing to certain parts of his day when he can feel private. Addicting as it is, it does not interfere with his life. He does not indulge in wanton Alison thoughts wantonly.

No, he does not. *He is not obsessed.*

Not most of the time, anyway. He is becoming used to being a complicated, contradictory person, like most other middle-aged men in turn of the twentieth-century Scotland. He wonders if his sparkplugs need replacing, if he's losing more hair, if his penis is big enough, if he should buy those more expensive comfortable shoes next time, if he will ever sleep with Alison again, if his father is getting more sex then he is, if the pork chop he chewed last night was too tough or are his teeth getting old, if he will ever stop being in love with Alison, if the dandruff that flakes off his wife's scalp is something she'd like to know about, if she will ever agree to anal or even oral sex, if he really wants her to anymore, if the garden needs attention yet, if his own birthday has come round again too quickly. Oh yes, Neal has had another birthday, and is now forty-four. A big deal? But this too has been gobbled up and is gone. The days flicker past in their predictability and their passing is not painful. What can time not obliterate? His love for Alison, of course, but it does not scream in his head every second of every day. He's too old for that kind of intensity, which is one of the reasons he can give serious thought to things like the toughness of pork chops.

His work is done for the morning and as he leaves the office to buy a roll and coffee, the sun comes out. So what, you might think, but this is Dingwall in late January and sun is an event. His hair lightens, a glint of red gold. And the air is a freezing bright elixir. He's inhaling iced coffee. Neal shades his eyes, feels a loosening deep inside, and decides to eat his roll on one of the seats outside Donati's. It's bird-shit covered from the pigeons who roost on it most nights, but this does not concern him.

He eats his roll slowly and reflects on his wife's good qualities, the way she makes her own Christmas cards every year, rarely resorting to glitter. The way she keeps their kitchen cupboards tidy, even the cutlery drawer, and he always knows where things will be. The way she tucks his pairs of socks into each other, neat little parcels. The way everyone seems to like her; in fact, now he thinks about it, everyone seems to like her a lot. All the social arrangements are made via her. They are referred to as Sally and Neal. Never, *never*, as Neal and Sally. He doesn't mind, of course he doesn't, but he notes this inequality in their popularity. It's interesting.

Yesterday there was another postcard from his father in Skegness. *Hey, wish you were here, son. Don't leave it too long. I know it's cliché but life really is hellishly short. Love from Dad (and Myrtle).* No word from his Buddhist mother in a long time. A celibate un-materialistic woman always on retreat. Somehow, she just doesn't count anymore, not in a maternal way. Things like Christmas presents and birthday cakes are long gone. Just the annual card, informing him that she's donated to some charity in his name. Did his dad's affair have to drive her to that? Well, at least someone benefits.

For a minute after eating, he lifts his face to the sun and closes his eyes. He feels blessed suddenly, and perhaps this is the first time since he turned forty-four he's aware of simply being above ground, not in it. A forgettable fact, being alive, but it is something, and he remembers now to give it its due. He pictures all the time he has left to live, as if it fills a container with a one-way valve. A clear Perspex rectangle.

He glances at his watch. Four more minutes left of lunch hour, then he'll have to rise, walk back up the High Street. Then one minute, thirty seconds left. Then he is rising, and walking. He can almost hear the hiss of time seeping away, and looks extra hard at the shop windows, in case he misses some little thing that turns out to be important.

He passes two boys who look familiar. One tall, one short. Early twenties. Arguing? But quietly so it's hard to tell. Certainly emotional. Their two voices are overlapping, low but fast and hard.

'Finn! Stop a second, man.'

'Aye?'

'What's your problem, eh?'

'What you talking about?'

'You never answer my texts.'

'What texts?'

'And you totally saw me Saturday, and just walked away.'

'You're off your head, William. Paranoid.'

Then Neal is past them and doesn't hear them anymore. His heart pounds, and without being aware of it, he automatically applies his old remedy. Thinks about the earth revolving and himself planted vertically on it. And about what used to be right here, on this street. Instantly feels happier. This is where horses used to be tethered while folk did their banking. That's where the original cattle market was. Down this lane is where Mary Queen of Scots hid, en route to a safer place. Whew! Much better. You know where you are, with history. Like a mantra, he silently says the names of places and people that are no longer here.

A Name is a Little Thing

She sits in The Swan again. Next day, same seat, by the steamed-up window. Weird, how even within a short period, one establishes routines. It's cheap, too brightly lit and uncomfortable, just what she needs. She has read, at last, the notices in the window, and is talking to Teddy MacDougall, the chef and café owner. He's about fifty, full-lipped, fat enough to have a bosom, and seemingly hairless. Quite a shiny man, when sitting directly under the fluorescent light, as he is now. He's smiling and Alison stares at him, transfixed, wondering how ugliness can spill over into beauty, just like that. And is that rouge on his cheeks? It might be, hard to tell.

She glances round the café again, just to make sure it really is as conventional as it appears. There are no black and white photographs on the wall, no sea-salt grinders, no balsamic vinegar bottles. Probably not rouge. Probably broken capillaries. Or he's blushing.

'So, down from the Highlands, are you? On what? Some kind of holiday?' Teddy asks gruffly, straight-faced through his smile, which is how he always greets new people. His café is full of regulars, mostly anti-social types who feel okay near him but uneasy near most other people in this trendy part of Glasgow. Teddy's regulars are frightened, for instance, of Costa. They read the *Sun*, love hamburgers, smoke Embassy Regals; in fact, the café stinks of Embassy Regals and hamburgers.

'No. Yes. Not really. I mean, who would come here for fun?' She lets a small giggle leak out, to signal it's a joke. She should just shut up.

'Why are you here then?'

'Just trying it out, like.'

'You mean one place is as good as another? Every where's the same?' As if he really wants to know.

'I didn't say that.'

'No.'

'But maybe. Maybe it is.'

'Hm . . .' He squints his eyes, as if he's considering the concept. Then suddenly the gruff dissolves. He leans forward on his elbows, and in a warm chatty voice, asks, 'So how *did* you get here, hen? What are you doing here? Tell me everything.'

She thinks, *What kind of job interview is this? Nosey bugger. I sat on the floor in my dark house eating out of a cereal box with the curtains drawn, ignoring the phone and when people knocked on the door I didn't open it. Then I drove to the Crematorium to pick up my jar of son, then I parked the car in Safeway's car park meaning to get some milk and bread but before I got to the door, felt like I shouldn't be leaving Calum's ashes on the back seat like that, just didn't seem right, so I went back and fetched them and then walked to the train station instead of Safeways, 'cause I'd decided to off myself, so perfect! But after five minutes realised jumping in front of speeding trains wasn't possible in a terminus. So got on a train instead. Didn't look to see where it was going. Didn't even have a ticket. Wasn't asked for one, either. Probably looked too loony to ask.*

'I got on a train,' she says out loud.

'Aye? Then what?'

'Then nothing. I got off the train. I'm here, I like it, thinking of staying. And I've been a waitress before,' she lies. 'I could start today, if you want.'

'£3.50 an hour. Thirty hours a week,' he says ominously, as if these are harsh and unusual conditions. 'The waitress I have is a student. Just wants to do weekends. So you would be Monday to Friday.'

'Aye, that's just fine.' A shaky note creeping into her voice – is her courage about to give out already? Traitor voice!

His eyes fill with a consoling expression. 'Really? That would be just great. But are you really sure, darling?'

The darling, which does not sound rote, is a jolt.

'Really,' she mumbles.

'What's your name, then?'

'Alison Ross. Well . . .' She begins to say something about her lack of work clothes, then closes her mouth and sticks out her hand, which he just looks at. The last waitress had been of the sleazy made-up variety and had eaten her way through most of his cakes every day before leaving with no notice and a chocolate gateau, and Teddy had felt demoralised because he'd liked her.

He regards Alison's hand to see if it might belong to another unreliable glutton. But no, it looks surprisingly reliable and un-gluttonous, as does her face. Grief becomes Alison. Fasting and walking have improved her circulation, and enormous amounts of sleep have eradicated her dark circles. She still has her perpetual crease of anxiety, her frown, but now it just makes her look sweetly serious. Eventually he takes her hand into his sweaty paw and shakes it.

'Nice to meet you, eh . . . Alice? Alice Roswell, did you say? Lovely name, dear.'

She does not correct him. A name is such a little thing, and yet. Lets the *Alice Roswell* hang in the air. Alice, a subtly different person from Alison, materialises suddenly, faintly, just out of the corner of her eye. Alice is simple, pure, feminine but never sexy. Alice does not swear. Her sense of humour is non-existent. People protect Alice. And Roswell is so much less common than Ross. People respect a Roswell, surely. Alice Roswell it is, then.

'Why don't you write down your phone number and address, and I'll show you the routine.'

'Ah.' She extricates her hand. 'Now. I was also wanting to apply for the live-in companion job.' His face looks blank, so she elucidates. 'For the elderly woman. Your mother, perhaps?' His face still looks full of dumb awe, wide-eyed, mouth open. It begins to make her uneasy, but surely that's a spark of intelligence in his dark lashed eyes? Yes, of course, he's faking it. Like a flirting girl. Dumb bald.

'Now how did you know about my mum, you clever girl?'

Alison/Alice smiles warily. 'Your notice. In the window. Below the help wanted notice.' She wants to take his pudgy hand and lead him to the notices.

'Oh! Right you are! I forgot I put that bit up as well. Been up for ages, that, I'd given up. I mean, who'd want to look after an old lady for fifty quid a week?'

'Fifty quid?'

'That's right, lovey. You'd get a roof over your head, like, and use of the house. It's in a nice quiet lane. But only fifty pounds a week. Can't afford more.'

'Well, I've no place to live yet, so it'd suit me fine meantime.'

'Good.'

'Have I got the job, then?'

'You bet.'

'Both jobs?'

'Aye. Why not?' He smiles broadly, revealing shiny teeth which match his shiny hairless head. He's almost blinding, and she pauses for a minute, letting all this light wash over her.

'And your mother?'

'I've been seeing to her twice a day for years now. Get her up, make her a cuppa. Get her some supper, help her to bed. She does most things on her own, but could use help with dressing sometimes. And cooking, washing dishes. Laundry. Bit of cleaning.'

'Okay.' She would be daunted, if she had any daunt in her.

'She's old, you know,' he warns. 'Pretty decrepit, in fact. I've been on the verge of checking her into an oldie's home, only I'm pretty sure she'd arrange for some hit man to take me out. Some guy called Jimmy, probably.'

'Really?'

'Oh yeah. She's crabbit, and if you boil her egg too long, she'll throw it at you.'

'Oh, I think I can cope with that.'

'She's got a mean pitching arm.'

'I think I'll manage. I'm a great catcher of eggs.'

'Well, Alice. If you like catching eggs, you'll love my mum. Go fetch your luggage, darling, and I'll take you over and introduce you.'

Alison, upon hearing herself called Alice for the second time, moves her shoulders as if she's shrugging something on, or off. She shakes his hand and leaves, promising to be back in an hour. Wanders in a daze for thirty minutes, then finds a charity shop and buys a suitcase for 80p – a beige plastic one. Pops the Nescafé of Calum into the suitcase, clicks it shut, and heads back to Teddy. Cannot believe she began yesterday in her own bed in Alness. Seems years ago. Right now, she couldn't tell you the colour of her bedroom walls.

'So, Alice, this all your wordly possessions then?'

'Aye. I travel light.'

'Good for you, sweetie. Let me take that for you.'

'No, that's okay, I'll carry it.'

'Don't be silly, I'll carry it. Time to close now, anyway. I'll just lock the door and we'll go and meet my mum. She lives about five minutes away.'

'I want to carry it, Teddy, honestly, thank you anyway.'

He lifts the case. Calum audibly slides from one end to another.

'What've you got in here, then Alice?'

'Stuff,' she says, blushing.

A quite long pause. Then: 'Right you are, none of my business anyway.'

She's shown her new room, the bathroom, how to work the heating, light the fire, pay the milkman, jiggle the television antenna for good reception. She feels blank, but is convincingly responsive. Lets the newness fill her. She notices the wallpaper in the hallway. It is very old, possibly as old as the house, a pre-war tenement. A pattern of small faded daffodils repeated on a blue and green tartan. She wants to stare at it; it seems to want to be stared at. What has it witnessed? Alice promises herself and it that she'll stare at it later. Strange, because Alison never gave a damn about the history of things.

'Lovely to meet you,' she tells Janet, who holds her hand far longer than necessary.

'Likewise, my dear. Likewise. Is my tea ready yet?'

The next day Alice walks to the More store and buys a pastel nylon nightie for £2.99, one that Alison would have hated. She buys knickers and socks in value packs of six, and two blouses, the first blouses she's ever bought. She also buys an unflattering skirt with an elastic waist. It has a floral pattern on a black background. She buys a toothbrush to cure her furry teeth, and then notices her purse is finally empty. Her bank account with its £1,367 is inaccessible; her bank card lies on the sideboard at home, along with her cheque book. The second morning in her new bed, still dark outside, she is woken by Calum's voice.

Mum!

In just his impatient demanding tone, age six or ten or twenty. She lays in bed and listens, with a queer alert feeling, to the echo of his voice. Since he could talk, his summoning *Mum!* has broken her dreams. Both his real voice, and his voice in her dreams. Hard to tell the difference some days. But now he's gone, his voice is so precious.

She makes her voice as normal as possible when she answers: *What?* Hoping to trick him back somehow. Then rolls over and tries to slip back into that particular dream.

'Married?' asks Teddy later, while laying out strips of bacon on the grill.

'No.'

'No kids?'

'No.' Pause. 'Well, I used to.'

Teddy raises his eyebrows.

'A son, but he died. Does that count as having kids?' It's like learning a new language.

'I'm so sorry. Yes, of course he counts,' says Teddy.

'Well, okay.'

'Name?'

'Calum,' she mumbles, coughs, looks at the oven behind Teddy. In a louder voice: 'His name was Calum, okay?'

'You must miss him terribly. Can't imagine how you feel.'

'Yes.'

'Can I ask how he died?'

'Car crash.' She puts the fork down and leans over to untie, then re-tie her shoelace.

Teddy makes a squeamish noise, then exhales audibly. 'Was it a drunk driver? Black ice?'

'Uh, no. No. Not exactly sure how it happened.'

'That must be worse. And when? When was this terrible event?'

'About three weeks ago. The fifth of January.'

Silence, bacon frozen mid-turn.

'Fuck, Alice. Excuse my language, but fuck.'

'Yes. Well, will I do the pans now? The sink's full.'

Alice splashes greasy water over her skirt. She's never been good at languages. She has a terrible memory for new meanings of words, new sequences of words, but she remembers her son well enough. And pretty much all the time.

Neal Remembers Calum

Events take a long time to sift down inside Neal. They settle down, then they flurry up a bit, then they settle down again. His mind is not exactly like a junk drawer, but pretty close. He mislays emotions. He sits at his desk with a cup of coffee, and in between answering the phone and writing down ad details, he remembers Calum. It's like being visited by him. A surging wave, the office floats away, and the old days are exposed on the beach in all their flawed loveliness.

He remembers not just the Ribena smell and his scabby knees, this time he remembers the sound of Calum's voice, calling him Dad. The way he never stopped even when he was corrected, sometimes sharply. He thinks of the way Calum's eyes always lit up when he saw him, and one spring morning in particular when he smiled with peanut butter all over his mouth. He remembers wrapping a large bandage around Calum's knee, after another fall off his skateboard; the way Calum didn't cry but seemed proud of his injury. They'd felt close, united in their . . . their what? They'd both hated the series of men in Alison's life. Those men who smiled so often, but rarely looked them straight in the eyes. Loud drunken laughter behind her closed bedroom door, used to send Neal and Calum out of the house. Or they'd hole up in the sitting room, with the telly volume up high. Never a point in remembering their names; not likely they'd still be around next month.

Neal burns his tongue with scalding coffee, quotes rates for lines, and remembers the exact way he felt when Calum reached for his hand. Honoured. A child liking him. It had meant he was a good person. A warmth pours into him now, as if Calum is still liking him.

'Neal!'

'What?'

'I said, do you want a cup of tea? I asked you twice. Are you alright?'

'Sorry, Margaret. I was just . . . thinking. Yes please. Just milk, no sugar.'

'You think I don't know that by now?'

Yes, Neal's mind is slow and echoing. Images drop slowly, like soft things, like marshmallows into fire – innocuous, ignorable, but once they hit the flames, sizzling into caramelised nuggets. And now Finding-Alison is shifted from the back burner to the roaring adrenalin-fired front burner. He swallows his tea in gulps, winds up a phone call about an ad for a VW Golf 1600cc with Panasonic CD player and infinity speakers. Hangs up, and before the phone can ring again, quickly dials her number. She'll answer this time, surely. She must! When she doesn't, he gets up, grabs his coat and leaves the office without even nodding to smiling Margaret, sitting at her desk and who he's never failed to smile at. Her unnoticed smile freezes, then fades as she stares at his retreating back.

'Hmph!' she grunts, secretly of the same opinion as Sally, that middle-aged men are dangerously unstable. She'd hoped Neal would be different – he'd certainly negotiated his thirties like a mature adult, but here he is, with that demented charging ahead look. Selfish, the lot of them!

Neal gets in his car and heads north on the Old Evanton Back Road and, as always, has a little thought about the road itself and the ghosts he is driving through. This is automatic and only uses a few seconds, but is specific and vivid nevertheless. He passes two horses pulling a carriage, heading for Foulis Castle. Inside is Angus Beaton, who has promised to cure the dying Laird with the leeches he carries in a jar in his sack. Those three aristocratic ladies walking with their maidservants holding parasols are on their way to the Catholic chapel. The cattle on the down slope of the hill to his right, stumbling and panting, are being driven by the Bethune boys with sticks. And oh look, there are those barefooted men with Nordic voices and red beards, charging up from the shore again. And over in those woods, that running woman with a baby tucked into deerskin, slung across her back! Then at the stone bridge at Pealig, a young blond woman driving a silver Polo south pulls into a passing place to give way. Neal briefly waves his thank you as he passes, and she nods slightly.

She is not a ghost, she is Zara, the woman who'd loudly wept and ran out of the church at the funeral. The keeper of the A9 Calum memorial. But Neal does not realise this. Only thinks, in a distracted way – nice hair, familiar face, do I know her?

He turns the radio on, and it's that song again. *I feel it in my fingers, I feel it in my toes.* He turns up the volume. He doesn't like most contemporary pop music, but this is the Trogs rehashed by Wet Wet Wet, and just the right side of naff. *It's written on the wind, it's everywhere I go.*

By the time the song ends, he's in a soppy mood and parked in front of Alison's house. When her doorbell is not answered, he rings the three other bells in the terrace. Why hasn't he done this before? He feels like he's just woken up, and it might already be too late so he has to hurry. His eyes swivel to Alison's windows, but the curtains are still drawn. He stares at them. His hands are shaking, he is quaking internally. This is a race! An emergency! Although all of houses have signs of inhabitants, only one door opens.

'Can I help you? Alison Ross? Sure, I know Alison, lives next door,' says an elderly woman slowly. 'Lovely girl, Alison, so nice. Terrible about her son, though. Hard to believe. I mind when he was wee, such a handsome lad he was, and always so thoughtful of me as well, like the time he kept these steps sprinkled with grit he got from the yellow bins down the road. Fetched it all by his wee self in carrier bags, so he did, he was that kind. I always kept some Marathon bars, the wee ones, just for him. Say, why don't you come in out of the cold, the kettle's just boiled, what did you say your name was? I'm Dorothy.'

'Neal. I can't come in, sorry, uh, Dorothy. I'm in a bit of a hurry and just need to find her. Alison.' He points to Alison's house.

'Ah. No time to stop?' A cheated look to her face, her mouth twists slightly to one side, eyes narrow. The air from her over-heated house wafts out, old lady breath micro-waved. A tinge of urine.

'Do you know where she is? I've been phoning, but never an answer.'

'Now, I'm afraid I haven't seen poor Alison since a few days after the funeral. That reminds me – are you not the mannie she went off with that day?'

'Me?'

'You look just like him. We all saw her drive off with this red-haired mannie, and she never even showed up for the reception.' She leers, just a second's worth of leer, but enough to make Neal queasy.

'Did she not?'

'No, she did not,' she enunciates so clearly, Neal wonders if she's drunk. 'She did not return till early the following morning. I mind her taxi pulling up at dawn.'

'Is that so?' This is exciting news – a piece of Alison's recent history revealed! So, she'd hired a taxi from Golspie. But then, in Neal's state, even seeing the word Alison written somewhere is exciting. Hearing the word spoken out loud is exciting. Being this near her house is exciting. He is a tuning fork vibrating to anything Alison.

'But do you know where she might be now?' He's begun to breathe shallowly, so as not to inhale the old lady air too deeply.

'No. I assumed she was staying with friends. Or sister, more like. Sorry, I can't tell you where her sister lives, but near by. Her name's Chrissie. I'm sorry, I don't know Alison that well, but she's a fine neighbour, and I'm sorry for her troubles.'

Neal, for the first time, wishes he owned a mobile phone. Of course, his dad already has one. He'll need to get one soon. And a CD player for his car. And a home computer. Maybe internet. Maybe a digital camera too. Maybe even a DVD player. He's been resisting for a few years now. It's not that he's against technology; he just feels a little tired at the prospect of learning new ways when the old ways seem sufficient. Everything seems to be accelerating so quickly. He's a historian, he knows about change. The way it comes in bundles and bursts, in complex knots, never the slow steady trajectory. But it's one thing expecting it, altogether different to be living through it. And what the hell has happened to wire coat hangers? Wooden cotton spools?

Typewriters and their ribbons in sweet little boxes? He stopped looking for a second, and *whoosh*, all gone.

He drives to the payphone by the bank on the High Street. Parks his car and while crossing the road notices a pleasing yeasty smell in the air, remembers the distillery nearby. His younger self stirs under his skin, with this olfactory prompt. Feels focused, energetic. He calls directory inquiries, phones Chrissie. A little girl answers the phone.

'Hello?'

'Hello, is your mum there?'

'Aye,' as in *of course she's here, stupid!*

Pause.

'Hello, I said is your mummy there?'

'I just said so, didn't I? What're you, thick or sumpin?'

Pause.

'Can I, uh, talk to her?'

''Spose so.' Sounds of phone slamming against wall, then silence.

Neal stands in the freezing phone box, shifting his feet to keep the circulation going, and listens to the tiny distant voices in the phone. None of them sound urgent. Has he been forgotten? He suspects the pattern for his quest has already been set. Rush! Then: delay, delay, delay, delay, delay. Five obstacles for every success.

It begins to hail; particles of ice pound the phone box. Ratatatatat.

'Hello?' An adult voice at last.

'Chrissie?'

'No, I'll just get her. Mum!' Neal has to adjust, remind himself what generation he resides in, because for a minute he thought the wee girl could be Chrissie's. But wait a minute – she could be. Chrissie must be no more than forty-five.

'Yes? Hello?'

'Chrissie? Sorry to bother you, this is Neal Munro. You might not remember me but I used to live with your sister. Long time ago, at Brae Cottage.'

'Neal? Of course I remember you! Ali used to say you were her best friend.'

'She did? I mean, yes, we were great pals, but then . . . '

'And you took her off after the funeral – where did yous go?'

'She told you then, did she?'

'She didn't need to, we all saw yous two just head off north like that.'

'No, I mean, did she tell you where we went?'

'I'd hardly ask you if she had, no, she acted like Madame Mystery.'

'Ah. It's not what you think.'

'You've no idea what I think. One of yous could have had the consideration to phone me, but I'm no complaining. I was worried sick. We all were.'

'Sorry, Chrissie. We should have phoned. Sorry.'

'Please, no need. It's over,' she says in a tone that says it'll never be over.

'You've a wife, right?' she says.

'Aye. Sally. Her name is Sally.'

'Thought so.'

'Yes.' Damn! Sally! Good, sweet, safe Sally. What in the world is he doing?

Somewhere a baby begins to scream, and a woman's voice soothes it.

'But tell me,' Chrissie says, unfazed by his pause. 'How can I help you, Neal?'

'I'm just trying to reach her. Your sister. Do you know where she is?'

94

'No. I do not, as it happens.' Snippily.

'No idea at all? I've tried ringing, and . . .'

'Oh, she's not answering her phone. Or her door, come to that.'

'Me neither. I mean, I tried her door too.'

'I don't know any more than you, Neal. Look, I'll see you around, eh? Got to go now.'

'But you must have more ideas than me. I hardly know her. I feel terrible.'

'Well,' in a slightly less miffed tone. 'She said she might go stay over the west, stay with a friend, Kate, and until this morning I just assumed she'd done that. But she's not there either.'

'Oh dear. Are you worried? Isn't it odd she wouldn't tell you?'

'We're close, don't get me wrong, but you know how it is. We each have our own lives. I've got four grandchildren now, and one on the way. It might be twins, it runs in the family. Then I'd have six grandchildren.'

'Well, that's, that's just wonderful Chrissie. Congratulations,' mumbles Neal, because she seems to be claiming these children, this vicarious fecundity, with such pride. Plus, talking about her kids, she seems to have forgotten she hates him.

'Thank you, but it's no picnic I can tell you. Kids these days, they cost the earth. Have you any kids?'

'No. No, we decided to leave all that to everyone else.' The response he always trots out. It's so quiet in the box, suddenly. Neal glances out he sees snow silently floating down. There is a muffled sound to the traffic.

'Oh! Ach well, I suppose with no kids, you get holidays abroad and a nice clean house. Can't blame you for the choice.'

Neal lives in a not perfectly clean house and has never been abroad for a sunshine holiday. He can't, right now, recall choosing definitely not to have kids – had there been a conversation? Must have been. And he's certainly never yearned for kids.

'So. I better let you go, Chrissie. Thanks.'

'Aye, that's alright.'

'Just I've been worried about Ali.'

'Same, same. Can't imagine where she's been, where she is. I mean, you'd think she'd let me know, where she was and that. I even wondered if she was maybe with you.'

'No! Not me.'

'I think I'll go to the police.'

'Report her as missing?'

'Yes. Aye. Well, she is, isn't she?'

'Yes, it's a good idea. Will I come with you?' So, his instincts are correct. It is an emergency!

'Aye? Aye, alright then. You don't need to, but why not.' Though he can hear in her hesitation, there might indeed be reasons why not. Like why does he care now, all of sudden? Some best friend he turned out to be. But the words *missing person* – it makes him think of limp bodies in ditches. Lifeless eyes, bluish skin.

'I'll meet you at the Alness police station in an hour,' says Chrissie, before hanging up to the sound of infantile squawking. The way she says Alness strikes Neal as odd. Then he remembers that Alnessians pronounce it their own way – *Al*ness, whereas folk from Evanton and beyond tend to call it Al*ness*. Reminds himself to pronounce it respectfully. *Al*ness.

Chrissie is recognisably Chrissie. Her laugh is rough, her voice chain-smoker gravelly. He greets her without drama.

She greets him in a similar manner, as if it's been a few weeks not seventeen years, and they were never bosom buddies in the first place. They enter the police station.

'Hey there, Billy, what's the craic?' she says to one of the milling uniforms.

'You're seeing it, Chrissie. And what's doing with you the day?'

'We're needing to report Ali – she's no been home for ages.'

Billy sighs and tsks. 'Ali, Ali,' he says. 'Poor Ali. I'll just get the forms. Hold on.' He returns and they all sit in a small room. Billy writes for a few minutes. Neal presumes it's the details he already knows. Name and address.

'Age?'

'Forty-one. I think. Yes, forty-one,' says Chrissie.

'Last seen?'

'By me? It was, uh, let's see, the fifteenth of January. I'd been with her since it happened, then left her after ten days. I had to get back home. I remember now, she was in the bath. She said she might visit a friend in Gairloch for a while, have a change of scene, and when I couldn't get through to her later, I assumed she'd just gone and done that. Her car was gone, and her house locked.'

'So, missing for three days. Not very long, really. Has anyone else seen her since?'

'Not that I know of. She never went west at all. Kate, it turns out, is away down in Glasgow. I spoke to her this morning. She thinks it's very worrying, not like Ali, and I agree. And Neal here hasn't seen her either.'

Billy turns his attention to Neal. Frowns. 'Are you related to Alison?'

'No. An old friend.'

'Not a boyfriend?'

'No.'

'No?' Squinting his eyes.

'No.'

'Do you have any idea where she might have gone off to?'

'None, I'm afraid. It seems very odd, and well, worrying that she hasn't been in touch with her sister.'

'I agree. Very odd, indeed,' says Chrissie ominously.

'How about the *why*? Do either of you know why she might want to disappear?'

'Billy! Of course!' Chrissie says scornfully.

Billy's pen is poised. 'Aye. But for the record, like. Reason?'

'Bereavement. Calum. Just write down that her only son died suddenly in a car accident. They were very close. You *know* that, Billy.'

'On the A9, wasn't it? Terrible.'

'Aye.'

Pause. Then Billy squares his shoulders and says, 'Don't take offence or anything, Chrissie, it's just one of the questions we have to ask – see, it's on my list. Did Ali have any drug or alcohol problems?'

'I'm not offended, daft man. No, not that I knew of. Liked a few lagers, that's all.'

'Any mental health problems?

'Eh? Like was she crazy? Course she was. Demented with grief. You think she might've topped herself, don't you?'

'Suicide can be one of the explanations. On rare, very rare, occasions, Chrissie. I wouldn't worry about it, it's unlikely.'

Neal has a sudden image of Alison in the firth, water logged, grey fish nibbling on her fingers. He pales, blinks fast, swallows hard.

'Right,' says Chrissie, and her voice starts to wobble. 'Well, I've thought of it already myself. I'd say it was not so very unlikely, in her case. She's always been a bittie on the dour side. Not that she didn't crack jokes half the day. Just never seemed that content in herself. Bit of a loner, really.'

'Still. Let's hope not,' says Billy, looking down at his paper. 'Any health problems in general? Was she on any medication, for instance, or seeing the doctor about anything?'

'No. She was fit enough.'

'Do you have a recent photograph?'

'Aye.' Chrissie, to Neal's amazement, pulls a photograph of Alison out of her bag. How did she know she'd be asked? It's all he can do to not grab it, have a look for himself.

'Do you think she took anything with her? Have you had a look round her house, noticed anything? Missing suitcases, coats, passports, that kind of thing.'

'Actually, I've not been round her place. Though I have the key. Silly of me, I don't know why I didn't think of it. Here, do you need the key?'

'Aye, but I think it's better if you come with us.'

'Well, just tell me when. I can get off work.'

'Aye, fine Chrissie. Ta.'

Billy writes for another three minutes, frowning with concentration. Asks for contact details. For bank, employer and car details.

'Right, then,' he finally says, rising. 'We'll see what we can do.'

'What will you do?' asks Neal confidently, wanting to show Chrissie he's a useful type of man to bring along after all.

'We'll wait a few more days to see if she turns up. If she doesn't, we'll post this information with the other missing persons. We'll check the hospital and shelters. We'll interview her employer and co-workers. Talk to her neighbours. Ask her bank if she's used her account at all. The phone company, see if she's made any calls. Check out her car, see if it's been abandoned anywhere.'

'I see.' All these avenues to explore! Neal feels hopeful for a second. He'd not imagined so many ways of looking for someone.

'I know it's a worry. But ninety-nine percent of missing persons turn up after a day or two, maybe a week or two,' says Billy. He stands up, extends his hand to Chrissie, then Neal. 'We can only hope for the best. Probably she's not wanting to be found just now, but is fine. Just licking her wounds somewhere.'

Chrissie walks home the long way to make up for all the pancakes she ate earlier. Down the High Street, up one lane, then another. It's snowing quite heavily now, but there is no wind and it feels weirdly warm. The flakes cling to her hair almost decoratively. She walks and walks, breathing heavily. Then because she had ten pieces of bacon as well, she walks back to the High Street and repeats her journey. Binging equals brisk walks. Pauses by the bakery, then squares her shoulders and walks on. Past the café with folk sitting, drinking tea and eating cakes.

When she passes the church the second time, she pops inside because her feet are wet, there's no food to tempt her in a church, and besides she is suddenly too tired to walk. Not a thing she does often. In fact, aside from funerals and weddings, pretty much never. It is empty and strangely muted, given the traffic nearby. She sits, her face slumped, and catches her breath. Hasn't smoked in years, but still feels it. Has no thoughts beyond, *To hell with you, Ali! I do not need this!* Starts to breathe easier, calm down. Begins to enjoy a sense of detachment, in the quiet and shadows. Alone! Lets her eyes slide shut. Then an old man – a minister – comes in a side door and she opens her eyes with irritation. He doesn't notice her, and she can't help watching him. What's he doing? Aside from ruining it for her.

Henry goes about his business slowly. Lately, everything he does is in slow motion. He shuffles papers, stacks hymnals, straightens pews. Finally looks up.

'Hello,' he says.

'Hello,' says Chrissie.

'Can I help you?'

'No thank you. Just, you know. Sitting a minute.'

'Stay as long as you like. Not a nice day, is it?'

'Thanks, but I better go now.'

Chrissie gathers herself. Wraps her scarf round her neck again, and heads home. Reads the poster by the door. You Are Not Alone. *The hell I'm not,* she thinks.

Another poster: God Loves You. And You and You. *Well! That may be so, but it's unrequited love on a colossal scale.*

Henry sits in the front pew a moment. Imagines being Chrissie. He knows her vaguely, though not her name. He guesses she is not a believer. Allows himself to imagine being her for a minute. A nothingness after death. To sack God was to eliminate protection and purpose. Like orphaning oneself at a vulnerable age. The world, not a cosy place after all. Stark and scary. How can Henry imagine this so easily? Because since Calum's funeral, he's been unable to think of anything else. His deep dark secret. He did not know Calum, not really, yet that particular funeral had felt the saddest he'd ever conducted. After watching those boys, those pallbearers, he'd felt their godless version of the world slice right through his chest to his backbone. He saw how it was to live godlessly.

Yes, Henry is having doubts. Has his religion, his life's vocation, just been a rather sweet but childish security blanket? He thinks of a bumper sticker he saw recently: What if the hokey cokey really *is* what it's all about? No heaven or hell. No reward for good behaviour, no chance of seeing lost loved ones again. No divine witness to all his endeavours. This makes him shiver of course, but not just with fear. He shivers because thinking this way is also strangely thrilling. Life, as a one-shot deal, is actually kind of exciting.

But what is he thinking? This way of thinking cannot be good for him.

He closes his eyes and says the Our Father silently. Tries to think about each phrase, and let it be real again. Feels a deep ache, a homesickness for his faith as it seeps away. Then he starts reading the hymn book, singing in his head. *Oh let us thanks to God give, Jesus died so we may live.* The phrase is one that's always comforted him, but today he thinks of another interpretation. It's obvious. Grief makes us live more deeply. Knowing we will die makes sense of life.

But Jesus died for our sins? Now that was a harder nut to crack. He used to be able to imagine a specific human being called Jesus. That he existed once, he still believes, but right this minute, Henry's Jesus is not very spiritual at all. If he was not the Son of God, who was he? Maybe just a poor bastard who happened to be born in the right place at the right time, and then about thirty years later, be in the wrong place at the wrong time. Maybe it just grew out of proportion then. Famous because he was famous, like the Mona Lisa. Or Shakespeare, who Henry secretly suspects is overrated to the point of no return. But if Jesus wasn't the son of God, it certainly wasn't his fault millions burdened him with the weight of that role. Talk about pressure. What if he was just a decent bloke? Said a few offhand philosophical remarks, did a few casual kindnesses that snowballed. Maybe he just had a knack for sounding clever, and happened to be born with charisma in a town full of ugly people.

Anyway, thinks the new cynical Henry, what's the big deal about dying for other people? People have always sacrificed their lives to save others. It's one of the better things about the human race. Probably since apes noticed that the occasional selfless act ensured the survival of their group, and the selfish apes over in the next cave were all dying out. Millions of people have died so others could live. So how was Jesus different? Maybe he wasn't. People always need scapegoats and heroes in equal measure, and maybe Jesus fit both bills, but unwittingly. Accidentally. Not a clue his name would still be revered twenty-one centuries later. Poor bastard, dying so young. High price for fame. He feels sorry for Jesus now.

Henry, considering the possibility of no God, feels sorry for everyone, including himself. What a strange precarious thing, life without God. *Lonely.* Could he ever get used to it? He feels so old today, incapable of change, and yet. And yet.

Neal parks his car in the snowy car park, prepares to go back to work. Checks his face in the rear-view mirror. He doesn't feel like himself, and wants proof. Yep, same eye wrinkles and aging neck, same thinning red hair. He tries to imagine Alison somewhere warm and safe. Licking her wounds, as the policeman had said. But licking wounds brings death and the grey fish back into Neal's mind, all wet and just the kind of thing that happens.

Janet's Wet Skin

Alice is amazed. Or as amazed as anyone can be who doesn't have an emotional life whatsoever, whose heart has hollowed out. With almost zero effort she's imposed a structure on her life again. Or perhaps it's the other way around. Since she's done nothing to invite a life, would have happily lived in a vacuum, would have happily *died* in a vacuum, life has gravitated to her. Sucked itself in, filled in the gaps of her unguarded apathy. And for all this structure, she had to look no further than Teddy, nearly the first person she'd talked to in Glasgow.

Has it been luck, or is this something about the world she hadn't realised? Maybe her amazement is naive, the result of spending her life in her birthplace. Maybe it's common knowledge that almost every individual can become the door for someone to walk through and create a whole new life. That all you need is that one friendly person. That the universe is pulsating with potential lives. That you can move as far as you want, as quickly as you can – wherever you stop, that is where your life will start to grow again. No particular single life with your name attached to it, waiting for just you. This thought makes her feel a bit stoned, as if a slight wrong turning on her way home from work might slip her into a whole different life yet again. Such a profound change of circumstances should not be so effortless.

She can clearly picture her old life as if it is still there with her in it, just up the A9, intact and unaware. Like an exhibit in a museum. She can even smell it, feel how it felt to be Alison. Chrissie on the phone, nagging her about something stupid. The toast burning again, must bin that toaster. The Thursday lager lunch with the girls from Virgin. Vivien's orange neck and Shirley's cigarette dangling while she yackety-yacked. The constant drone of voices, both in the call centre and in her headset. Eight hours of talking about things she didn't care about, to people she didn't care about, till her own voice was hoarse. It was white noise, and cut her off from thinking anything at all. She can clearly see her favourite yellow chair in the staff lounge. The butts over-flowing in that tin ashtray, and the clock with the hands that seemed to move so slowly when she was working, so quickly on her breaks. The supervisor glaring if she was one minute late, for Christ sake.

But now all of these things are like a place she visited briefly, two or three times perhaps, in her childhood. She was not so firmly rooted in it after all, and now she is not there at all. She feels nothing, not even a vague affection. Do many people build new lives out of random events? Chance meetings and impulses and accidents? And are such lives less valuable, less legitimate than planned logical lives? It seems likely that what has happened to her is not uncommon. Like a million people, like Alness itself, she has crumpled to nothing, then re-invented herself.

But what to do with this knowledge? Alice would like to know. Then decides it's probably wisest to just work with what she has, with where she is, with who she has become. What else is there to do, but be quiet and make the best of things? Her new life doesn't involve a lot of talking, provides a lot of time for thinking. Her tasks are menial, and Monday to Friday amount to roughly twenty-five a day.

7:00: Escort Janet to toilet, help her on and off toilet, wiping bum if necessary.

Insert Janet's teeth. Slippery, yellow things attached to pink plastic.

Escort Janet back to bedroom, turn on radio for her. Radio 4.

Kitchen: Boil eggs, make white toast and weak tea.

Bedroom again: Help Janet dress.

Comb her hair, check room temperature.

Small talk, shouted, about the weather. About two minutes worth.

Follow Janet slowly into kitchen, arrange chair (where she'll spend most of the day) so she can reach the remote and telly guide.

Witness the sliding of the egg and toast into prune-wrinkly mouth, listen to mastication and swallowing.

Clean crumbs and egg yolk off Janet's cardigan.

Have two-minute goodbye conversation. Yes, I have to go now. Yes, Teddy is fine, not sick. Yes, he's a good man, you raised him well. Yes, I am coming back. No my name is not Elisabeth, I am Alice. Yes, the remote is here, and the heating is not broken, it is working and it is on.

11:30: walk five minutes to work.

Wait on tables at The Swan.

Talk to customers about weather.

Say thank you at least fifty-three times. Remember not to shout, as is her habit at home (home?!), Janet being a bit deaf.

Talk to Teddy, wash dishes, set tables, fill saltshakers and sugar bowls.

Lunch break at 2:30, read papers left by customers.

Eat anything. Whatever Teddy put in front of her. Whatever is not selling much that day. Yesterday's donuts.

Work till 4:00, home to escort Janet to toilet again.

Heat tins of stew for Janet, followed by weak tea and a Mr Kipling cake. Bakewell tart, usually.

Sponge-bathe parts of Janet's body – torso and feet on alternate days, face and hands every day.

Put Janet's nightie on her.

9:00: Escort Janet to her bedroom, settle her in bed.

Read Agatha Christie or Maeve Binchy loudly till she falls asleep, her old lady breath wafting her moustache hairs in a hypnotic fashion. Hypnotic to Alice, anyway. She sits some evenings and just watches the old face.

Brush her own teeth, undress, climb into bed. Sleep, a while.

She has twice gone out on Saturday nights, after Janet is in bed. Gone to neighbourhood pubs and ordered a pint. But weirdly, the stuff tastes vile to her each time and she cannot finish it. More proof of utter alteration of her character. Alison loved nothing more than a pint or two, but Alice is a teetotaller. What the fuck? Or, in Alice-language: Goodness me, what on earth is happening?

Mostly she spends her weekends in her room, or downstairs with Janet, watching television. Janet always naps in her chair half way through watching a late morning show about cooking, and Alison takes charge of the remote then. Mutes the commercials about haemorrhoid cream, chairs that tip arthritic grandfathers out, life insurance for pensioners. Watches old movies, and sometimes she falls asleep in her chair too. She is so sleepy these days, all the time.

'Here, are you married?' asks Janet one evening, while having her chest and back sponged by Alice. They are in Janet's bedroom because it's warmer than the bathroom tonight, and towels are on the floor around her. Janet keeps her eyes closed for the sponging, and often talks. She feels less naked, eyes closed. Such a nuisance, the way her joints won't even allow her to wash her own body. But the gas fire is lit, and a sensual pleasure comes from the soft wetness of the sponge, and its circular movements. Her skin feels thirsty.

'Married? No,' says Alice, wringing out the sponge. 'Were you ever married?'

'Ha! Course I was, long enough to get Teddy started. Three whole months. Couldn't abide it.'

Alice laughs for the first time in weeks. Other people's maladjustments to life had always pleased Alison. Moments like these, she feels her old self – that happily grumpy rather shallow hedonistic person – so near her heart lunges as if an old friend has unexpectedly walked in the room. But no, it's gone already, just a flicker that was all, and she is back in her new strange self.

She gently washes then pats dry Janet's papery skin. It doesn't repulse her because, unlike Alison, Alice is not squeamish in the least. In fact, she likes to touch Janet's skin, and in her new contemplative way, to think about all the Janets still encased somewhere inside. The infant Janet, and the schoolgirl, the young mother, the middle-aged woman. A historical monument, this old woman. Janet is the only person she touches now, and some days she looks forward to this evening bathing session. Alice sprinkles some talc, then slips a clean cotton nightgown over Janet's head. What cannot be put right by a good warm bath and talc and clean cotton bedclothes? Well, aside from the sudden death of an offspring.

'And why was that? Why didn't you like your husband suddenly?'

'Oh, it was his voice,' says Janet, after a moment. 'I'm fussy about things like that. Voices and laughs. Didn't realise it at the time, of course, just married the bugger, didn't I. Then wham bam, three days later I hear him laugh. Hadn't properly noticed it before. His laugh was so sudden! So barking! I went off him right there and then. Once I get like that, there's no shifting it, it's a case of irreversible disgust.' She rolls her r's so hard, she spits a little. 'So I cut my losses and sent him packing.'

'Quite right, quite right,' agrees Alice. 'Who could live with a horrible laugh?'

She settles Janet into bed, tucks her in. The fire sputters conversationally, and the rain hammering against the window makes the room seem even cosier.

'So, did you ever fancy someone longer than three months?' asks Alice, but Janet has dropped into one of her sudden sleeps and Alice tidies up the bedroom and then the kitchen. She moves slowly, washes the dinner dishes, dries them and puts them away.

Later she stands at the dark window in the kitchen and leans her forehead against the glass. Lets it cool her. Then hears an extraordinary sound. It can't be what it sounds like. She looks out onto the wet dark street, and there he is. There's no traffic, there's suddenly no rain or wind, and in the middle of the street there's a boy, about ten, who is bouncing a ball down the street. It makes a hollow rubbery noise, and the bouncing is so steady she finds herself tapping her fingers on the glass to the rhythm. The streetlamps cast a yellow light – depressing, unflattering to every object but the boy. The boy is lovely. Especially it is lovely the way his walk is so light hearted, despite the dark and the lateness, the dangers of being in the middle of the road. Alice begins to open the window, to shout to him, Get out of the road! Shouldn't you be home? Must be near your bedtime!

Three young women, stiletto-heeled and scantily clad, turn the corner, strut their stuff past the boy. Shrieking and giggling, drunk. At first the boy just grabs his ball and freezes, then as they pass, he turns too, facing Alice. And then he mimics their strut and swagger, with his skinny ten-year-old body. Lifts his heels off the ground and becomes, for a second, a parody of a twenty-one-year-old girl on the pull, his shoulders swinging, his head tossing non-existent hair. It is so surprising, Alice stops breathing. The top of her head feels agitated, as if a breeze has lifted up her scalp and tickled her grey matter. And suddenly everything, not just this boy and the giggling girls, but everything inside this house and outside this window seems a slow parade of beauty and sorrow. Beautiful sorrow, sad beauty, back and forth, beginning and ending, all at the same time. The unbearable is borne every minute, and the loveliness of life is borne too. In most cases, secretly, because how can anyone really know what another person is feeling? (Alison would never have thought about this.)

She watches the boy till he steps onto the safety of the pavement, and turns the corner at the end of the street. The second he's gone, the rain returns, and the wind. The air howls with it, the house complains back loudly with whistles and groans. She opens the window and drinks in the wild night. Ah! Out of the sludge of her days, this moment. She feels time rush around her, like this wind, and the wind is everything that has happened and is happening. Here I am, looking out this window and remembering Calum, and that boy, those girls, the sound of that ball bouncing, and maybe the main truth about life is that it's temporary. Maybe *that* is the beauty. Nothing lasts. Not even love, despite what the songs and poems say. If it did last, it wouldn't be so precious. (Alison would never have thought about this either. If this were a television programme, she would immediately switch channels. Find a soap, or a reality show.)

Then the phone rings, the kettle boils, and she tucks this moment, wrapped up in her awareness, into a safe place. Private, but accessible should she need it. Oh, who is she kidding? Of course she'll need it. Probably tomorrow, in fact.

A9

Roads are not still. They may seem solid, permanent, the only unchanging thing in a world of motion, but that is illusion. If the A9 between Inverness and Scrabster had been recorded on film since it began then viewed at high speed, it would wriggle about on the screen like a worm. Curling through villages, then looping around those same villages. Meandering through inland glens, then suddenly shooting over new bridges instead. Twisty roads becoming straight, dizzy roundabouts popping up like varicose veins. Lay-bys appearing then disappearing, then appearing again a mile further. Single tracks morphing into two lanes.

Roads never stay the same. They are constantly eroding, while at the same time they are constantly in the process of improvement. At least that is the intention. The assumption being that we all want to get somewhere else quicker than we did yesterday.

Zara is late for work, speeding south on the A9. She approaches the memorial and outwardly seems unaware of it. But in her mind, the Calum's Accident movie begins

112

again. She cannot even think about Calum without it happening. Over and over, always slightly different.

Calum is shutting his car door, in that unnecessarily forceful way young men have. Puts on his seatbelt, starts the ignition, heads down the A9 with that new blue Nokia sliding about on the passenger seat. He checks in the rear-view mirror to see if that spot on his forehead is still there, and it is. He frowns, briefly fingers it. Notices that the road is not icy but is this close to being black ice. He can tell because of the way the steering wheel responds so easily, so quickly. He is intuitive about his car, and the tiniest change registers in his mind. Yep. The road is degrees away from an ice skating rink, but he's okay. No traffic, no rain to make the road more slippery, the sky is a calming blue. The phone begins to ring and he gropes for it, at first keeping his eyes carefully on the road. It eludes him, and he glances over, stretches his arm further. He hears his own voice shout *Zara!* No, no. It's *Mum!* he's shouting this time. *Mum!* He sounds frightened. And also pissed off. Very.

She passes the memorial as the movie finishes. It only takes a few seconds these days.

'Happy Valentine's Day, my darling,' says Zara out loud. 'Miss that ass. Nicest ass in the universe,' she adds tearfully. She is alone in the car and can say anything she likes.

The floral tributes are long gone and it is still too early for Zara's efforts to be noticeable, but people who knew Calum now think of that bit of A9 as the Calum Place. Some prefer not to look as they drive by. Others look fearfully, and each time with that terrible sadness again, and a version of the movie Zara sees. Some nod quickly but solemnly; others slow their driving and look hard, as if expecting to see something.

Some of his friends (but not Finn or William), the pallbearers, meet regularly now. Have a pint, or kick a football around. They like to talk about it. About Calum, about the funeral, about the A9, about that particular spot.

The ones who drive, drive more carefully. For a while.

Part Four

March, April & May 1996

Neal and Sally Drink Baileys

Neal is putting the dishes and cutlery into the dishwasher, while thinking about Alison and Calum as usual. These thoughts override, ride through at a fast gallop, everything else he thinks about these days. Do people essentially change? He used to think not. Now he wonders.

He avoids the mirror while shaving these days, almost shy. The pornographic daydreams have waned, thank god. They just made him feel squalid. It turns out Neal doesn't actually enjoy impersonal arousal. In fact, it kind of scares him, and instead of sex, now he remembers grocery shopping with Alison, and Calum's nine-year-old voice asking, 'Will ya come play footie in the rain, 'cause it's cool fun to slide in the mud, innit, Dad?'

Remembers an incident involving a tooth under a pillow and a stoned tooth fairy.

He pictures Alison sleeping as she had that Golspie night, her slack face, her sad odour. The way she'd wanted to be ... expunged, somehow. That is the Alison, the damaged desperate Alison, that his love can get its teeth into. In a way, he sees her now more vividly than he had at the time, when he was too distracted by the surprise of her. But then Neal has always been chockfull of delayed reaction.

Alison! He calls her name silently, frequently. It's a wonder he doesn't forget sometimes and shout *Alison!* out loud in the middle of Tesco, or at work. He has to keep shouting her name, otherwise, how will he ever find her? He has something important to tell her, but where the hell is she? And what is he going to tell her? Something, something lodged in his throat right now. She is somewhere right now, or her body is. Things change, but nothing disappears completely. She could be eating chips and watching telly somewhere right now. Or she is not eating chips and watching telly, she is dead, in the firth. Chips for some other living thing. Incorporated into the body of some grey fish. It's very possible, indeed probable, he will never see Alison again.

The dishwasher is turned on now; it emits a rhythmic liquid swishing noise, which Neal quite likes. It's soothing. Almost as good as Rogie Falls, the Skiach, the waves at Rosemarkie. He sighs, wonders if he is going insane.

He remembers the winter Alison moved in. It'd all happened quite suddenly – one day she was the landlord's daughter, motherless single mum, distant and glowering, and the next day she was at his door with a black bin bag in one hand and her other hand dragging her weeping five-year-old son. Neal had just stood there, staring at her.

'Look, Neal, would you mind if I bide here a whiles, I can use the spare wee room at the back. My dad's being a cunt, to be honest. Not having it anymore. Calum will no wake you, he's quiet in the mornings, honest, he's only whinging now cause he's tired, aren't you, pet? There, there, we'll go to bed now, and hey – I'm sure you could use having a lassie round the place, hey? Not that I'll be doing your washing up or anything.'

118

'Okay.'

She'd laughed harshly. Stepped past him into the hall.

'So that's great, right, well good, that's settled.'

Calum, who'd paused his whinging, recommenced in a higher decibel. Like a dying cow. Snot was running into his mouth, he was completely beyond caring. Neal had watched her drag Calum into the room that only contained an old mattress on the floor and an even more ancient quilt and pillow. No sheet. She'd turned her head just once to nod and mouth *thank you*, over the howls. Smiled briefly, then the door was shut, and Neal could clearly hear the sound of two crying voices behind the closed door. But he wasn't alarmed or angry. No. He was bewildered. And embarrassed, because the place was a tip. And excited, because Alison was sexy, in a young, buxom, jaded way.

Then much later that night, she'd emerged. Offered Neal a joint, laughed about her situation. The nagging uptight dad, the bedwetting Calum, her boring job in the paper shop. It was nice to have her there. Everything about the house felt warmer.

That night Alison crawled into Neal's bed for the first time, woke him and didn't say anything. Just crawled under the blankets, curled up away from him, and he'd held her silently till she'd fallen asleep. Watched her face, her pale eyelids twitching in some dream, her plump breasts and dark nipples plainly outlined in her white cotton t-shirt. He could have wept with longing.

And that was that. She didn't like to sleep alone, but she obviously didn't fancy Neal at all.

'You dinna mind, do you? Only it's just lovely to sleep with you some nights. Let me know if you start minding, or get a girlfriend or something.'

'Aye. Alright.'

Alison brought a whole social world with her, and the house was often full of young women in Indian print skirts with sequins, or faded jeans with dozens of patches. Air thick with patchouli and sandalwood. And unlike the girls who on the surface embraced feminism but spent all day making tea for their long-haired lovers and effacing their selves, Ali and her friends were a rambunctious, confident lot. Giggling and chattering and getting high, always leaving the sink full of cups and mugs.

Did Neal mind? He did not. Not one bit. But when all those young men started visiting Alison, well, that was a different matter.

Neal sighs. Sally is ironing in the sitting room so she can watch *EastEnders*. Neal watches with her for a few minutes, then gets up and stretches self-consciously. He doesn't really need a stretch, but wants to camouflage the importance of this question:

'Where's that old box of photos and things?'

'What? What old box?'

Phil is shouting his cockney rage in Albert Square, while Pat heaves her bosom and sweeps her front steps.

'You know.' He yawns artificially. 'From when I moved in. You put it somewhere. My old stuff.'

A lull on Albert Square and Sally turns to focus on Neal.

'When you moved here? You mean, seventeen years ago?'

'Aye. Remember? It had my stuff in it. From the old days.'

'Ah.'

'Do you remember? You must, Sally. I think it was the box that said Spanish Oranges on it. White, with green letters. I can see it.'

Sally is the archivist of all domestic articles; their whereabouts and state of repair are at her mental fingertips. A pair of garden shears bought in 1987? His own P60s? The TCP? Neal relies on her utterly.

'Let me think, Neal. Wait a minute.' She closes her eyes and visualises their less used storage spaces. Under the stairs, the small crawl space loft, the garden shed.

'Why are you wanting it, anyway?' Opening her eyes. Does she sense something?

'Oh, just, you know. Curious. Been so long. Thought I recognised some of the faces at the funeral. Got me to thinking.'

'Oh, Neal. As if you'd ever look any of them up. What are you like? You only knew them a little while, and never gave them a second thought, after.'

'Still . . . that box had some records in it, too, I think. Stackridge. Al Stewart. Hawkwind. Lothar and the Hand People. Tubular Bells.'

'As if we still had a record player! Heavens, Neal, are you having a mid-life crisis? I've been reading about that, in *Cosmo*, it says all men get this menopause thingie too, and what you . . .'

'I think it had my Furry Freak Brothers comics too.'

Sally sighs. 'Whatever, Neal.'

'Look Sally, do you know where the box is or not?'

'Yes.'

'Where?'

'Gone. I chucked the lot years and years ago.'

'You what?'

'I probably even asked you. You were never bothered about old rubbish like that, Neal, or I would have saved it. How was I to know you'd have this . . . this urge now?'

121

'It had photographs and old address books, and things. It had my bellbottoms with the paisley insert.' He is whining, much to his humiliation.

'So? What are you wanting those things for? You can buy bellbottoms now, it's all come round again. If you can get them in your waist size. You can probably even get Stackridge on CD.' She narrows her eyes at him, gives him her wifely x-ray. 'Honestly, look at you. I'm sorry, I am, but what *is* your problem, Neal? What exactly is on your mind?'

Neal flinches – his mind is full of Alison – but Sally suddenly zooms back into *EastEnders*. Frank is kissing Pat, even though they're divorced and he tried to kill her a few hundred episodes ago. It's been a particularly wearing day at the returns counter. If she hears one more woman insist she has never worn that party dress, she will scream. She is too tired to think, too tired to talk. She needs television, and especially she needs to see if Grant Mitchell will get caught this time.

'Nothing, I just . . .'

'Shhh, Neal. Go put the kettle on, if you don't want to watch.'

'Jesus, Sally. You threw my stuff away. That was my stuff.'

But he puts the kettle on, and because he's cheated on his wife, he's not even angry by the time it boils. Guilt removes his entitlement to anger. On the fridge, held by a magnet, is the latest postcard from his father. The photo is of a man's hand clutching another bum. Orange skin with white bikini line. *Hey You! Waiting for you to visit! It ain't the Rivibloodiera, but it'd be a change from Dingle Dell. Hurry! xxx, the twa lovebirds.* Lovebirds indeed. Nothing is more vomit-inducing, thinks Neal, than a parent in love. He makes two cups of tea, grabs the biscuits, and carries them through.

'Thanks,' says Sally.

Neal sighs and drinks his tea. It has to travel past a painful lump on its way to his stomach. He can feel the shape and weight of this swelling. It is Ali-anxiety, and a sudden acute yearning for things he never thought he'd yearn for. Like the second track on the first side of *Songs for Beginners*, Graham Nash. And Sally is right, he might even have given permission to chuck out the box. The only reason the box had existed was because he'd been too lazy to sort through his stuff when he moved. Easier just to bung it all in a box. But now? Everything has changed. The amount of money he'd pay to see that box again is astronomical. Would make Sally consider booking him with a shrink on the sly, never mind what the article said in *Cosmopolitan*.

He sips his tea, half a mind on the prattle of the Albert Square residents, and the other half visualising the contents of the missing box. Sometimes it worries him a bit that he can't really remember how it felt to be young in the sixties, the seventies. When he sees hippies portrayed on television or movies, they always seem such an uncomfortable mixture of naivety and self-indulgence. Naff! But right now, with nostalgia pouring into him, he does remember. What had it been like?

For Neal, after his particular adolescence, it had simply been a relief to be with people who didn't make him feel apart. Maybe that was what it all boiled down to. Not just a common cause or rebelliousness, not just that pushing away of a whole generation of war-bred parents, but a sense of not-aloneness. Even now, visualising them all, his hippie friends from the seventies, from Brae Farm Cottage days, seem more charismatic and beautiful than any group of A-list Hollywood stars. He cannot recall feeling bored with any of them. Had they really been so beautiful, so interesting? Yes, he thinks now. Yes, oh yes. They'd been that lovely.

123

Were all young people beautiful to themselves? Probably, he admits to himself. But there'd been something different, he still feels, about that period – it had been like a party everyone had been invited to, no matter what your accent, religion, appearance. No matter if you had hair the colour of flaming carrots. The only ticket you needed was to be between fifteen and twenty-five. A huge, messy, loud, anarchic, tolerant gang and no one under thirty ever went to festivals or concerts. From a historian's point of view (which is to say Neal's), hippies had been a quirk – their sheer numbers gave them clout, and the times had handed them the common denominators of Viet Nam, economic ease (Nigg!), the Pill and marijuana. A heady cocktail, and even though it's sad getting older, he feels sorry for everyone born after the fifties. Then instantly feels ashamed, for wasn't it typical of his generation to think they'd invented something special?

He remembers some square black and white photos, stuffed into an old envelope. Some faded colour Polaroids too. Calum as a kid, in his too-long flares, skinny arms dangling from a too-small t-shirt. Ted and Mick with their strange Burmese cat, posed in the doorway to the one-roomed bothy they had altered into two rooms, with an arched doorway. Half-blind Eddie with his lopsided smile and squinting into the sun, wearing a tie-dyed t-shirt. Mandy, rolling a joint on the Tea for the Tillerman album cover, with king-size Rizla rolling papers and bits of card rolled into filters. Mary and Jen, shirtless in the garden on a hot afternoon; it was the summer everyone decided to lose their modesty. Alison between them with no shirt on either, her pillow breasts round and perfect, nipples like, uh, well, a bit like pink round jelly sweets. A joint in her hand, and her eyes on the photo taker, himself. No big smile, but such a haze of relaxation. So what, her eyes said. Here we are, and this is us. Here. Now. Want a hit?

Another photo – Calum sitting by himself in the corner by the fire, reading a *Beano*. Above him, a poster advertising Glastonbury. A peace-sign sticker in the corner.

Memories of photographs are like a silent film, and Neal supplies the soundtrack. Dylan, Lennon, Nick Drake, John Martyn.

Then, unbidden and unwanted, come memories not recorded on film. He remembers scary moments, when he wondered what he was going to do with his life. The nights he lay awake miserable, certain he would remain chaste till he died, an old wanker. If he ever got the hang of masturbation. Other men seemed to regard a daily wank as normal as brushing their teeth. They all got off with pretty girls, but he never even got off with himself. Oh, those girls with long straight hair and fringes that fell over their eyes, so they were always shaking their heads to see! Why did they never fancy him? He was a freak (not the cool kind), idealising his group of friends, never really belonging.

And what about those hours he used to spend trying to get lifts? Hitching to Dingwall in the pouring rain, car after car passing, drivers not even looking. And the times before he found the confidence to stop accepting every joint, times of getting too stoned, not being able to talk, having to go lie down till his mind quietened. Times when even the music seemed discordant and scary. Not always a happy-go-lucky party, then. Not for everyone, not all the time.

Still, if he wrote a Twenty Years Ago Today column based on his own life, it wouldn't list those bouts of getting soaked at roundabouts, those nights of insecurity, like the lists of war casualties and lost grey kid gloves. He wouldn't want anyone to read about those bits. No, he'd write a column listing the loveliness of his friends instead.

But where are they all now? He's been as careless with them as he's been with the box. Like Alison, they're probably all still around, but dispersed, disguised. A tribe in hiding. Maybe they'll re-emerge in their eighties, stop getting haircuts, taking baths, drive the staff in old folks homes demented with their loud music and demands for stronger drugs. They'll be so annoying!

'Sorry, Sally.' He's fond of his wife. She sits in the chair that has been her chair since it entered the house. Her eyes are tired and kind. In fact, he feels a surge of fondness break through his disappointment and exhaustion. It floods through his veins. Or is that the sweet tea raising his blood-sugar level? So hard to tell metabolic changes from love.

'What about?' *EastEnders* has finished, and she turns her attention to him.

'For shouting at you. About the box.'

'It's okay. Doesn't matter.'

She's like his oldest favourite pair of shoes, the ones he hasn't the heart to get rid of even though they let the water in. They're so soft, maybe one day he'll wear them again. They used to feel like a second skin.

'How was work?' she asks.

'Fine. Did Fifty-Four Years Ago Today. Tail end of War. Ads for Servants. Tonics for baldness and general torpor.'

'Tonics for torpor, eh? Fancy a bedtime drink? Glass of Baileys?' In the old days, a code for imminent sexual advances, but usually from him, not her. Coming from her, it might not be a code for anything.

'Uh, sure, Sal.'

She gets the drinks from the kitchen, and Neal wonders when they did it last. Not that long ago, a week, and then he wonders how many times they've done it altogether and what the average per year is. He tries and fails to remember any specific time. Not even the first kiss. He can remember it occurring – in his old Renault, her apologising for her breath smelling of garlic. He remembers feeling grateful. He'd clung to her, felt rescued. But what had the first kiss felt like? Had the surface of the earth become unstable? Had ordinary objects altered, become unrecognisable? No. All their amorous activities blurred into one sufficiently passionate but unmemorable act.

And then he thinks about time and how it used to go so slow, and events did not blur together. That last summer with Ali lasted about twelve years, yet Neal has trouble accounting for entire decades now, which makes his life feel, well, it feels blurry. At this rate, he'll be old and dead by tomorrow afternoon, latest. And his entire life flashing before his eyes will take no more than three seconds. *Phwet!!!* Gone.

Sally is not back yet – thoughts about time seem to take up no time whatsoever. She's just opened the bottle. Neal tells himself the reason he has so many vivid memories of those early days is because he'd been happy then. Ah, now, watch him closely – here comes another summer memory, pulled out of some sentimental file. A day before the sun was cancer-giving scary; a date-less day of doing nothing much. Drinking tea out of a tea-stained mug on the front steps of the cottage; barefoot, and hardly any clothes at all. No shirt, and a pair of cut-off jeans. The way his skin felt baked right through to the bone, and his muscles felt fluid and powerful, even in repose like this. Doing nothing. Killing an endless July afternoon. Ali just pottering in the garden. Calum pushing his Britain's combine harvester through some dandelions. Neal's entire being had been tingly with untapped possibilities. He should think about the past more often, it improves his looks. More relaxed, dreamy, a slight smile tugging at his lips, and a certain promising light in his half-closed eyes.

Sally brings the drinks – generous dollops slosh around in thick short glasses, ready to do the business, and Neal snaps out of his handsome-making trance. He drinks his Baileys.

'Come here, you,' he says and pulls Sally onto his lap.

A wife! How extraordinary to have a wife. Even more extraordinary that he can act like the kind of man who pulls his wife onto his lap. Like he's finally overcome his ginger hair and joined the mainstream human experience. This is good.

They brush the Baileys off their teeth and get into bed. He lays a hand on her thigh, slides her nightie up a bit, moves his mouth towards her mouth, but then she says she's tired, maybe in the morning, maybe some other night. He considers nagging her a bit, reminding her she quite likes it once they get going, but decides against it. Anyway, he's not that keen after all, as it turns out. Goodness, he's actually relieved! Is he tired of all this? They roll away from each other, bum to bum, and Neal's last thought is that he hasn't a clue what his wife's last thought is.

When he wakes, his first thought is this: Must find Alison. *Must find her.* Over breakfast, he listens to Sally talk on and on about her new haircut, which she is unhappy about, and he is intensely annoyed, *intensely annoyed*, she is not Alison.

He phones Chrissie when he gets to work, but no one answers.

Chrissie reaches for the phone, but the line is dead. Typical! She is slow these days, but then praying takes up so much time. She had no idea. No sooner does she start to visualise the people she wants God to look after then she goes off in a daydream. Gets nostalgic. Worse than looking through old photo albums. So she is slower now in general, but also more refreshed. Ever since that snowy day she'd reported Ali as missing and later stopped in the church. The old minister had irritated her and she'd left, but on the walk home she'd felt lighter somehow, despite the ten pieces of bacon and dozen pancakes and syrup.

And as she'd approached her own home, just out of curiosity, she recited the only prayer she knew by heart, The Lord's Prayer, to the beat of her own footsteps. Said it three times, and during that time did not fret about Ali or want to cry about Calum. Prayer as a displacement activity. Imagine Heaven, she orders herself, and up it flashes, all warm and cosy. Calum running over a green hill towards a rainbow. She doesn't care if it's true or not. It's legal, doesn't cost anything and it works.

But it's her secret, her new faith, and she guards it as if she's having an affair with a married man. She knows well enough what her daughters, what her pals, would say if they knew. Poor old Chrissie, off her head! Must have been losing her nephew, that did it. Must have been the shock. But she'll come to her senses, just wait. You know Chrissie, always going overboard, then hating herself. A binge kind of woman. Shame on her, but bless. As if Calum's death and Ali's disappearance were infectious viruses that lowered her immune system, allowing some toxic belief to creep under her defences. As if all she needed now was a good dose of antibiotics.

They would never get it, but as far as Chrissie's concerned, right now God is ace. Immortal souls! Who wouldn't want one? It's a win-win. If eternal life is true, then life is less heart-breaking. If it is not true, then at least she'll have got through these sad days with less pain, less depression. It's like discovering her Tesco Club Card points entitle her to free shopping forever if she'll only use them on the right days, in the right sequence, while doing a tap dance and eating a banana with the peel on. Distracting, even silly and embarrassing, but hey – what's she got to lose?

As for Jesus. Well, he was hot, obviously. She visualises brown eyes, medium height, broad shoulders, scruffy sandals, hippie hair. About twenty-four. Soothing voice, not a fussy eater, moderate drinker. Fatally attractive to women without trying, without caring. Serious magician, a proper miracle worker, Daddy's right-hand man. But fun, too. A man's man, lots of pals. Extremely popular kind of guy. Never boring, so a sense of humour, obviously. Self-mocking probably. Peter and Paul teasing him about the girls, like Magdalene. Feet-washing and loaf-multiplying were probably in-jokes. *Dude, cover your feet*, probably meant: *Danger! Female groupie approaching.* Basically, George Clooney with a beard and without a libido.

She replaces the phone with a sigh, closes her eyes and silently recommences her praying. Out loud, since she is alone in the house. Her husky voice whispers, '. . . on Earth as it is in Heaven; give us this day our daily wishes, I mean bread . . . this is what she looks like, God.' She squints her closed eyes, visualising her sister. Needing to talk to Ali is what she mostly uses God for. 'Her neck is probably not that orange anymore. Hair probably longer. Please look after her, if she's alive, and get her back to me. Tell her I'm worried sick, but tell her I'm not pissed off anymore. Tell the silly bitch to ring me right now! Sorry, sorry. Not angry, really.'

Pause. Sigh.

'If she's croaked, then still look after her, and tell her I'm asking for her anyway even if she is dead. Tell her I've lent her car to one of her nieces, as her own car needs too much done for the MOT, but she promises to look after it. Oh, and please do not tell her I am praying to you, right? Under no circumstances can Ali know I believe in you. I am serious. Stop defending yourself, you're not really getting it. No offence, God, but she'll think I'm taking a day off my senses. In the name of the Father, Son and Holy Spirit, amen.'

Then she combs her hair, puts on some lippy and goes to the minister's house, which is right next door to the church, a short walk away. She wants to ask him a prayer-related question. A bit like going to Citizen's Advice, that same expectant, slightly impatient urge to pick an expert's brain. No time for chitchat, just tell me. Knocks briskly on his door and waits. Knocks again, and once more.

By the time Henry opens it, Chrissie has gone. He stands there on the empty doorstep, looking vague, distracted. Not praying takes up so much time, and he is slow these days, slower than ever before. He thinks too much, and too hard.

This morning he's thinking about his father, a man he has not thought about for decades. His father's shoes, the way they were so shiny and black, and the sound they made when he entered the house every night. Heralding the end of the female-dominated phase of the day. He doesn't often think of his father, because he was only five when his father died. He remembers odd things, like the shiny shoes, and the tobacco smell of him. Old Holborn, he's since decided. There are black and white photographs of course, and these are what he was looking at when Chrissie first knocked.

131

Dad in army uniform, with two other soldiers, standing in front of a pub. A cocky look on all their faces. The wedding photos, the bride and groom sweetly serious, looking older than their twenty years. His parents, his sister and himself, on a picnic at Rosemarkie beach the summer he died. His father holding an infant awkwardly, with his own name and birth date in pencil on the back. His mother's young handwriting.

He can't recall the death itself, but he remembers a red tractor and a toy farm they were given by Auntie Phyllis about that time, and now he thinks it might have been a treat to console them. Toys to distract the children while the adults got on with the wake, the funeral arrangements, the whole packing away of a life.

But it's not those perfect little cows and sheep or the tractor with a steering wheel that turned that he's thinking about now. For the first time, he's not thinking about his own age at the time, but about the age of his father. He'd never asked, and never worked it out from his birth year – always felt his father was his father, and therefore a grown-up man. But now he sees his father was a boy. He was twenty-five, the year the flu epidemic swept over the Black Isle. Apparently Henry had it first, but recovered. He doesn't remember. Maybe he gave it to his father? No, no point in thinking like that. It was an epidemic, for heaven's sake.

He stares at his own self in the photographs as if he's a stranger he'd like to get to know. Looking for clues, willing to be sympathetic to any evidence of kindness, any hint of the way his life was going to unroll. He wants to like this boy, forgive him for not understanding the enormity of his loss. For quickly accepting his father's absence, for being distracted by the new red tractor. Now he thinks of it, he's sure a tiny plastic man came with the tractor. Yes, in a blue boiler suit, with a red hat. But his dad, what were the colour of his eyes? Only twenty-five, same age as Calum. A kid! With all the things every life has – a particular set of habits and quirks and dreams and memories and plans and moods. A favourite jumper, a dislike of tinned peas. A unique shape, just like every life has a unique shape, and its own particular momentum.

His father would have woken in the mornings of the week before he caught the flu, thinking about his day ahead, and maybe vestiges of any dreams he'd had. He'd have risen from bed, and perhaps think about leaving off shaving for a week, see how a moustache would look. His wife, Henry's mother, might have shouted at him again to hurry up, his eggs were getting cold, and he would have entered the cold morning kitchen scratching his face, and there they'd be: his young wife, her hair still in curlers; his baby daughter crawling on the floor; and his son, Henry, looking up from his boiled egg and soldiers of toast, a smile in his eyes. He'd have felt loved, but it would be such an ordinary feeling he wouldn't take note, just sit and spread marmalade on his toast. Just another day, no thoughts of death in it, and a week later he'd wake up with a fever, and a throat that wouldn't swallow. And now, a blink of time later, no living person remembers the colour of his eyes. His mother would know, but she's dead and the dead don't count anymore.

It is definitely lonelier without God and immortality, definitely harder work to be alive such a short time. Atheism puts more responsibility on the living to treasure lives, to remember them.

Henry closes the front door and slowly returns to the kitchen table, where the box of photos is spilled out.

'Who was it?'

He startles, as if his wife hasn't been in the kitchen all the time. She's quite deaf, so never heard Chrissie knocking.

'No one. No one was there.'

'That's funny. Never mind. Henry, I was thinking of going to Tesco today, we're out of milk. We're out of lots of things, in fact.'

She can still drive, unlike Henry, whose sight is too poor now. Luckily their frailties do not overlap yet, a fact that tickles them both. If they time it right, by the end they'll be a single competent (but very wrinkly) person.

'Alright, dear.'

'Do you want to come? Might do you good to get out.'

'No thank you.'

'Well, there's a bit of ham from last night in the fridge. For your lunch.'

'Thank you. I don't feel very hungry, but I might have it.'

'Henry. You never eat these days!'

'Alright! I'll eat it! Stop fussing!'

'Fine!'

So off she goes, bundled into her pink quilted coat, and her heart lifts as she heads down the A9. He's been worrying her a lot these last few months. So distant and polite, and tossing and turning all night.

She decides to treat herself to lunch in the Courtyard Café, and afterwards maybe buy that expensive red velveteen dressing gown she spotted in Cormacks last week. She loves her dear old Henry, of course she does, but my goodness, marriage is a long haul and she could use a day off some days.

Alice Has a Haircut

It's her day off. Alice is in her bedroom, her new bedroom that has nothing of her old life in it. The brown plastic container of ashes purporting to be Calum sits on the table by the window. The Calum Jar, as she refers to it. Calumjar. Caljar. One day, it'll be caja, small c. One day it will be forgotten somewhere, spilled heedlessly, mistaken for strange desert sand, for the sweepings from a cold fire, for anything but an accident-prone boy who hated talking and loved to run even on windy days.

She's cutting her fingernails, and then her toe nails. Clip clip clip, the brittle dead bits of herself flick onto the carpet. Along with long nails, facial hair also seems to be surfacing as taboo, no matter how deep her despair, how broken her heart. This morning she shaved her moustache and chin hair with a cheap disposable razor and wondered why on earth she'd messed about with creams and tweezers all those years.

She's sitting on her bed, on the candlewick cover – possibly the last bed in Scotland without a duvet. There's a wavy mirror above the chest of drawers opposite her. The chest of drawers is dark varnished wood, but not solid wood like oak – it's thin nasty veneer, and the varnish is flaking in places. It's the kind of furniture that is tossed daily on skips everywhere, along with hulking wardrobes and Danish coffee tables. Furniture that has had its day, and deserves to have had its day. Actually, very like the furniture in that ugly hotel room in Golspie, now she thinks of it. But it suits Alice.

Alice is a little tawdry too. Her clothes conceal anything attractive about her figure, her hair is lank and her face often looks blank. She is sweet but she has no taste, has Alice. She has had her day.

When she finishes her nails, she gets down on the floor and begins to pick up some of the bigger bits of fingernails, the dingy half-moons that might hurt her bare feet. Under the bed she notices her cheap suitcase and for no reason except it might be more fun than picking up fingernails, she decides to open it again. Have another look at one of her acquisitions. She'd not really looked at it properly that first day. Inside are two side pockets, and when she slips her hand into the first one, she finds a ring. This is the kind of event that has begun to seem normal to her, and her heart does not skip a beat. She's immune to surprise. The band is thin with wear. The stone is a small blue one, probably glass, she thinks. Yes, definitely a bit of cheap jewellery, but worn for many years. She holds it in her hand and thinks of the hall wallpaper, the faded daffodils and tartan. She puts the ring on and stands up. Imagine getting married. Imagine being married!

Her eyes graze her reflection in the mirror. Then return to study it. She frowns at her freckles, which now her fake tan has disappeared are more startling than ever. Skin like a speckled white egg. Then she notices her hair. Oh dear. Her blond shoulder-length hair is not only unwashed looking again, but it has an inch of dark roots. She badly needs a touch-up, and remembers suddenly she had an appointment for the seventeenth of January. She thinks for a second of Belinda, her hairdresser. How no matter what was happening, she always felt better after Belinda's ministrations. Belinda would've taken all this in hand, and not just the hair. Actually, so would her sister Chrissie. *Chrissie! Help me, Chrissie!*

The impossibility of Belinda or Chrissie rescuing her makes her feel panicky. Then she reaches for the nail scissors and begins to cut. First shank of hair to fall is nine inches long. She cuts right at the beginning of the blond, close to her scalp. Waits to feel horrified, but no – nothing. Then she smiles, or grimaces. Whispers, 'Oh dear!' and hacks away. Twenty minutes later, the floor and bed are covered with blond hair, hiding the fingernail and toenail clippings. It'll take a Hoover to sort out, too many fine hairs to settle on a brush and dustpan.

She looks at herself in the mirror. Is rather pleased with her uneven handiwork. She looks, for once, how she feels. Flayed. Hacked at. She rubs her hands roughly over her scalp till her hair stands straight up.

'What do you think, Calum? It'll do, eh?'

You look like death, Mum, so you do, answers Calum's voice, that old smile hidden in it.

Yes, Alice has started talking to her son again. What's more, he's started to talk back. And it is such a relief, after not speaking to him for two months. How on earth had she imagined she could live without talking to him again?

Alice goes out for a walk, gives her newly exposed scalp an airing. When she returns to her room, anticipating fresh cleanliness and order, a familiar smell catches at the back of her throat. Masculine sweat, fresh and pungent at the same time, as if from some wholesome exertion. She inhales as deeply as she can. It evaporates so quickly maybe she imagined it, but the setting sun has pierced the clouds and her room is momentarily bathed in light.

The Way the Clock Ticks Upsets Neal

Neal stands in the kitchen, bathed in the refrigerator light. There's a vague smile on his face. His guard is down, he's trundling through the minutes, mind on what to nibble. Thinking back on the column he wrote earlier. The fact that at one time, the Royal Hotel could accommodate three hundred cycles and their riders. How many riders to a bedroom? Were Victorian cyclists so thin they could squeeze three to a bed? Sally enters the room. She's been upstairs, making thumping noises, but this is the first time he's seen her since he got home from work about half an hour ago.

'Hey,' he says, not looking at her, reaching for some cheese.

'Neal. Listen, Neal.'

'What?' Something in her voice, his blood runs quicker, and he slowly turns.

'I've got something to say,' her voice high and tight. Damn, where has he heard that tone recently? He almost says, because he believes it to be true: *So do I. I love Alison Ross.* Those are the words that are rising even now. But Sally has staked out this moment, and his words remain swallowed.

'Aye? What's that, then. What're those bags? Are we going somewhere?'

'I'm leaving you, Neal.'

Neal laughs. Straightens from the fridge, a chunk of orange cheese forgotten in his left hand. Laughs again, giddily.

'What's so funny?'

'You're joking, right? Leaving me.' His head feels light. '*Sit down, Neal, I have something to tell you.* I mean, this is a joke, right? Right?' He feels his face burn.

'No. Not a joke. Now listen, Neal.'

'What would you go and do that for? What's wrong? We never even argue. I thought we were doing just great. We *are* doing just great. '

'Oh come on, Neal, you know.'

'Know what?'

'You know. I know.' She blushes too. '*I know.*'

He laughs again. It's too cliché, too ridiculous. She's watched too much *EastEnders*. They have a fine marriage.

'We have a fine marriage, Sally. You've been watching too much *EastEnders*. Our marriage is not perfect, not a, a, a laugh a minute, but what do you expect?'

'Well, I expect my husband to not jump into bed with other women. Actually.'

Neal opens his mouth, closes it. A pain jumps into his gut, sharp and wicked and offers a surreal distraction to the conversation.

'What do you mean?'

'Actually, what really shocks me is that you, Neal Munro, are capable of it. In fact, if I hadn't proof, I would have bet anything it was a lie.'

'Sally. What are you talking about?'

'Neal, did you or did you not stay at the Golspie Arms the night of that young lad's funeral?'

'No!' The cheese drops to the floor. 'No!' But he can tell by her face he's just failed the first test.

'No?'

'I can explain, Sally. It wasn't like that.'

'Oh?' In a tone both insinuating and cynical. Not her style, but she is surprisingly good at it.

'No!'

'Aren't you going to ask how I know?'

A pause.

'Okay, Christ, what well-meaning friend decided you should know such rubbish?'

'Why should I tell you? You don't tell me much. But as you asked, it was friends plural, not singular. First of all, Isobel.'

'Isobel?' He keeps his tone of voice natural, though the room is very unnaturally spinning.

'Isobel who cuts my hair.'

'Izzy?' Saying the word Izzy makes him dizzy.

'Izzy, who cuts my hair, asked how I liked Golspie.'

'Golspie?'

'Yes, fucking Golspie. Now bloody shut up and listen to me!'

'Sally!' Her swearing shocks him almost as much as her accusation. Sally has always been curiously demure in her language. The world is dangling at an unprecedented angle. Wait, he wants to say. It's not too late to stop this, rewind this conversation, go back to safety. But Sally is a nice, principled woman, so he has to listen.

'Isobel's wee sister is a cleaner in the Golspie Arms. She saw you leave that morning. And, naturally, assumed I was there too. Told her sister.'

'Your hairdresser, Izzy, told you all this?'

'Well, she didn't mean to stir it up. In fact she got quite flustered when she realised I hadn't been there. Even Rebecca heard.'

'The postie?'

'Aye, well, you never expected to keep a secret in a place like this, did you? She uses Belinda, the hairdresser who uses the chair next to Isobel. Anyway, I acted like I knew and it wasn't a big deal. Told her that Izzy misheard and I'd actually been staying at the hotel too, and we left separately. I mean, she'd love to see me made a fool of. She's never respected me.'

Her tears begin to fall now, and Neal hates himself. He also feels embarrassed. Self-hatred and humiliation struggle for supremacy. Oh dear, oh dear.

'No, not a fool, Sally. Sally, sit down sweetie.'

'Don't sweetie me, you, you, you fuck!' Her voice cracks with the effort of choosing the right swear word, and Neal has to add fear to self-hatred and embarrassment. Layers and layers of unpleasantness. A small pain above his left eye, like a pocket of blood, has begun to pound. Gut still aching away.

'Ah, Sally, we didn't, like, *do* anything. She was just that sad, and well, we used to have this thing where we'd just cuddle up in bed and sleep. Nothing else.'

'Who are you talking about? Your slapper?'

Neal's face says it.

'That woman? It was the boy's mother? Alison?'

Oh yes, by now over 250 people within a hundred-mile radius know that Alison and Neal spent that night together, but they have not told his wife. Sally's informer Izzy was not at the funeral and only knew he'd been at a hotel. If she'd known the truth, she would not have told Sally. Izzy feels awful right now, just awful. Ross-shire gossips, that's to say all Ross-shire residents, have their standards, and betrayed spouses are always shielded.

'Oh my god, Neal! How could she? How could you! Oh! Oh! The very night of the funeral, not dead a week, and *oh dear Jesus.*' These last three words are uttered from her guts, low and full of gravel.

'But Sally,' says Neal, genuinely terrified by her Exorcist voice. 'You're not listening, nothing happened, we just held, I mean, lay and nothing happened. It wasn't planned.'

'Don't lie to me, Neal Munro.' She stops crying, but her voice is all over the kitchen, and she blows her nose loud. Neal moves to her, arms out.

'Don't touch me!'

'Listen, Sally. Let me explain.'

'No, I don't want to know any more!'

'Alright. Fine.'

'Just go away.'

'Fine.' He walks towards the stairs.

'No! Come back! Tell me everything.'

'Everything?' Over his shoulder.

'Everything. I want to know the worst.'

Neal pauses, frowns. 'What's the worst?'

'Did you, in fact, well, *did you*? You know.' She sniffs.

Neal comes back into the room fully.

'Have sex? No. Not sex. I told you.'

'No? No sex? *The truth*, Neal.'

A very long minute passes, sucking all the oxygen as it goes.

'No sex . . . as such,' he finishes in a desperate whisper.

Sally wails, her first proper adult wail. Lifts her face and wails like a banshee.

'Sally, it was once. That's all. Just the once.' No point in telling her about that second time, was there?

'So, you did do it,' she sobs. 'Why are you smiling?'

'I'm not smiling. It was just the once, Sally.' Neal manages to defeat the nervous snigger that keeps wanting to leap out. God, what is wrong with him? He wants to fall on the floor and giggle hysterically. That wail was just so funny!

'I can't believe it. You lied about it just now. Even now, you still lie.'

'How does it help anything, to know about something upsetting you can't change? I didn't want to upset you.'

She wails again.

'Any more than you are already, Sally. We never did it before or since. Honest. The first time I've ever done it with someone else. All these years I've been faithful.'

'How am I supposed to believe that, now, just after you admit you lie to avoid upsetting me? How can I believe anything you say?'

'Sally, calm down.'

They are still in the kitchen, the cheese is still on the floor.

'I don't love you anymore,' she says in between spasms of dry speechlessness. 'How can I ever trust you again? It's all over, after all these years, it's over. Oh, oh, oh! You've killed our marriage. You're a cheat and a liar. Oh, oh, oh!'

He can't help noticing his wife, while weeping, is quite unattractive. He feels repulsed, which is a relief after fear, embarrassment, giddiness and self-loathing. And he stoops to pick up the cheese, feeling a sudden need for some semblance of caring about things like food on the floor. Puts the cheese back in the fridge.

'Listen, Sally. We'll have a cup of tea.'

144

Her sobs subside, and they finally move from the kitchen into the sitting room. It's like a choreography of self-consciousness, both of them stiff-limbed, awkward. She sits. He sits. Both cross their legs at the same time, in the same direction.

'I'm still leaving you, Neal.'

'But it's your house, Sally.'

'You're right. You should go. Will you leave, then?'

'No. Are you crazy? No! We should both stay and figure this out. Fix it.'

'I'm leaving you.'

'Please don't even talk like that, Sally.'

'How can I ever trust you again?'

'Just calm down for a few minutes. What a fright you're giving me.'

He springs up, darts to the kitchen. While he fills the kettle, drops the bags into the pot, arranges the two mugs, his mind frantically works out a defence.

'There are worse things, you know, Sally,' he calls through the open door.

'Worse things? Worse than what?'

'Worse things than a one-night stand after seventeen years of marriage.'

'Wait a minute. Are you saying this is now my fault, because I am making a mountain out of a molehill?' Neal studies his hands, which are holding the milk and sugar.

'Christ, Neal, if it was such an accident, so innocent, why didn't you tell me?'

'Shit, Sally. I told you why. I didn't tell you because I didn't want to hurt you. You see? We're kind to each other. That's something. We're a nice couple, us. Everyone thinks so. We have a fine marriage.'

'No. No, Neal. I'd say lots of folk think we *used* to have a fine marriage. You screwed around, then lied about it. Two major chuck-able offences. I don't even know you. You're a stranger.' She looks at him fearfully, as if to demonstrate his strangeness.

Neal pours the tea, brings their cups through.

'Sally, I can't believe you'd walk away. Where would you go?'

'Oh, not far. My life is here, even if my marriage isn't. To Dingwall. I'll stay at Emma's for a bit. She's away in London for the week anyway.'

'She knows?'

'Aye, she knows a bit. I called her this afternoon, told her I'm needing a wee change, that we're not getting on. That's all.'

'She'll never believe it. I mean Christ, Sally, we never even argue. She's never heard us so much as disagree with each other.'

'Yes. Well. I expect she's heard the gossip too. There was a noticeable lack of surprise when I told her.'

Neal notices neither of them touch their cups of tea. Feels himself sweat, a sour, panicky sweat that makes him uncomfortable in his own skin. His mouth and stomach, obviously behind the times, tell him it's teatime and he's hungry.

'Let's go out for dinner, Sally. A nice Indian. Screw the cups of tea.'

Sally rises, grabs her coat and suitcase.

'Screw you!' Getting surprisingly natural at swearing in just one hour.

'Where are you going? You have to go to Emma's right this minute? What's the hurry? Hey! Where are you going? Come back here, Sal!'

She doesn't slam the door, but it feels like she did. The air reverberates, and Neal empties out. His eyes are open but see nothing. He sits on the sofa, his arm resting on the warm indent of his departed wife.

I have been careless again, thinks Neal. *Catastrophically careless.*

Later he gets into bed and notices things he normally does not. Without anyone else breathing nearby, the clock ticking has increased in volume. It's like an attention-seeking foreign accent. It suddenly occurs to him that he has not apologised to Sally. That's the one thing he has not done. He is so stupid!

'I'm sorry,' he whispers into the empty room.

The ticks are not impressed, and tick on loudly till he gets up, and shoves the clock under the sofa cushions.

Teddy is Impressed with Alice's Haircut

'I think it's lovely,' says Teddy, sweeping breadcrumbs off the floor of his mother's kitchen, while Alice opens two tins of beans and pours them into an old pan. The back of her neck is very pale and very slightly in need of a good scrub.

'It is not lovely, my boy,' says his mother, who is sitting in her special high-backed chair with foot support and two strong arms. 'It makes her look like a concentration camp survivor. Or one of them chemo folk, you know, with their hair all falling out. You're a right fright, Alice.'

'No, she's never. It's an improvement, look at her.' Then he speaks to Alice. 'You look younger now.'

'Thank you,' says Alice, stirring the beans with a wooden spoon.

'Are there enough beans for me too? I might as well eat here.'

Alice pops two slices of white bread into the toaster. 'I assumed you were staying,' she says, giving his comment about rejuvenating haircuts one second of thought, and it pleases her. There's no denying, still a glimmer of vanity.

'Aye, you sit here, my boy,' says his mum. 'Alice! Fetch another chair from the sitting room. You sit here next to me, Teddy. Alice can get another chair.'

In the few seconds it takes Alice to enter the sitting room, which is never used and never heated, her pleasure evaporates, and she's worse off than before. She plummets past the craggy precipice she's been clinging on to. Help! Did she really expect a reprieve? Fool.

But then she hears steady footfalls out on the pavement, loud enough to carry through the stone walls, loud enough to compete with the distant traffic. Someone is running hard. She moves to the window, but the street is empty, save a black taxi, engine idling. The footfalls stop. Something in the night sky flickers and she looks up. A large white bird, maybe an exceedingly healthy seagull, is gliding over the rooftops of the houses over the way. It is unexpected and beautiful. She imagines slicing through the chill night air, yet not moving a muscle of her own. Silently carried on the wind. She stares till it vanishes. The sky is so dark she wonders how she saw it at all.

'Alice?'

'Coming, Janet.'

She hauls a damp ancient chair out of the room.

'What did you do to these beans, Alice? They're all runny.'

'Not my fault, Janet. They're Tesco Value beans.'

'Well, don't buy them again, my girl.'

'Fine,' even though she has, in fact, not bought them. She found them in the cupboard.

'And grow your hair out again, will you? You look like a lad, no a lassie.'

'I'm hardly a lassie.'

'Are you no? You look like one to me.'

'That's because you're such an old biddy,' says Teddy. Janet laughs crudely.

'Anyway, you look like a lassie to me too,' says Teddy loyally. 'Two against one. You are.'

'Not.'

Alice runs her hands again through her cropped hair, still not used to it. Then she lightly touches the tips of her hair with her palm – it feels feathery. She likes the way it feels.

'Ah, Alice, I know fine you're no just a carefree lassie, I know about your trouble,' says Janet, un-chewed beans visibly rotating in her mouth.

'I told her about Calum,' says Teddy. Not apologising.

Alice stops touching her hair, stares at her plate, the watery beans sogging up her toast.

'I would've guessed something like that, anyway,' says Janet. 'You always look that lost. It's a terrible *terrible* thing. Just terrible, so it is.' She looks at Teddy, as if to reassure herself the terrible thing has not happened to her. 'To survive your own wean like that – it's no right. No right at all.' She wipes up the last bit of bean juice with a bit of bread, shoves it in, chews with her mouth open.

'Mum,' says Teddy in a warning tone.

'Well, will you be wanting some pudding, then?' Alice gets up, her beans only played with, her bread massacred.

'Aye, open a tin of pears, and we'll have the double cream, if it's no gone off,' suggests Janet. 'Do you not have other weans back home? Surely your family will be missing you.'

'Shut up, Mum,' says Teddy tenderly. 'You sit, Alice. I'll make us a cup of tea, eh? Better yet, I think there's a bottle here somewhere. Mum, where's that whisky? A drink's what we need.'

'Top of the cupboard. You do the honours, son.'

Teddy pours out the drams. 'Sláinte, girls!'

Teddy knocks it back in one, Janet slurps it while making little noises of pleasure, and Alice takes one sip and gags.

'I don't have any,' she says. 'Any other kids.'

'Just the one, then. Like me,' says Janet.

Alice nods, puts her glass down and leaves it there. Watches Janet's mouth move, then Teddy's mouth move. Thinks about that seagull and the way it glided in the dark and then disappeared.

Melissa Mannerley's Engagement

For days, he can't stop thinking about Sally. Sally this and Sally that. All the wonderful things about Sally. A month passes. Then another, with just brief phone calls and hasty visits to collect things. A maddening series of blurred encounters. He wills her back, phones her, and one evening, summoned, she returns, bag in hand.

They talk and talk. It's eerily like the start of their relationship. They're careful, polite, shy. They laugh at each other's jokes. He cooks a leg of lamb, watches a video with her, makes love to her, and he thinks *good* – it's just been a blip of mid-life madness.

'I've been so stupid, Sally.'

'True. Foolish too.'

'Aye, foolish.'

'In fact, a complete and utter wanking bastard. '

'Steady on.'

'Have you missed me?'

'Missed you? Course I missed you, uh . . . Caroline?'

But it's a charade, this bantering. In the middle of the night, he wakes to hear her weeping. A muted whimpering and swallowed sobs. He wakes the next morning to find Sally at the kitchen table, and her bags are packed again.

'I don't understand,' he says, exasperated. 'I said I'm sorry.'

'I know. And I'm glad. I believe you. But that doesn't undo it, Neal.'

'But, Sally, Sally.' He looks around, and thinks: Sally chose that sofa! And those cushions – wedding presents from her relatives. How can she abandon him, force him to live alone amongst her soft furnishings? Then the sudden lurch.

'Have you met someone else? You have, haven't you? Who have you met?'

Then Sally cries so hard – yes, remarkably, self-controlled Sally has become a champion crier – she can't speak at first.

'I haven't met anyone.' But she has, she has! Of course she has. Or at least she has noticed someone. Passion is a virus, it's contagious, and even before she knew about Neal's dalliance, his libido had rocked hers.

'Don't you get it? There's no one. I haven't got anybody!' She cries with heart-breaking regret, because she is certain she will never kiss the man she's recently noticed in the library, the one who makes her feel dizzy with yearning on a scale she's never felt before, and it is simply impossible now to settle back with Neal, with his quiet conventional lovemaking. This stranger in the library gives her vertigo whenever he's in view, just like in a damn novel. An entirely novel sensation.

'Ah. So you're looking, then.' He hears his own peevishness, can't help it.

A pause, a booming envelope of silence, into which the sound of the washing machine drops like a suddenly noticed, but welcome, guest.

'Not exactly. Just natural, at times like this, to wonder if there's someone else who might be, well, better for you. Me, I mean.'

'What do you mean?' And he means this. It has never occurred to him to look for a replacement wife. God knows, it was a bit of a long-winded miracle just getting one wife.

'Neal. Darling.'

Darling? She's never called him darling. In an instant he realises he prefers the angry, hurt Sally to the patronising one. She's growing in stature by the second, and he's shrinking into a demoralised blob. Who the hell is Sally?

'It isn't just the fact you slept with her. That was a symptom.'

'It was? Of what?'

'Of a relationship that was never right. Come on, Neal.' Sally sighs now in a calm, wise, *irritating* way. 'Not even from the start. We could've safely carried on with our mistake till we died. Made the best of it, like a lot of folk. Nothing really wrong with that. But I think we should go out and try to find people who bring out the best in us. Don't you think we should be brave? Risk loneliness?'

'No. What a stupid question. Scrapping all these years, for no good reason.' He blushes.

'Leaving you doesn't mean those years didn't exist. They're not scrapped, silly. Just I want to end it now, alright?' She blows her nose. Blushes too. They are a pair of pink soggy adolescents. Soggy and sizzling at the same time.

'Go on, then. Just go!'

He turns his back till she leaves. Does not respond to her goodbye. Spoiled bitch.

Of course by the next day, he softens again, softens in the empty rooms. The state of the bathroom, the toilet bowl especially, panics him. But she does not answer his phone messages. Both of the women in his life have jumped ship! The minute he really wants them, really loves them, they vanish.

Nothing feels easy anymore. Nothing, nothing, nothing, not even work. He is slow and distracted the next day. Maybe it's not Alison and Sally. Maybe it's simply change that is the enemy. Whether it's in the background or foreground of his life, he doesn't like it. It makes him cranky, then afraid, then cranky again. It tires him. He types clumsily and when he makes a mistake, he deletes the entire line, not just the wrong letter. He pounds the keypad.

15th March 1955: FORTY-ONE YEARS AGO TODAY

* La Scala Cinema is showing The End of the Affair with Deborah Kerr and Peter Cushing, as a double feature with The Deep Blue Sea starring the fabulous Vivien Leigh.
* Glenview Distillery upgrades their storage, using new purpose-built sheds.
* Miss Melissa Mannerly of Alness and Mr James McIntosh, also of Alness, wish to announce their engagement to be married at Christmas. Melissa, who works at Lovely Locks, will be creating synchronised hairstyles for all ten of her bridesmaids, as well as colour-coordinating their make-up and dresses.

And oh, dear, the very idea of ten matching bridesmaids, perhaps a vision of lavender and pink, and a perspiring kilted groom watching them all troop up the aisle in a church full of over-dressed and over-perfumed spectators –

it's too much. Not funny, no, Neal is not laughing – the old Neal would have laughed quietly at the tackiness, been scornful of the extravagance, but he's not even within a hair's breadth of laughter or scorn.

Neal thinks this image is *sad*. Unbearably, utterly sad. As sad as cracked plastic carnations on a muddy grave. As sad as a mascara-smeared hen-night girl with a cowboy hat, tottering down the street alone. As sad as a small-town High Street at the end of a rainy gala week, with tattered banners fluttering overhead like reminders of better days. Ah, Neal is suddenly awash with sadness.

And touching too, to think of this couple who, forty-one years ago, actually thought celebrating their marriage was worth all this effort! What hope they must've had. What trust in the future.

But wait a minute. He knows this couple. This happens now and then, and always gives Neal a queer thrill – like finding a recent demise while out perusing a graveyard full of ancient headstones. Of course! The McIntosh family, down the end of Castle Street! One of their daughters keeps getting busted shoplifting in Markies, according to Sally. So, they survived ten overexcited bridesmaids at least long enough to produce a petty thief. Good for them!

Maybe Sally and himself should have tried that, instead of their pallid registry office affair. Gone to town with it. Engraved invitations, hired kilts, a custom-made cake. Maybe they should have had a kid; even a wee brat. A heap of brats. Anchored themselves down a bit more.

Neal considers this for a full five minutes, staring at but not seeing his monitor. Then he shakes his head and shuts down the computer. Looks around in surprise. Where's everyone gone? Why has he not seen them go? (He has seen them go. He's even said goodbye to some of them.)

Neal goes home and spends the evening putting off going to bed. He watches telly, flicking restlessly through the channels. Actually enjoys *EastEnders* for the first time, can't understand why he used to think it terrible. It is fascinating. It's high art. He eats biscuits, toast, bowls of cereal, till he feels full. He'd cook, but all the pots and pans are dirty in the sink, and the sight of the cold greasy water depresses him. Maybe he'll buy a pair of rubber gloves. Maybe he'll break the cardinal rule of no pans in the dishwasher.

He drinks a cup of tea. The Baileys has long since been finished, and he hasn't the heart to buy more. He looks for the new Neil Young to put on, can't find it, thinks to himself – *Damn it! She's taken away more stuff!* Picks up a book, puts it down. He used to read novels, quickly and with absorption, when Sally was about. Now that he has no interruptions, he finds he can't concentrate on anything for long. He misses that need to escape.

Neal, in his boxer shorts and t-shirt, sprawling on his sofa, notices that he is getting thinner. Then notices that he hates being alone. Hates it! Especially at night. He hears things. The way the house creaks and seems to breathe. The way a branch scrapes the roof. His neighbour's door slamming, a car starting. Late last night he heard loud running footsteps on the pavement outside and almost called the police. He lay there, hardly breathing, wide awake for a full hour afterwards. *I am a wimp*, he tells himself now, and he has no defence. *It's true*, he answers himself. *I am pathetic. And passive. And pre-historic. All the P things.*

I will not survive this.

He considers getting a dog, and he's not a dog person in the least. He wonders if another woman will save him – bound to happen, isn't it? He's only forty-four, and according to *Guardian* Soulmates, even redheaded middle-aged men have a chance. The world is full of single middle-aged women desperate to be a wife, or at least a hussy. But he's never made a move on a woman, not really. Always safely waited (mostly futilely it has to be said) to be persuaded. He has no idea how to go about seducing a woman, in case none of these rampant women make a move on him. How is he even going to meet one of these women who might want to seduce him? And meet one he must. It's either that or get a dog. And then, since there's nothing on the television now but news and sport, and he has taken to avoiding his own bed, he closes his eyes and thinks about Alison.

It's obvious, he tells himself. She'd never fancied him in the old days. She'd had sex with all the boys, but not Neal. But then his reward had been her friendship, hadn't it? He'd been the one she'd wanted when things were bad. She'd trusted him because he never presumed, never expected sex as the price of a cuddle. And she never went off him because she was never on him. 'You're my teddy bear,' she said once. This had seemed an insult, as if he was not a man at all. But now he thinks it was probably this trust that had led directly to Golspie, and she'd not wanted him to be a teddy bear then. Had she? Okay, here comes a belated bit of sexual imagery after all, but only enough to drift off to, not enough to require action. Just the comfort of her pillow breasts, the curve of her lower back.

He's at the very last outpost of wakefulness now. Eyes still shut, he pulls up the old quilt he's taken to leaving on the back of the sofa, covers himself, but neglects to turn off any lights. Need a remote control for the light switches, he thinks. Then he sends himself off to sleep by summarising his recent past. Reminds himself how he got here, as if these

158

events are stations his train has shot past and now he has no idea where the train is heading. He clings to the only certainties, like bits of breadcrumb, in case he has to find his way back.

The story so far, then:

Calum died.

Golspie hotel, made love to Alison.

Alison disappeared. Might be dead.

Sally gone too now.

And tomorrow he'll begin the Ninety Years Ago Today column, even though the deadline is not till Thursday. Ninety years ago ... it'll be the Great War, and roads snowed in for weeks, and maids needed in the big houses, 3d a year ...

Not much of a lullaby, but it does the job. His mouth is slightly open, body curled in foetal position, his hands tucked between his thighs. Relaxed for the first time today. He so obviously needs to get some sleep. He's frightened every waking minute.

The next day is better, and the next, and the next. He starts to feel like his old self. But for no obvious reason, he has a terrible day a week later. A day like a continual slap in the face. A whole mocking series of slaps. And then that day leads to another bad day, in fact things seem to be getting worse, not better. He's falling apart. He has no social life. Sally seems to have taken it with her, along with her Jackson Browne tapes, which he does not miss, and the kitchen knives that cut half decent, which he does miss.

Is it really over between them? How can it be? Surely civilised marriages that putter along for years don't go out with a bang, surely they only know how to putter. He feels sluggish, that the momentum of life is not matching his own internal rhythm. It's all a bit too fast for him. He will never catch up, never understand what's happening while it's happening.

Like Henry the old minister. Henry hits the ground running every day, also sluggishly, also astounded at the speed of change. At the callous nature of change. His small church is fuller on Sundays now. No one needs to stand in the aisles, but it's still quite full compared to the old three-pews-filled days. Flowers, well there have always been flowers, but who's been concocting such an extravagance of blossoms and festooning them in every corner? And what angel plays the organ so passionately? Is he dead now, and this is what heaven is? A wish fulfilment hallucination?

But no, there is no heaven anymore, remember? God is gone and his soul is a nothingness. An empty house with coat hangers and empty Coke cans on the bare floor. *Don't tell anyone!* He wakes every morning full of naughty secrets, like a petty thief or a peeping tom, and every day he goes through the motions of faith. Of course, he's a terrible actor, and he gives the truth away in a million ways he's not aware of.

His wife picks up every nuance but says nothing because she's hoping it's just a phase, and least said soonest mended. Men and their moods.

His spiritual wobbliness should have alienated his already pretty scanty flock, but no. His qualms have made him more popular. Psalms with qualms. His church, where gentle doubt is now at the helm, has become more welcoming, and the word has spread. Worried that the truest fact in the world is that you can rely on no one? That on the day of your death, no matter how many people surround your bed, you will be alone? Come to that church in Alness, the one just off the High Street. Henry will not argue with you. He'll invite you home and his wife will make you the loveliest cup of tea, and no one will ask you to pray with them. You can talk about your troubles, and before you know it, you'll see a funny side. Or a funny side to something else altogether.

Sunday morning, and he does it again. Henry without his faith is naked, and shivers in the pulpit. Regards his congregation silently, eyes full of unshed tears. Church is the one place he doesn't laugh. *Look at them!* he orders himself. Look at their faces. All they'd ever wanted was to know they weren't alone. And look, there's Chrissie in the front row. Bless. Poor lass, her nephew dead out of the blue, and her sister likely a suicide.

He has instant access these days to all sorts of feelings, and he understands exactly why Alison would put a rope around her neck and kick away a chair. His own neck tingles, as if it has been his neck, and he feels the blood rush back into his heart, as if it has been his heart that was almost so cold it could not go on.

A9

Midnight, but not dark. Not once you get used to it. Zara should be cold – she left her jacket at home – but she's not. Her cheeks are pink, her eyes shining. She sits on the ground by the road, very still, and not far away twenty-eight rabbits munch on shoots of grass and dandelions. The A9 is rabbit city from midnight till dawn. So far, they've not munched on her growing tribute to Calum. The shrubs have all taken. There's proof of life in everything she planted that pitch-dark mid-winter night. The gaps between them are filling up.

She sits cross-legged and talks away as she always does. This, right here, is the magic place. The place that might contain, somehow, if she listens hard enough, the vibration of his last heart beat, the last sound of his voice. 'Course I still love you, you idiot,' she says, and her hands absentmindedly pat the earth, almost exactly where Calum is, in a sense, still dying. The extinguishing of light and sound and sensation begins to happen again. There's his voice now, the panicky *Mum!* The syllable torn from him involuntarily, and perhaps not meaning Mother. Meaning: *Help!*

If you asked Zara if she believed in life after death, she would instantly say no. A girl of her times, she knows deep down there is nothing but the present, no soul, no heaven or hell. And yet, this aching hope that there remains something of Calum, some version of a listening ear, a receptive heart, a witness to her A9 verge gardening.

The Cherubim yellow roses she planted are becoming famous. Perhaps because they are so early blooming, perhaps the sheer abundance. Or maybe just the surprise of them, blooming on a bit of waste-ground by the A9.

Memories are short. Now there are only a few people who will never be able to pass this place without thinking of Calum, and one of them is 184 miles away. Zara is the only person in the world who knows how these roses smell at midnight. She tries and tries to describe that smell, but can only come up with the mood the smell puts her in. Whenever she is near them, which is about once a week around midnight when the scent is headiest, she is filled with nostalgia. Not just for that fish and chip supper in his car, and the first greasy kisses that followed. Nor just for sitting in those corner seats in The Com and feeling the electricity flicker like tongues between their holding hands. Those were fine memories, but the nostalgia she feels when she inhales those yellow roses is for her future. The future that she'd imagined so often, containing Calum. There it still is, unwinding itself out in front of her with its unique shape, but where Calum should be, the future has collapsed like a punctured balloon.

Zara lives with her parents. She feels a little old to be living with her parents, but after university didn't quite know what to do next, and her job in the call centre is low paid. In any case, her parents seem glad of her company. They don't know about Calum. Never even met him. Got to have some secrets, living with parents. What if they'd broken up? Or they'd disapproved of his lack of education or indeed, lack of employment? So much more complicated, once parents are in the picture. Zara packs her trowel and secateurs, and heads home with a half dozen roses. Her mother will think they are beautiful, and Zara will easily lie about where they came from. It's not a big lie.

Part Five

June to October 1996

Alice Forgets the Bacon Butty

Alice may not have many material objects from her previous life as Alison, but she does have her memories. Especially of her son. She replays them all the time. She's a fairly bright woman, is Alice, and she thinks she can do this while she does anything else. She moves expertly through a continual landslide of memories. Dozens of Calums flood in all day long. Calum, aged five, bringing her some wild flowers – bluebells from the bluebell woods at Kiltearn. Calum, aged eight, dancing in his new suede moccasins. Calum, frowning jealously as she tells him about a new boyfriend.

She can even chat to customers, take orders for bacon and eggs, hamburger and chips, two milky teas and a plate of toast while having a conversation with her son that began eight years earlier.

'So, Calum, who do you want to invite to your party?'

'Neal.'

'I mean kids.'

'No one.'

'Surely there's lots of nice boys and girls. We could do pass the parcel and musical statues.'

'Nope.'

'Calum! Give me some names, here. I want to give you a bloody party.'

'I don't want them.'

'Why not?'

'They won't come.'

'Don't be daft. Why wouldn't they come?'

'They just wouldn't, that's why. No one has birthday parties anymore. Are you insane?'

'Miss! I asked for black pudding with my eggs, remember?'

'Sorry, so you did.'

'And we're needing more sauce here as well.'

'Right away.'

So she'd taken him to La Scala to see a Disney film about a talking dog. She seemed to be the only adult, the place heaving with kids. All laughing, throwing popcorn, spitting, screaming, all the way through the movie. Most a fair bit younger than Calum. Had he outgrown this? Was she missing a beat? She sat by her son and they were like a tiny peaceful island, but it was a not a peaceful feeling. Her heart ached all the way through the show, and on the way home, when he tried to crack a few jokes, get her to laugh, it was all she could do to not cry.

'This soup's cold, miss.'

'Sorry, is it? I'll get another bowl.'

'In fact, I'll just have a wee word with the boss, if you don't mind.'

Alice is smart, it's true, but perhaps juggling the past while waitressing is beyond even her. Another year, another birthday. Dinner at the local Indian, just the two of them. A delicious, if silent, meal.

'Well, here's to you, Calum. Eighteen!'

'Aye.'

'Did you enjoy your dinner?'

'Aye.' Then, 'Thanks.'

'Fancy a pudding?'

'Nah.'

'Full up?'

'Actually, got to go now. Some mates are picking me up to go out.'

'I said two burgers, one egg and chips. Not three burgers, no bloody egg and chips at all. And where's our plate of toast, anyway?'

'It's coming. Uh, was it white or brown?'

'From here? You could have said. But great, that's great. What's your plan? Inverness?'

'Aye.' Looking a little shifty, a smile in his eyes.

'And?'

'And you're right, Mum. Inverness. Maybe clubbing.' Suppressing a giggle.

'Are you high again, Calum? You've got that face.'

'I wish.'

'Jesus. Well, have fun, son. Be careful and have fun.'

She heard the car before she saw it – deep thumping music and an angry male voice singing something about a bitch. And from her seat inside, she'd watched as he hopped into the boy-racer and joined three other boys, all looking about twelve, only stretched out and not cute anymore. She'd waved superfluously as the car revved up and sped off, swerving skilfully around the parked cars, leaving a thick exhaust cloud. That noise, that sight, seemed the epitome of young virility. The modern equivalent of young men tearing their shirts off and pounding their chests and roaring their fledgling manliness, while fighting dragons and bloodthirsty armies. Fuck you, everybody! Did you hear me? I said fuck you! And by the way, you over there: fancy a dance later? You think I'm hot, don't you? Don't you? Please!

'*This sauce bottle's nearly empty, can you no just gie us a new one, hen?*'

'*Aye, no problem.*'

'*You said that five minutes ago.*'

'*Did I?*'

And for no obvious reason, a memory that has stuck of four-year-old Calum, scabby-kneed and sunburned, picking dandelions one spring afternoon, wearing that Superman t-shirt and cape that Neal brought home one day from Woolys. God, he'd worn that cape to death. In the back garden, offering her a dandelion seed head, perfectly round and fluffy. She remembers telling herself to remember this scene, because he had jam around his mouth and the sun shone through his hair like a halo. Click! A mental snapshot.

'Blow, son,' she'd said. 'Make a wish first, and give it your biggest blow.'

'*Never mind that, and never mind bringing me a bill either.*'

'*Fine. Whatever. Sorry.*'

He puffed and spit, but not effectively enough. Half the seeds remained.

'Ah, well, never mind, Calum, your wish will come true anyway.'

'I never made a wish. Can I watch Sesame Street now?'

She cannot think of this scene without immediately singing in her head: Sunny days, sweeping the clouds away, on my way to where the air is sweet. Can you tell me how to get, how to get to Sesame Street?

His death, of course, is on a continuous loop which she tries not to stare at, but which spins out his last moments in slow motion for eternity, and which she watches out of the corner of her mind's eye. Like Zara, she's written, directed and produced this film. And like Zara's, it changes slightly with every viewing. Today, his car hits the concrete and the front half crumples like silver paper. Only it screams, this metal that crumples like silver paper. His face is frightened, so frightened it regresses to a panicky five-year-old, and then it too – this face with his freckles and that chipped tooth and his wonderful blue eyes – it screams too, and crumples.

But why did his car go off the road at all? No other traffic, a clear bright day. Why? That is the haunting, maddening part. Some days she visualises a dog straying onto the A9, or his tyre blowing out, or a sudden steering wheel malfunction. On particularly surreal days, the car itself has a death wish. If it wasn't for all these movies, she'd no doubt be a more efficient waitress, but Teddy doesn't mind.

'I think you'd be better off without that one,' says one customer, nodding his head in Alice's direction. She's staring into space, while another customer tries to give his order. She walks away without writing anything down, or indeed acknowledging the order.

'Away with you, she's that great,' says Teddy. 'You've just to got appreciate her finer points, pal.'

'I'd rather appreciate the finer points of a bacon buttie, like the one I asked for. Three bloody times,' says the customer.

Teddy glances over at Alice, who is now waddling dreamily, rather like a rubber boat on lazy wavelets, over to an empty table, carrying a plate of food for herself. Well, if a few customers don't like Alice, there are at least a few dozen who do. Aren't there? He sighs, returns to the kitchen. The girl has to eat, he tells himself.

And she eats with gusto. She scans *The Herald* while methodically eating a hamburger, right till the very last greasy morsel. Without looking, she reaches out till her hand finds the plate of equally greasy chips and begins to consume these the same way. Without awareness, without haste, without taste; she eats blindly, and now she's reading the advice page with the same vacant interest. A letter from a woman who wants to know if it's normal to put on weight upon reaching menopause. Alice has not had a period in . . . well, ages. And she is getting – well, there's no other word for it – fat.

The advice columnist confirms her suspicions. Yep. No more periods equals no more waist.

'Nearly finished, are you?' asks Teddy. The café is filling up again.

'Yeah.'

'What do you think of my new shirt then?'

'Nice.'

'You didn't even look.'

'Sorry. It's very . . . nice.'

'Do you really think so?'

'Yes. Truly. Too nice for here.'

He turns sideways, sucks in his belly, squares his shoulders and pouts. The shirt is taut over his belly, like skin. It looks expensive.

'Teddy, are you gay?' It's just occurred to her, and her voice is a little louder than it would be if she'd thought before speaking. The absence of decent food and coffee and tasteful decor make it so unlikely, but there you go. Stereotyping, even in her pit of depression. Teddy smiles, blushes slightly, and says, 'What a question!'

'Well?'

'I suppose I am. A bit,' he says, shrugging half apologetically and raising his eyebrows, as if admitting to a fondness for something embarrassing but innocuous. Reading *Hello* magazine, or watching *Coronation Street*, or cheating at Monopoly. 'Trying to be, anyway. Bit of a late bloomer, it turns out.' In a very low whisper.

'Well, I think that's . . . nice.' Alice smiles vaguely while wiping grease off her mouth with her hand. The world is shifting a little again, she can feel it, but this shift is not unpleasant. It's alright. It makes sense.

'Weird thing to call it, eh? I mean, look at me. Hardly jumping for joy, am I?'

'Hey, hey. Hardly anyone jumps for joy anyway. And it could be worse, you could be gay in the Highlands.'

'True.'

'Listen, the shirt is perfect, Teddy. But the shoes.'

'I know. They kill the shirt, don't they?'

He walks to the mirror above the counter, frowning, and she puts her apron back on and waits on a table of four young men. They all want the same thing, BLTs on white and cups of tea. When she returns with their orders, she spills a cup of tea and it quickly runs off the table onto their laps. They all stand up and roar with laughter, just when she's expecting angry shouts. Their laughter, throaty, reckless, reminiscent of Calum – feels like a flood of goodwill rising to buoy her up. A solid surge of life itself. But it's not solid; it does not last. And when the boys leave and their table is cleared, there is no trace of vitality, no promise of anything. Alice returns to the kitchen with their plates, absentmindedly nibbling on their left-over chips.

The next day is Sunday. It's been a wet June, but it's very spring-like today, and Alice spring cleans her room. This is accomplished in about eight minutes, due to her minimal possessions, but still – the weather is making primal demands, and she takes stock. She empties out her chest of drawers. Her meagre, inoffensive clothes lay clean and neatly folded on her bed, ready to be replaced in the drawers, newly lined with pages from the Sunday supplement. The brown plastic container of Calum has gravitated to her bedside table, not for any sentimental reason, but because the other table is too wobbly, and it sometimes falls off when she opens the window. The prospect of spilled ashes on the floor is appalling. She still regards the container with as much ambiguity as she had on the first day, when she'd tried to leave it on the train, yet been unable to leave it alone on the back seat of her car when she went shopping.

She's not a sentimental person. Never visited her mum's grave at Kiltearn, though she'd loved her mum more than most twelve-year-old girls. Life seemed sad enough without seeking out reminders of a previous sadness, and besides, what connection was there between her laughing pretty mum and a lump of granite in the ground? Zero, that's how much connection, and she feels the same angry way about this jar, which arrogantly claims to contain her son. Calum, the silent runner, the dry joke maker and lover of Snicker bars, in a plastic jar?

Yet there it sits. Not in the bin.

Janet has seen it, but not commented on it. Janet respects grief, and in fact, likes Alice better because she holds her loss so closely and quietly. Janet, like most people who reach their eighties, has hidden a fair amount of pain herself. Not even Teddy knows about the right leg of her Freddie Campbell, which was all that remained of him after the Germans bombed the Clyde third night running in the winter of 1942. How she'd felt when she came to and had to lift Freddie's leg off her chest. Or what she later did, to sort out the baby Freddie planted in her. Teddy has never even heard his mother mention Freddie. She's told him plenty about his own father with the unfortunate laughter, and the way she snuck off from him in the dead of night, Teddy by then amounting to about three dozen cells. And she's told him about the kinds of illicit jobs she took for a while. But for Janet, these are, curiously, not painful secrets. Some secrets can be aired and some cannot, and that's all there is to it.

It's still June outside, a brilliantly hard blue sky, and Alice opens her window to let in the air. In it rushes, with the sound of birds nearby, and these things stir her. She dumps the contents of her bag on the bed. She throws away old receipts, bus tickets, coupons, video cards, an old lipstick down to the pink nub. Opens up and reads a scrap of paper, folded into the side pocket. Oh aye. That poem Kate from Gairloch slipped into her condolence card, and which Alison had scanned and slipped into her bag. Never read it. Alison didn't get poetry. Alice sits on the bed and reads.

Mangurstadh

I send you the hush and
founder
of the waves at Mangurstadh,

in case there is too much
of the darkness in you now

and you need to remember
why it is we love.

John Glenday

She frowns. She remembers that Mangurstadh is a beach on the Isle of Lewis. She and Calum went there once, on a camping trip with Kate and her toddler daughter Mhairi. An empty sandy beach, bordered by high rocky outcrops. Sheep had dotted those scrubby hills. Cow dung on the beach, and some driftwood. *The hush and founder, the hush and founder. . .* the waves sucking back, and crashing again? Maybe. It's like a word puzzle, a riddle, and Alice's brain aches in a pleasant way. She says the words aloud, very softly, and with their utterance comes the sensation of sand between her toes, and the vibrations of those waves, hushing and foundering. Whooshing and thundering. The clamour and spray. The way her hair felt, sticky with salt. Ten-year-old Calum, half naked, screaming as he scurried as close as he dared to the waves. The waves relax her even now, as if they are literally scooping out her sadness and whisking it away to a deep, cold place that doesn't care. In, out, in, out. Giving and taking, pushing and pulling, hurting and pleasing, staying and leaving. Breathing in and breathing out; first breath, last breath.

Alice, frowning very hard now, thinks, *Pretty much sums it up, doesn't it? Life sucks and blows a bunch, and then you die.* Kate's husband has cancer, not the kind that can be fixed; maybe this poem is something she administers to herself. As medicine. A tonic. Alice closes her eyes, a slight smile in her heart, too weak to make it to her mouth, which is pressed tight in concentration. The air full of salt, the gulls wheeling, Calum and his hysterical giggling.

Why it is we love . . .? Has she forgotten why she loved? But what is the answer?

There had been a full moon in that late afternoon sky, oh yeah. A very pale orb, and when she remembers commenting on it to Kate, it seems odd she didn't make the connection at the time. The queen of gravity, coolly observing all the ebbing and flowing she caused. And from there, it's a millisecond's leap to Alice putting her own sad self on the surface of that moon over Mangurstadh beach. Queen of the moon. What? No, more a clown, her. Absurd sad clown on the moon, yeah, that's more like.

But imagine the earth from the moon. Her watching self, her Calum, Kate and her lovely naked baby – small as ants, then poof! Gone, just the jagged outline of the coast, and a dot of white for the sand. Then a quick zoom down (because moon clowns can do whatever they like), and there are those beautiful children in their beautiful bodies. Is there anything as beautiful as a child's body on a beach? Alice's eyes fill at the same time her smile finds an entrance to her mouth and eyes.

But why is it we love? And why do we need to remember this? It feels like the answers must be obvious, must be hovering just outside her brain, but: No idea, thinks Alice. Not a smidgen of an idea.

After a few minutes, she blows her nose, slips the poem carefully back into her bag, and recommences sorting out her bag. Looks at an old newspaper photo of Calum in the Fyrish Hill race. Neither foot touching the earth, his face a blur of concentration. Nevertheless, there is something peaceful in his face as he hurtles mid-air. It's as if he's trying to fly, and maybe more: that he believes if he runs a little bit faster he really will fly.

She places this on her table, thinking – *buy frame*. Then studies a tampon, puts it back in her bag. She likewise replaces her new library card, some cash, her lipgloss, and then she stares at her old car and house keys. Adds *buy envelopes* to her mental list. Then suddenly, as if the answers needed her distraction to creep in sideways, Alice raises an arm, opens her hand to address the poet, like an anxious-to-please student to her teacher: Yes! I know! I know why it is we love. Because without love we just . . . *float*. Like . . . me, here. Like those dandelion wishes Calum tried to blow. And why do we need to remember this? Because it's hardly worth living, being a dandelion wish, yeah? Am I right?

Aye, answers the John Glenday in her head. *A+*. He is bearded and fat, wise and kind. His eyes are the warmest brown. He smiles and says, *Floating dandelion seeds are just wisps of potential. Better the ties of love, Alice. Better those terrifying ties.*

Alison is Not Inside a Grey Fish

Neal feels a little insubstantial on his own, as if he is floating, unanchored, but the Sally vacuum is filling, slowly. He has stretched all his routines out a bit, till there are few gaps in the old Sally spaces. His days pass easily, mostly.

But early one early summer morning, the phone rings.

'Hello?'

'Neal, it's me, Chrissie.'

'Hey Chrissie, what's up?' He yawns, scratches his belly, tries to fill the kettle while cradling the phone under his chin.

Alison's sister has taken to phoning Neal a fair bit lately, now it's been established that they both secretly think Alison is probably inside some grey fish. When her car was found in a car park near the station, they'd hoped for a while this might mean she'd taken a train somewhere. But no movement on her bank account, and no missing clothes, suitcases or passport has forced a less optimistic conclusion. Right now, Chrissie's voice sounds mystified, excited.

'Listen, Neal. You will not believe this. Alison's house and car keys have just come in the post.'

The words take a few seconds to sink in.

'Did you hear me?'

'But that's fantastic news, Chrissie! Thank god.'

'Aye, she's alive, at least. Thank God, as you say.' Chrissie's eyes smile, noting the irony of hiding her truth in speaking the truth, so to speak. He'd answered her prayers so efficiently, but damn, wasn't she also good at praying to get such a fast result? And such a novice too. Who needs ministers, anyway?

'A note? Did Alison send a note?'

'No, but the handwriting on the envelope is definitely hers. Maybe she's not wanting to talk just yet.'

Chrissie is quoting God, actually. It was Him who explained about Alison not wanting to talk just yet. So sensible, God. So perceptive. And He won't mind her taking credit. He'd not want her cover blown.

'Still, you'd think a note – just to say where she is.'

'Neal, she'll get in touch sometime, I'm sure.'

'What's the postmark?'

'Glasgow.'

'Glasgow! Okay. That makes a kind of sense. Who does she know there?'

'No one I know. Kate goes there sometimes to see her daughter, but she hasn't seen Alison.'

'Oh. Well, it's still brilliant news.'

'Aye. You're right. It's great. Can't believe it, actually.'

Alison is not inside a cold grey fish!

But it doesn't cure everything in Neal's life, merely punctuates it with flashes of hope, slow at first but increasing in frequency, like this:

He forces himself to eat a bowl of Fruit 'n Fibre with cold milk, which is what he always has now since Sally left and no longer makes porridge. (Alison is alive!) The noise they make in his mouth seems a little loud this morning, but he manfully finishes the bowl. Notes that anxiety resembles the symptoms of falling in love, for he could not eat much for a while after Golspie either. Odd that the two events – making love to Alison and being abandoned by Sally – should each reduce him to Fruit and Fibre. The cleverness of this observation, and the news of Alison's aliveness, cheer him so much, he almost has another bowl. (The world contains a breathing Alison!) But then he notices the time and all the cheer leaks out. Late again, and anyway he still doesn't know where Alison is, and to be honest, it is a little humiliating that she has not contacted him.

He gets to work late, feeling shaky. (Alison is alive but never thinks of him!) Margaret the receptionist gives him a worried look, which he ignores. She's noticed he's lost weight, that his eyes are empty and his skin tired and dull. He looks like a man bereft of a wife. *I bet he feels exposed*, thinks Margaret. Men need wives to be barriers between them and the world. In her opinion, a single middle-aged man is practically naked.

'Are you alright, Neal?' asks Margaret in such a patronising tone, Neal immediately gives her a huge brittle smile.

'Yes indeed, Margaret, I'm fine. I'm great. I am just perfectly great, okay?' (Irritated by Margaret, and Alison does not love him, but she is alive!) 'How are you, Margaret? Are you alright? You look a little tired.'

She doesn't answer, just gives him a pitying look that says *you can't fool me, mister.*

Damn, she can see right through me, he thinks. (But Alison is alive!) He feels raw. He accepts a cup of coffee from Margaret, and splashes some of it over his lap. Black coffee on his new Gap khaki trousers. His own clumsiness is so familiar, he's

181

not really surprised. (But Alison is alive!) The stain will never come out. (She doesn't love him, but so what!)

Alison must be alive, or has been alive enough recently to post the keys, and this accelerating fact, as it flutters down inside Neal, alters things.

Margaret reminds him primly, that he has seven days of holiday which he must take or lose. Why not take today off? Why not, indeed?

So Neal says a cheery cheerio to the gloating Margaret and gets in his car. Puts on *Rubber Soul*. John Lennon singing 'Baby You Can Drive My Car'. He's not shaved for a few days; he seems to be growing a beard. His chin itches in a pleasant way – that is, he enjoys scratching it. He stretches in his seat, and that feels good too. (Alison is alive!!!) He gives his wife a quick thought, but it still hurts, so he stops. Sally thoughts could ruin whole minutes, whole days.

But look at him: Neal has faced the bogey man of loneliness and not died. He lives in Sloth City and not become ill. His idealised lover is not dead, and so can resume muse status. If Neal could bottle this feeling, it would be banned within days. It's that wonderful. The road is wonderful, his car is wonderful, John Lennon is still wonderful after all this time. Ah! Wonderfulness!

He passes two boys who look familiar, and they look like they wouldn't agree with his wonderful diagnosis. Who are they? Their faces, pale and serious, tug at something unpleasant in his memories. Then he is past them, and it's alright to be wonderful again.

'You going to Stevie's birthday do?'

'Nah,' says Finn. 'Busy.'

'It'll be good craic,' says William. 'At the National. You should come, Finn.'

'You going?'

'Aye.'

'Think I've got something else on that night.'

'Oh well. Fancy meeting up tonight?' asks William. 'A pint somewhere?'

'I don't know.'

'Just a quick half?'

'Nah. Sorry. Working late.'

Pause.

'I still can't believe it about Calum. Can you?' asks William.

'No.'

'I miss him. Weird, 'cause I didn't see that much of him. You miss him?'

'Yeah. Sure. Well, actually, it's more like I keep thinking I see him.'

'I keep thinking about him. Remember how he peed himself during story time once. Miss MacKenzie. Mind her? Mind her changing his trousers, and pretending he's spilled his juice on them?'

'Aye,' says Finn, looking over William's left shoulder at nothing.

'And the time he won all those races on sports day, mind that? His t-shirt had like a hundred stickers on it, and he wore it for weeks after.'

'Aye?' shuffling his feet now.

'Rosskeen. He was Rosskeen and I was Dalmore. What were you, were you Dalmore too, or were you Averon?'

'Can't remember, sorry. Sorry.'

'You okay, Finn? You alright?'

William moves slightly towards Finn, and Finn steps back. Checks his watch, face reddening.

'Got to rush, late again.'

'Okay. Okay. Bye then, Finn. See you.'

'Bye.'

The boys are heading in the same direction, but now they've said their goodbyes, Finn half-runs so he doesn't walk alongside William.

Yesterday, in the heat, all the rowans started shedding blossoms, and the pavement is littered with them today. It's an annual phenomenon, these pretend snowflakes, and they rise up around the boy's footsteps in little white flurries. William stares at Finn's back, wistfully, and Finn's face is pink, confused. Neither notices the rowan blossoms.

At home, Neal makes coffee and considers the day. It's not even ten o'clock yet. The day stretches out, an unexpected reprieve from routine, and seems longer somehow than a weekend day. Why has he not taken all his holidays? What is wrong with him? It is also a beautiful day, the sky is so blue it looks fake. White clouds scud across it like . . . like in *The Simpsons*. A Simpson sky.

He finds his hiking boots and drives west to the foot of Ben Wyvis. Walking up the mountain is not an ordeal. Neal has always been a walker, and his legs are strong. He paces himself, stops several times, walks slowly up the steep steps at the top. It takes him two hours and a bit. He strolls slowly on the flat plateau at the top and notices the Cairngorms, the Firth, the empty glens to the west – but it's the inner view that compels him. That makes him smile, weary and exhilarated at the same time. What does his love for Alison feel like now? If he never sees Alison again, she will still bring him this joy. Without doing a thing, she gives him access to his own heart.

And somewhere un-fishlike, her heart is beating.

Beating Hearts

It's been such a cold wet summer, the sudden sun is an assault on the senses. Young men who work in offices are swinging their jackets over their shoulders, walking with their heads up, checking out the talent. Middle-aged men with short hair suddenly wish they had long hair again and whistle old songs to themselves, and smile small bemused smiles. Dozens of women momentarily close their eyes and lift their faces to the sun, tilt their heads to let the sirocco breeze reach as much of their necks as it can. Everyone, from the adolescents loitering outside Our Price to the old ladies working in the charity shops on Sauchiehall Street, feels younger than they did yesterday, and without exception, they all remove at least one item of clothing. Collectively, Glasgow sighs into this reprieve of a day, and the wind indifferently whips all these urban sighs away to the sea.

Alice is on one of her walks. She crosses over George Square then heads down Buchanan Street to Argyle Street. Not to shop – she rarely shops – but because this is one of the routes she walks. She jaywalks across Argyle Street and a car almost clips her; she gives a little yelp and jumps onto the pavement. The driver beeps and shouts from his open window, 'Watch where you're bloody going, hen, why don't you!' But the *hen* comes out in a nice way, as if he likes her. That's the kind of thing this sun can do.

On and on she walks, left foot, right foot, left, right, and within minutes she's somewhere else. She doesn't want to remember but remembers nonetheless, another day like this when the wind had real warmth in it, and they'd all piled into Neal's old van and headed to Loch Achilty. Calum, Neal and herself. All the way to the loch, they played a tape full blast. What was it? Blondie? No, it was 10cc. *I'm not in love, it's just a silly phase I'm going through.* She was between men again and it was a relief to just be with Neal and her son. Relaxing! She'd rolled a joint, lit it and smoked it all herself. Never needed company to get high in those days, though it's been years since she fancied a joint – dope just began to make her paranoid after a while.

She remembers they parked in a lay-by and walked along the loch shore till they came to a place out of sight of the few houses. It was hot, further from the coast and therefore hotter than Alness. They all took their clothes off. She hadn't felt naked, not in an embarrassing way. They'd skinny-dipped before, and sometimes even used the toilet while the other one was bathing. Calum must have been only six or seven, not modest yet. The afternoon was blissfully primitive: they ate sandwiches when hungry, drank Irn Bru when thirsty, dozed when sleepy, and swam when they felt too hot. The water was dark, peaty soft. Once a school of tiny fish slid against her legs and she hadn't minded. A timeless afternoon of laziness and calm. Till clouds moved across the sun and a breeze came up. The water rippled with it, and she felt her skin rise in ticklish goosebumps, her nipples harden, her mood descend. She thought of her dad, his unhappiness and cruelty. Her pretty dead mum, the way she used to always let Ali help her make bread. That huge yellow bowl and their four hands pounding the dough. The most recent boyfriend, the way he'd looked at her with dead eyes for weeks before dumping her. Even while fucking (and yes, there was no other word for it), always the dead eyes.

Alice shivers right now, recalling this long-ago afternoon on the loch shore. The happiness, which she did not know was happiness at the time, which was too slow and ordinary to stand up and be counted as happiness; and the subsequent frightening mood dip. She remembers how Neal, who must've seen, must've been watching, handed her over his shirt. She'd put it on, his large, soft red tartan shirt, and wrapped it around herself, and that is how she feels right now in this warm wind on a Glasgow street. Still stark naked, naked to the bone and shivering, but momentarily distracted by sensuality, by warmth, by the illusion of protection. Not much, not a solid safe feeling, but a good-enough-for-now feeling.

It's the first time she's really thought of Neal since the Golspie hotel. He's been summoned by a climatic change, and she slows her walk. Alice halts, raises her face and closes her eyes instinctively, not to savour the sun or wind, but the memory of Neal's shirt. Oh! If only memories like these could be safely folded up and re-aired when needed. Not just fleeting images, all blurred and compressed, but the whole experience. Re-live those times properly. Calum had been so happy that day. In fact, now she thinks of it, Calum had always been happy when it was just the three of them. He'd hated all her boyfriends. *Hated them.* Right pain he'd been, sometimes, cramping her style, putting blokes off her with his glares and tantrums.

When she opens her eyes, she finds herself still on Argyle Street. The wind is still warm, she feels tireless. She walks past the lower end of Central Station, under the overpass and into the meaner end of the street. The pawn shops, the sex shops, the men walking slowly with no goal in mind. Finally she comes to a junction, and when she crosses, the pavement veers away from the road. There are many cars here, but no other pedestrians, not a single one.

She hurries till she finds herself walking between grey tower blocks of council flats. It feels like she's entering a dangerous forest. The street is in shadow. She walks quicker, and is quickly, within minutes, completely lost. There are still no people in sight, though George Square is a mere quarter mile away and heaving with people. Presumably, there are hundreds of people here too, but they're hidden behind locked doors and boarded-up windows. She feels watched. As she walks, the wind whips up carrier bags and crisp packets, and even empty tins of Tennent's. It doesn't feel like such a friendly wind here. A small scrawny dog, half Corgi by the curly tail, appears from nowhere and follows her half-heartedly, every so often dropping behind, then scurrying back to her side.

'I've nothing for you,' she warns him, hearing her voice out loud for the first time in hours. It cheers her like an old friend, this rusty sound of her own voice. What else does she have of her past now, but her own body and its emanations?

'Nothing. Not a sausage.'

She comes to a chip shop, which – miracle of miracles – despite the chain-linked windows, is open. She buys some chips and a battered sausage. Eats the chips greedily and gives the sausage to the dog. Then she lets her internal compass lead her back to the heart of the city, which today is located precisely at the top of Sauchiehall, where a dark-eyed man is playing a wild fiddle, an ancient Celtic air gone mad, to a large crowd. Office workers on their lunch, shoppers out of shopping steam, pensioners out for a constitutional, and babies who have no choice about things like destinations – all this humanity is gathered together temporarily in a cluster. No one within this crowd feels lost or lonely because *they* are the heart of the city.

Of course, there is a multitude of such hearts everywhere, and they change every minute; with every breath they shift and alter, till they beat in a different way in another location, maybe even just a block away, thirty minutes later, a wee bit further towards the river, the cinema, the clubs, the corner of a room in a fourth-floor flat. The world is dotted with hearts. Like stars in the sky.

On her way home, with the day still nice and trying not to end too early, Alice is noticed by someone from the Highlands. Her old friend Kate from Gairloch, with her glowering eighteen-year-old Mhairi. Between them, they carry seven carrier bags of new clothes and shoes.

'Is that you, Alison?'

Alice looks caught, says nothing. Experiences deep irritation.

'Alison! Hey, it *is* you, isn't it?'

'Hello Kate. Hey Mhairi.'

Mhairi grunts: 'Hey.' Yawns.

Kate squints. 'Hey Ali! I wasn't sure it was you. You look so different.'

'Do I?'

'Well, yeah! But you look great. Honestly. Short hair suits you. And nice shoes.'

'Thanks. But I'm getting so fat, look!'

'Don't be soft.'

'Eh?'

'Sorry. You look great. Look at me – middle-age spread gets us all in the end.'

'Aye. Well.'

'Everyone's looking for you, Alison. You should ring Chrissie. She's dead worried.'

'Aye. Well. Keep meaning to.'

'Will you stop fidgeting, Mhairi?'

'My hands are killing me, Mum. We should've taken a taxi, like I said. It's cheap here.'

'Oh for heaven's sake, put your bags down for a minute and stop whining.'

Mhairi sighs melodramatically, rolls her eyes in disgust, and Alice suddenly realises why Kate and Mhairi seem so odd to her. Losing a child has begun to seem normal, so the weirdness is that Kate's child has *not* died.

'What are you doing here anyway?' asks Kate.

'Just, you know. Stuff. Work and that.'

'Fancy a coffee? Let's have a coffee somewhere, Ali.'

Mhairi sighs again, looks pointedly at her watch.

'Will you stop fussing, Mhairi? Come on, Ali. A coffee.'

'Sorry. Bit late, you see,' Alice blurts, looking at the sky just above Kate's shoulder.

'Well, keep in touch, girl.'

'Yeah.'

Kate hugs her hard. Alice's arms remain limply at her side, then she briefly squeezes her old friend and swiftly walks away with a muffled, 'Bye, Kate. Take care. See ya, Mhairi.'

'Don't forget to ring Chrissie. Everyone wonders where you are, Alison.'

But Alice gives no indication she hears.

Janet Disappoints Neal

'I know where Alison is,' Chrissie tells Neal over the phone. She's called him at work, and he turns from the computer to pay attention.

'Kate, an old pal of hers, phoned me up. Said she'd seen Alison down in Glasgow. Didn't look anything like her, really, she said, but it was definitely her.'

'She talked to her?'

'Aye, she did, and it was her right enough. Luckily Kate kind of followed her home.'

'You're joking.'

'Well, I don't think it was that on-purpose sneaky, like. She hadn't planned to spy on her or anything. Just that Ali acted so strange. She gave me the address of the house where Ali went.'

And for this, Chrissie has given up chocolate éclairs forever. That was the bargain, as of yesterday. Every day, a different bribe to God. If you give me Ali back, I will give up Rioja, milk chocolate with raisins, gossiping about workmates, criticising my eldest about spoiling her kids. Always, the carefully specific sacrifices, in case her bluff was called.

* * *

The next day at dawn, after the quick bowl of Fruit and Fibre, Neal drives south instead of going to work. He doesn't phone in sick. Work routines have kind of slipped off the radar, and in the last two months Neal has missed four days of work. The old Neal was punctual and reliable. Weirdly, it gets easier and easier not to care. Nothing horrendous has resulted, so far.

As he passes Dunkeld, a train thunders past on the way north to Inverness. He gives it a glance, but does not see, of course, Alison or Alice looking out the window, thinking of her sister.

Whoosh!

They slide past each other at a relative speed of 156 miles an hour.

And perhaps something passes between them, for there is a palpable quiver in the air of Neal's car suddenly, and he presses harder on the accelerator. And in the train, Alice/Alison shivers, and begins to eat a pear. She isn't hungry, but she needs to rid herself of excess energy. If she was still a smoker, she'd smoke now. She's restless, impatient. Is she approaching normality, as she approaches her old home town? It looks like it. Crunch, crunch, and she notices it's not a very juicy pear, but finishes it anyway. It's something to do, and it's been a long time since she's noticed the taste of anything.

Maybe she'll get pissed tonight. That would be a good thing to do. Find Chrissie and have a right old session. She's not been pissed since . . . since that bottle of whisky by herself that terrible day. Damn, she misses getting drunk. She hopes her stomach allows her to. Is it an ulcer? What a drag it is, getting old.

* * *

Neal is in Glasgow, his old home town. He's not thinking of it that way – he's lived just as long in the Highlands as here, and it's changed him, softened him, even altered his accent – but the shape of the buildings, the smell of the river and city, the colours, the accents all answer something in him. This is where he grew up; his tribe claims him still.

Because he's not prepared for this, because this is almost an accidental visit, he's slightly slowed by the nostalgia of street names, park landscapes, shops. By the man selling the *Evening Times* on the corner, calling in a flat tone, 'Evtimes! Evtimes!' And nowhere is a reminder of his failed marriage. Glasgow pre-dates Sally. He hadn't noticed the strain of being surrounded by reminders, till right now, here.

He finds the right street, parks his car. Realises he's faint with hunger and badly needs a pee but decides to plough on regardless. Alison, just find Alison. He knocks on Janet's door, and after two minutes she opens it, leaning heavily on her walking frame.

'Uh, hello, I'm looking for Alison Ross. Is she here?'

'Alison?'

'Aye, Alison Ross.' He speaks loudly, in case the old lady is hard of hearing.

'I'm afraid you've got the wrong house. No Alison Ross living here.'

'Are you sure?' He checks the address written on a scrap of paper.

Janet cackles. 'Do you not think I'd know who lives in my own house? How could I not know? Did some girl gie you a fake address? Aye, girls these days.'

'No, it's not like that, really.'

'Never you mind, pet.' She shuts the door.

★ ★ ★

Alice/Alison is still on the train – Neal had driven faster and not stopped, unlike her train. As they pull out of Aviemore, Alice goes to the toilet and tells herself she's Alison. 'Hello, Alison,' she says in a low voice, and tries out an Alison smile for the mirror. But she gets off the train at Inverness, face wet, and waits three and a half hours for the next train back south. She cannot, she just can't. Not even for Chrissie. Not yet.

She sits on a hard bench and rests her hands on her stomach and thinks her life is over. She's been gone too long, not only from Alness and Chrissie and everyone she knows, but from herself. She is Alice, and she lives alone day to day. A boring menopausal fattie who doesn't drink or have sex. Who stares out of windows and notices odd things and thinks odd thoughts. And she doesn't care what she looks like, aside from facial hair. She is a blob, a sexless loner, and that's just the way it is now. She rings Teddy from a payphone to tell him her change of plan, but mostly just because she has a sudden need to hear his voice. Of course, he is full of questions she has no answers for.

Teddy Asks That Question

'So,' says Teddy, apropos of nothing, as he begins all conversations, and sometimes ends them, apropos of nothing. Alice assumes he has a perpetual stream of internal conversation and now and then opens his mouth to let some out, mid-stream.

She is sipping her morning coffee, leaning against the chrome worktop, letting her eyes scan the front page of a *Sun* someone left behind. Her aborted trip to Alness was three weeks ago, almost forgotten already. What a close call! Teddy dries his big rough hands on a towel, which he swings over his shoulder, then sashays to the fridge for some milk.

'When did you see him last?'

'Who?'

'Calum.'

'Calum?'

'Your son, right? Calum.'

'Calum? The last time . . .'

She looks dazed. Her swift walk to work has done its job, and she's narrowly averted collision with sad thoughts; leapt heroically over them, and kept moving. Let the centrifugal force of her movement scatter them all. But watch out, here they come again.

'Sorry love, don't answer if it upsets you. Just I was thinking you might want to talk about it. But just tell me to mind my own business.'

'That's okay, Teddy. Let me think. Hmm . . .'

But she's only pretending to think. She knows the final scene by heart, it's ragged with perusals. It was five days after Hogmanay, it was a mere seven months ago – could such a small slice of time really separate two such vastly different realities? Her mind, for the millionth time, automatically leaps to the conclusion that all she has to do is turn back time. A simple achievable act, turning back the clock. Surely she's done trickier things before. Then in the next millisecond, her mind bites hard on time's irreversible flow. That old bugger.

The last time.

Morning. About seven-thirty. She'd knocked on Calum's bedroom door, got no answer, peeped in. The room smelled of tobacco and socks, a textured sweet smell. He was still in bed of course. Outside the window, a wet dark morning, like countless other January mornings. It always seemed to be getting darker or only slightly less grey.

'Oh. Hey, Mum.'

Seemed awake, more awake than if she'd just woken him. Had he been lying there, thinking of things? What things? He seemed okay. A little more secretive than usual perhaps, but okay. He never told her anything. Nothing that really mattered, anyway. She had no idea how he spent his days, since that last job ended. Nope, to the last, Calum was a mystery to his mother. Nevertheless, she felt they'd been close, in a non-confiding way.

'Morning, son. Just thought I'd check to see if you need

anything in the sales. I'm having a look round at lunch break. Another jumper maybe? There's some fleeces reduced to ten pound at Markies.'

A lie. Just wanted to check on him before she left was all. Needed an excuse.

'Right.' He got up, pulled on his jeans over his boxers, and shuffled into the kitchen. He was wearing his black Simpsons t-shirt with Under Achiever and Proud of It. She followed him. He filled the kettle, switched it on.

'So. Do you?'

'Do I what?'

'Need anything. In the sales.'

'Nah. You're alright. Thanks anyway, Mum.'

The kettle boiled and he washed out two mugs. Alison could tell from the lack of steam in the cold room that the water was cold. She wanted to ask him to let the water run till it was hot, wash the mugs properly, but refrained. Mustn't fuss too much. One of her constant yearnings, so constant it was unnoticeable, was to conjure up a young woman for Calum – someone to pull his best side out – someone to wake him up, to snap him into his life. Nag him to wash up properly.

'You okay, Calum?'

'Course,' he barked. His face flushed dark. Did her concern irritate him that much? Emasculate him? She wished she hadn't asked. Made small talk instead.

'So cruel, having sales just after everyone has spent far too much already.'

'I suppose.' He yawned, and she noticed he needed a shave. Also noticed he looked better with just this amount of shadow, better than the clean-shaven look. Wondered if this future girlfriend would think the same. He looked at the television, as if wanting to turn it on.

Oh god, *was* he unhappy? He seemed more morose than usual.

'Look, I'm wearing the cardigan you gave me. I love it, Calum. It's so warm.'

'Good.' He turned to her and smiled, slow. A true Calum smile, right from the eyes, and her heart filled. Her boy loved her, so he did.

'It looks nice on you, Mum. I knew it would. Goes with your eyes.'

Then she smiled back, and for a second they both beamed at each other. What had been going on that last morning? Normally they hardly spoke, but here he was, acting depressed, then complimenting her! Smiling! Such small things, smiles and compliments, but from Calum at eight in the morning, monstrously enormous. Something was up. Something was wrong. Or was it?

'What're you up to today, then? Anything exciting?'

'Nah. Same old, same old,' he mumbled.

'So, have you thought any more about applying for that cheffing course?'

'Nah. Don't worry. I've got some ideas, some plans.'

'Early bird gets the worm, Calum. Whatever your plan is, do it soon.'

'Uh huh.' Leaned towards the telly, switched it on, and at the sight of her unemployed, unshaved, unmarried son sitting there watching a morning chat show, her mood plunged. When oh when would this nagging sense of helplessness end? When would he begin his life? His presence in the house was increasingly a weight on her.

'Okay?' he asked, eyes on the screen.

'Aye.'

A pause. Calum never seemed to think pauses were voids to fill with words. That thoughts were things that could be aired for no reason at all. He sat, seemingly content, while she rummaged for more subjects.

'Quite a nice Christmas, wasn't it? I thought that turkey was awful though. Maybe try duck next year. Or skip the whole thing.'

'Bloody Christmas. Yeah, whatever, Mum.'

'Might take back that skirt Chrissie gave me. Hope she doesn't notice.'

'Aye. Money's better,' grunted Calum economically.

Pause, while she tried not to think of the dozen gifts she'd wrapped for Calum, and none of them money.

'Well, that's people for you,' she said weakly. 'And Christmas.'

'Yeah. People. Christmas. Sad, innit?'

And minutes later, she was driving to work in the murk. On the back seat was his new shirt she'd offered to return to the shop in return for a larger size. The shirt was one of the presents she'd given him. When he'd unwrapped it, she'd the impression he didn't really like the shirt and he hid the fact to protect her. The idea of Calum patronising her was strangely comforting. Isn't that what adult sons did to their doting mothers? And he might go to college one day – didn't that sound healthy and exciting? And surely he'd marry one day, settle down, be a daddy. Most boys did. There were always two views to take of things – how it appeared, and how it felt from the inside. From the outside, he seemed a typical boy with his life ahead.

'The last time I saw Calum? I kissed him on the cheek while he watched telly, and I drove to work. I didn't usually kiss him, though I always used to wonder if I should more often. Or could. I mean, who ever touched him? His cheek felt cold and rough. I kissed him because I tried to, now and then, in case we ever got back to the way we were when he was little.'

'Did you hug him?'

'No.'

Alice recalls the exact way Calum had looked, sitting there in front of that stupid telly. His face was like, well, no other face like it. It was Calum's face, not to be repeated in nature again.

'Doesn't matter. Well, that's good then,' says Teddy, reaching for the paring knife to begin slicing onions.

'Good?'

'Good that you had a nice last time with him. No fighting. Nothing bad. Nothing to regret.'

Teddy smiles and Alice does not.

'No, no regrets. Except maybe the hug.'

'Hugs aren't everything. You didn't say anything mean to each other.'

'No, nothing mean. But I wish . . . I wish I'd spent more time with him, done more things with him. Talked to him more.'

'But it sounds like he was a normal lad. Not big on talking, us lot.'

'Still. I remember one evening. I was on my way out to the pub with some pals, and I asked if he would be okay for dinner, and he said, "Sure, on you go, Mum." I keep thinking of him sitting there in that empty house on a Saturday night, watching *Top Gear* re-runs. I should have stayed in, kept him company. It should have been him on his way out to have fun, not me. I was so selfish.'

'Shush. Just a normal mum. And a normal son.'

'But I used to get so angry at him, Teddy. You've no idea. His endless mess everywhere. Cups and plates of old food in his bedroom, filthy clothes on the bathroom floor, mud tracked all over the house. The way he never turned off the telly or the CD player. I'd come back to a house with all the lights on, telly blaring, and no Calum. Once I said it was about time he pissed off, he was only using me.'

'I'd be angry too. Anyone would. Kids!'

He turns to toss the onions onto the greased skillet, and asks, 'Where was he off to that day, anyway?'

'Don't know. Nowhere special, probably.'

'Probably a pal's?'

'Aye. Not far. He never had much petrol.'

Teddy wipes his hands on his apron and wraps his arms around Alice. She doesn't respond.

'Sorry, darling. Really sorry I brought it up.'

'Nah, it's okay. It's good to say his name out loud, actually.' And this time she smiles a little, and returns the hug.

Neal Hugs a Pink T-Shirt

It all starts with Margaret at work, because Suzie Thomas is her second cousin. She figures Neal and Suzie have a lot in common. She's from Glasgow too, came up in the seventies to work at Kishorn. Divorced, no kids. Lives in Fortrose now, which is kind of like a coastal Strathpeffer, Neal's town. They are both in their mid-forties, neither believe in astrology or God, and neither has had sex in a while. Margaret knows Neal will never go on a blind date, so she tricks him. Poor dear man, but there's no other way to help him. She invites him to celebrate her birthday at The Mallard, and when he turns up, Suzie approaches him smiling.

'You must be Neal. Margaret asked me to let you know she'll be a little late.'

'Oh?' He hadn't really wanted to come at all.

'Yes, she'll try to come later.' She notes his hair and thinks, *She never said ginger. But nice blue eyes. Or are they green?*

'Who else is here?'

'Just us, so far. Fancy a drink?'

'No thanks. Why is it just us?'

'Go on. I'm having a gin and tonic. Flu. Everyone's sick with the flu.'

'Oh. An orange juice then. Thanks.'

And when their drinks come and Suzie has paid, she suggests they sit down. They find a corner, and Neal looks uncomfortable and drinks his juice quickly. Suzie frowns a little. He's not as good company as Margaret promised. Bit boring. Didn't offer to pay for their drinks and hasn't asked her a single question about herself. But then she notices that he's noticing her very tight, very low cut pink t-shirt. Her nipples are pressed against the cotton about twenty-four inches from Neal's mouth, which begins to salivate like a baby despite the fact he has no particular liking for Suzie yet. Neal has lost control of his own mouth.

'Aye, I knew she'd be this late. She was in a proper tizz about something, alright,' she says, smiling.

She begins smiling a lot. Leans forward so when she giggles her breasts bulge even further upward till they seem to be leaping over the table to him. And it goes on from there.

It isn't difficult. He's lonely, shy and sober; she's lonely, confident and a little drunk. She asks for a lift home when it becomes obvious Margaret is not coming. She offers him a whisky, which he accepts though he hates whisky. They sit on her sofa, he drinks the whisky as if it's needed medicine, and she presses those breasts against him and kisses his mouth. Her lipstick tastes awful, like a perfumed candle. Then, before he has time to worry about anything, they're both naked in her bed, quietly humping away. Suzie is his third lover, and Neal is her sixty-seventh. Not that she keeps track.

In a way, the vision of her nipples squashed into her pink t-shirt has stayed with him because now, in the dark, he seems to think of her entire body as pink – feminine, soft, open, perfumed. Suzie is just very, very . . . *pink*. And open. And making love with her feels remarkably like scratching a very itchy place. If it is a counterfeit of the real thing, so what? It satisfies.

Maybe his dad has been right all along and all his problems are simple ones after all, with a single simple solution. All he needs is a decent shag. And he is calm afterwards. Not invigorated, not scoured out or stunned, but just relaxed. It's happened so easily, so effortlessly. It seems the odds of pulling, so to speak, have improved substantially since he'd been a young man. His last thought is that he'll phone his dad tomorrow. And then he drops into a solid sleep, as nourishing as a decent hot meal.

A Bad Day

Janet likes a decent hot breakfast, none of this Rice Krispies nonsense. She wakes up every day looking forward to her soft-boiled egg, bacon and toast. But this morning she waits in vain. She waits for her cup of tea, waits for her medicine and vitamins and waits for help onto the toilet. Then hobbles to Alice's room to scold her. The door is open so she enters the room. The curtains are drawn and Alice is under her candlewick cover, but she's not asleep. She stares at the ceiling with hard shiny eyes. Janet opens her mouth to say, 'Get out of bed you lazy cow.' But Alice's eyes are too strange. Feral. Janet feels timid for once.

'Alice, dear, are you alright?'

Alice slowly turns her face to look at Janet, expressionless.

'Are you ill, pet? It's way past getting-up time, you know. Is your alarm working?'

Alice closes her eyes.

'I'll ring Teddy, that's what I'll do,' says Janet. 'I'll be back with Teddy. You just stay here.'

Twenty minutes later, Teddy arrives with his apron still on. The café has been open for an hour, and a regular is looking after things.

'Alice? Mum said you were poorly. Alice?'

Alice's eyes are open again, but this time instead of hard and shiny they're soft and shiny.

'Do you want some paracetamol?'

Alice shakes her head. Her lips press hard together.

'I'll get you a nice cup of tea, then you can tell me all about it, eh?'

When he returns, Alice is sitting up on the bed, an old cardigan over her nightie. She sits on her hands, then slips her hands out to sip her tea. Grimaces.

'Oh. You don't take sugar, do you?'

'Aye.' Clears her throat. 'But that's alright. It's fine.'

'I never remember, me.'

'No, nor me. Anyway, it tastes fine. I'll get dressed in a minute. Meet you at the café as soon as I see to your mum. Sorry. Is she alright?'

'Oh aye. She's enjoying this little crisis – amazing what she can do when she thinks someone is worse off than her. Now. Tell me. Did you just wake up feeling like crap, or has something happened?'

Alice sighs, looks at the window. 'It's just a crap day, Teddy.'

Her voice swims about the place a bit, over the bed, around the floral walls. Her chin dives down.

'Is it? How? Sun's out, look at it. Don't you like sunny days? August is usually wet, this is lucky.' He opens the curtains.

She flinches as if the light is painful, or his words sharp stones. He mentally reviews them.

'Is today an important day in August?' He whispers, 'Alice? *Is it an important day*?'

She nods. Blows her nose.

'Ah. The fourteenth of August, was it? His birthday?'

She nods again, her face crumpling.

'Oh dear. Oh dearie dear.'

She slumps back on her pillow. Her crying is a painful hoarse inhalation. The exhalations are silent.

'Now, now,' he says, and slides onto the bed with her. Pulls her into his side. Tucks her head into his shoulder. Teddy being gay makes this extra comforting. He reminds her of someone . . . but Neal wasn't gay, was he? Obviously not. But same uncomplicated feeling.

'There, there.' And after ten minutes, he says, 'Now tell me, Alice. What did he love doing?'

More blubbering. Teddy strokes her head.

'Come on now, it might help. Tell me. Tell me what Calum loved, pet.'

She hiccups. 'Playing.' Hiccup. 'Stupid computer games. Drinking.' Hiccup. 'Lager.' Hiccup. 'Dole day. Scary movies.'

'Anything else?'

She swallows the last of the hiccups and says, 'Running. I think he loved running best. He said once that nothing mattered when he ran. He didn't have to talk.' She says all these words into Teddy's shirt.

'And his favourite foods?

'Why?'

'Just tell me.'

'Pizza. Chips. Chip butties. Those expensive energy drinks. Oh, and Snickers. He loved a giant-size Snickers bar.'

'Here, use my apron, blow hard this time.'

After five more minutes, Teddy raises Alice up, smoothes her hair and says, 'We've got to go now, so get dressed. I'll just phone the café, tell them we'll be in after lunch.'

'Who will look after it?'

'Who knows? Sam's there now, and he's no got a place to hurry to, so he may stick around all day for the extra cash. Up you get, there you are. Look, here's your clothes, you pop them on like a good girl. Wash your face, and I'll meet you downstairs.'

Alice manages to do as she's told, but barely. Moves like an invalid. She does not brush her teeth, glance in the mirror, wash her face. She pulls her jumper over her nightie and tucks the rest of the nightie into the ugly elastic-waist trousers she's taken to wearing. She slips her trainers on, but forgets about socks, and leaves the laces untied. She goes down the stairs to Teddy, who knows what he's doing. He's sorted out his mum, found a pair of trainers to wear and he's waiting for Alice with a carrier bag. He wordlessly leads her outside.

'Where are we going?'

'Running, of course. I know just the park.'

'Running? I can't run, Teddy.'

'We'll only run a wee while, don't worry. We'll wait till we get there, and we'll only run a wee ways, then we'll have a lovely picnic.'

He walks quickly as he talks and pulls Alice by the hand. Drags her on, then off the train at Hillhead Station. They arrive at the Botanical Gardens. Follow a path that leads away from the greenhouses and towards the river. Soon runners begin to pound past them.

'This is the place,' says Teddy. 'They all come here to run. They're all mad, like.'

A woman jogs so close to Alice she almost trips, and Teddy holds Alice firmly by the upper arm and guides her to the grass verge.

'Now. Alice.' He looks her right in the eyes. 'Why not still celebrate his birthday? You're glad he was born, are you not?' He holds her away from him, holds a hankie to her nose, waits till she blows, then without saying anything else, begins to slowly run away from her. He turns when he's about twenty feet away, jogs on the spot and shouts, 'Come on, fattie!'

Alice's tears are a torrent now, and her nose is running again. It's as if he died yesterday.

'Come on, Alice. Get a move on!'

Alice walks towards him, more to not lose him than anything, but he speeds up and begins to run girlishly away, albeit a very heavy middle-aged girl. Two shaved-headed men in pink Lycra shorts pause to watch him. Then suddenly, he's almost gone from sight and Alice whimpers. She shifts up a gear, and runs. It's easy at first, but quickly becomes hard. She's out of breath.

'Teddy! Teddy, slow down. I can't do this.'

He slows till she almost catches up, then he sprints again and is gone.

She looks around. The park is unfamiliar. She can't remember exactly how she got here. Somewhere a dog growls menacingly. The sun's too bright. For a minute, the glare becomes something more, and everything reflective near Alice glows intensely – an old spoon lying abandoned on the grass, the sprinkler system, some beer tins, a large puddle. Half a dozen men in long orange robes head towards her, their voices an incoherent drone that echoes. Did Teddy spike her tea with acid? Her head begins to buzz, to ache, and she runs. This time, she is too afraid to care about anything but regaining the sight of Teddy. She is too far from herself and so afraid even her bladder trembles.

She finally spots him sitting on a bench by a pond. He's taking things out of the carrier bag. Two chip butties, now cold. Two Cokes, two Snickers. She collapses next to him, says nothing, only pants. When her breathing slows, Teddy opens the tins and passes her one.

'Here's to him.'

'Okay,' she whispers.

They both drink. And then Teddy eats both chip butties because, even though this is better than staying in bed, it's impossible for Alice to swallow food.

Neal and Pink T-Shirt at the Indian

Finn and William are on the same bus, sitting one row apart on the 25A to Inverness. Both, coincidentally, eating chips. Finn looks behind him briefly because someone has turned their music up loud, and he acknowledges William with raised eyebrows.

'Hey,' says William.

'Hey,' says Finn.

'Alright?'

'Aye. You?'

'Aye, sound.'

'Good.'

Then Finn turns away again, and William looks out of the window at nothing. When the bus arrives at the station, Finn walks away first. Quickly, without looking back. He walks past The Raj, where Neal and Suzie are toasting each other with pints of Tiger.

Life is so much better now for Neal, with Suzie and sex punctuating his days. This is the third time he has taken Suzie out to The Raj and already it feels like a tradition. They order what they always order. He has lamb jalfrezi, and she has chickpea korma. She's a vegetarian, plus some other dietary things he can never remember.

Neal makes an effort at conversation because Suzie has demanded it. It does not come naturally, and earlier in the evening he primed himself with conversational gambits. The earthquake in Kuwait, the unseasonal cold rain. But somehow, probably because he doesn't really care, these subjects fade when he reaches for them now. Current news just doesn't seem that interesting to him. He enjoys the thick hot flavours of his curry, the crisp cold Tiger beer. At some point, he becomes aware that Suzie has stopped talking. Looks up to find her watching him with an expression that has already become familiar. What exactly it means will come to him in a minute.

'Lovely food here,' he says nervously.

'Yes. It is. Very. Lovely,' she agrees.

'Sorry, did you ask a question and I didn't answer?'

'Yes.'

'A while ago, was it?'

Later they go back his place. They've both noticed, but not commented on, certain similarities in their houses. The same curtain pattern in the sitting room. The same brands of food in the kitchen, the same cafetiere. The same CDs and tapes by the stereo, the same kind of ground coffee. They even both have fathers who are on second marriages to much younger women. Suzie doesn't speak of their similarities because she thinks it might jinx things. Might make Neal self-conscious. Neal doesn't mention it because he doesn't visit many houses, so it doesn't strike him as unusual. He feels at home at Suzie's house but doesn't mistake it for home.

Look at the way they brush their teeth calmly, fold their clothes carefully, each enter the bed from their own sides.

Each reads for fifteen minutes, lying next to each other, then yawn in unison. Then they have semi-rigorous sex, missionary style, till both make convincing climactic noises. After, they whisper goodnight and roll away from each other and fall instantly into sleep, like puppies. They've been like this from the start. They've skipped the stage of excitement and talking all night and not eating much. Have already settled into the kingdom of convenience and common interests. They're good for each other. Aren't they? Like vitamin pills.

In the morning, over breakfast, she asks if she can stay all next week at his house, as her house is being rewired, and he says, 'Alright.' But with such a look, she rushes in with, 'Ach, don't panic, I've no intention of moving in.' She smiles broadly. Ever cheerful, ever light, is Suzie. 'I love my own space, love it,' she says. 'I'm never going to live with anyone. I'll be gone by the next Saturday, promise.'

'Alright,' he says again.

Then Chrissie phones. Her voice is a jarring note, a reminder of that restless intensity, of the way he's betrayed his quest. Suzie-sex has sedated him.

'Neal! Just seeing how you're getting on.'

'Fine, Chrissie. Sorry I haven't phoned for a while.'

'Nah, don't be silly, I've not called you for a while either.'

'No word, I suppose?'

'No. And you?'

'No. Nothing.'

'I wonder,' muses Chrissie.

'Wonder what?'

Suzie walks by him, glances at him with raised eyebrows. He shrugs back.

'Nothing,' says Chrissie, noticing his voice is a little different now – more outgoing? More polite? Perhaps he's not alone. She suddenly feels shy.

'Tell me. What do you wonder?'

'Just if she'll ever come back.'

'Oh.'

'But now we know she's alive somewhere in Glasgow, and it's up to her now, isn't it?'

'I guess so.'

'Why doesn't she want to see me, though?' Hedging her bets here, because she's also posted this question to God. Always good to get a second opinion, right?

Yesterday after church, she'd hung around till Henry was alone so she could speak to him. *Is there something like a long-distance dialling code for praying, to get quick replies to prayers? I mean, that's your job, right? Every job has perks, every employee knows cheats. I need to know where my sister is. If she's, well, alive. What's the point of religion if it doesn't answer stuff like that?*

Henry did not have the answers she'd hoped for, but he'd answered so slowly and sadly, his voice quavering, she couldn't be irritated. The surprise of an uncertain clergyman! It had cheered her, his transparency, his melancholy. Why should someone else's sadness make her own sadness lessen? But it did.

I'm not sure what to tell you, Chrissie. I think perhaps, when someone loses someone, especially a child, it's very difficult to accept. To know how to go on. Everything they look at will probably remind them of what was, and Alison probably felt a strong desire to escape. Be where she could be distracted and begin to cope with her life. I hope your sister is alright. Let's assume that she is, since we can't do anything about it. That she'll be home soon. Just hope, Chrissie, and try not to fret.

And then they made a date for next Monday morning. Just a chat and coffee.

Now she grips the phone too tightly, and Neal holds his phone tightly too, flinches slightly listening to the frustration in her voice.

'I'm her sister. Her only family now. Why would she not think to ring me?'

'I don't know, Chrissie,' says Neal.

'Oh. Okay. I'm thinking, maybe get Kate to take me down to Glasgow, show me the exact house she saw her go into? I mean, Kate might've written down the wrong address.'

Neal remembers the old lady at the door saying, *I'd know if someone called Alison lived here.*

'You could.'

'Would you come with me?'

'I don't know. No, probably not.'

After he hangs up, Suzie comes up behind him and nuzzles his neck. At first he finds it a little irritating, a little ticklish, but then he closes his eyes and pretends she's wearing that pink t-shirt again, from that first night.

A Bad Night

In the night, Alice wakes up in pain. Food poisoning, she thinks at first. Severe cramping – her period finally? She just makes it to the toilet before her bowels let loose. Hopes Janet doesn't hear, has taken her hearing aid out. She also pees – no blood – and is momentarily relieved.

She returns to her bedroom, gets into bed, and then the pain comes again. And five minutes later, again. And again, much sharper this time, with echoes of previous similar sensations.

Back to the toilet to vomit. She's emptying out at breakneck speed, she'll be inside out in five minutes at this rate. Damn, what has she eaten? She sits on the edge of the bath and rocks back and forth as the pain rolls through her belly and back. This is it. She is dying.

Good, she thinks.

Good, good, good. Death, come get me. Here I am. I am ready to roll.

But what about Janet? She better warn Teddy.

'Teddy,' she says when he finally answers his phone.

'Is it Mum? Have you rung for an ambulance?'

'It's me, Teddy.'

'What's you?'

She starts to tell him about dying, when the pain makes speech impossible.

'What's happening? Is that you moaning? Fuck. Fuck. I'll be right over.'

But she doesn't hear any of this because she's dropped the phone and is on the floor.

'Dying!' she moans with grim satisfaction. Makes her way back towards her bedroom, but for no reason goes into the airing cupboard instead. It's small, dark, warm.

Outside it's raining. Teddy arrives with the rain still running off his bald head. Looks for her downstairs and upstairs.

'Alice? Alice!' softly.

'Teddy!' she calls softly back. 'In here, Teddy!'

'Where's here?'

'Teddy!' she calls in a half-scream. The last syllable of his name gets the most emphasis, so he hears EEEE!! Races to the cupboard, where she is curled up under the towels.

'What the fuck are you doing in here?'

'Help me.'

'Aye, well I'm here.' He sits with her. Puts his arms around her.

'I'm dying, Teddy,' she whispers in a pause from pain. 'I just thought I should tell you, like.'

'No, no, darling woman.' He smiles. 'You're not dying, it's only a baby you're having.'

'A what?'

'A wean, Alice. How could you not know you were having a wean?'

'A baby? A baby? Are you off your friggen head? How can I have a baby, I don't even have a friggen boyfriend! Plus, I'm friggen menopausal! Frig!'

Alice never swears. Alison is rearing up again, but she's out of practice, and it's a few minutes before she can say fuck.

'Fuck, fuck, fuck.'

Another severe spasm; a moan so low, so guttural, three walls away Janet sits up in her bed. Just sits there, trying to work out an explanation. Street stabbing? Ghost?

'There, there,' Teddy says soothingly, since it's obvious Alice must be humoured. 'Maybe it's an immaculate conception. That's what it is, sure.'

A9

Among others, today the A9 is used by a lorry driver taking shellfish to France, a farmer taking ewes from Wick to the Dingwall market, two housewives from Bad Caull wanting to choose some new curtains at Arnott's in Inverness, a Harley Davidson biker from Germany seeing the sights, and one seventeen-year-old who was going to wait till he passed his test, but then just couldn't.

Drivers who notice Calum's memorial, well, they continue driving. Roadside shrines are not common, but they're instantly recognisable for what they are. Thoughts of death pass through these drivers for a second, and maybe one or two of them make different choices later in their day.

Tonight Zara is invisible, even to herself. It's that dark. Not a scrap of moon. She reads the ground and the plants like brail, her gloved hands moving roughly over them. She nods as she finds each thing she planted last January. They are all still there, just playing dead to trick the oncoming winter. The rose bushes, the birch trees, all leafless already. But what's this? A few Seraphim red roses, which she feels very gently. The petals feel like skin, cold but alive and vulnerable. Between the Seraphims and the yellow Cherubims, there have been roses blooming here for seven months.

She's exhausted and she's shivering. It's the coldest night since last April. 'Well, Calum, will you look at this place now,' she whispers triumphantly. She stopped apologising altogether a while ago. Just continues as if he has forgiven her and they are practically an old married couple now. She even bickers with him sometimes. His death has not succeeded in ending the relationship after all. It has a little while to run yet. Some days she feels just plain bored with him, and annoyed. 'I told you twenty times: I am not bossy, I'm just speaking my mind. What, you want me to keep my mouth shut? Piss off, you.'

And then Calum's car slides off the road again and again, and his surprise is always fresh. His eyes widen and his face trembles like a newborn. As vulnerable as a human face can be. Comprehension dawning, just, and his heart leaping in protest. *Not yet! Not now!* Over and over, his phone rings, he reaches for it, hopes it is her, the sun glints off the road, and over and over again, the crows on the wire, the broken bottles on the verge, the *Mum!* yanked from his throat. The ear-splitting metallic crunch and sense of leaving the surface of the earth momentarily. All this, all this, all this. Then nothing, nothing and nothing.

Part Six

October 1996 to February 1999

Alison is Back

'Mother's name?' asks the register.

'Alison Ross,' she answers clearly. Alison is a bigger person with a longer history, and so Alice succumbs, disappears. It's a seamless join. Teddy's eyebrows lift, but he says nothing.

'Father's name?'

Pause.

'Father's name?' Looks at Teddy, who looks at Alison.

'Neal Munro,' she says, in a rushed exhalation, as if he's been held captive in her lungs.

'Child's name?'

'Solas Teddina Ross. S.O.L.A.S.'

Alison chose Solas for three reasons. It sounds a little like Alice, her name for those lost nine months. It also sounds like solace, which is what new life can bring the world. But most of all, she chose Solas because *solas* means light in Gaelic. Alison pays tribute to light, in this naming, because this whole dark year light has been rescuing her. Impersonal, cold shafts of light in all sorts of places. Alison has begun to think the dead might reside in reflections in

223

puddles, in rays that shoot out from under grey clouds like banners of excitement. In people's eyes sometimes – that flash of light – when suddenly, despite themselves and everything around them, joy fleetingly grabs hold of their hearts.

Teddy gently rocks the baby, who obligingly sleeps and dreams milky dreams. He kisses her feathery red-blond hair tenderly, lets his lips linger.

'You want one too, Teddy?'

'Definitely.'

'Well, you should get one. Just get one. You'd be an ace dad.'

'You think?'

Solas shifts slightly, raising her tiny hands nearly to the top of her head, which is as far as they'll go. Then re-settles into her dreams.

Alison takes her baby when they're on the bus and nuzzles her head. Silently says, Here she is, Calum, here's your wee sister. Look at her, is she not just lovely? Aye, I know I'm a bit past it and she'll completely finish me off, but will you just look at her wee fingers? She's got your eyes, so she does, and she's your sister, and will you just look at her, Calum? I'll be showing her your photo soon, the Fyrish Hill race one, don't you worry about that, my lad.

Too right she'll finish you off, Mum. But do you not think you need a bit of finishing off? Anyway, she's brought you back to your mean old self, so no moaning please. And mind you get her the good trainers, not the cheap rubbish.

Course I will, son. Got to admit though, it is fucking freaky being a mum again. Like it's the first time, really. Some days I feel I haven't a clue. Some days I feel so scared I wonder if she'd be better off without me.

Don't be daft, Mum. She'll need someone to annoy later. To drive crazy and cost heaps and make messes for. Who better than you?

Aye, right. I forgot that bit of the job. Quite good at that bit, wasn't I?

Aye. You were aye dead easy to wind up.

Alison talks to her son more now than when he was alive. So strange, to just speak her mind to him. And even weirder, he has become a sympathetic listener. He is, it has to be said, quite good company now. She can tell him anything. And she has stopped worrying about him, too. In that place where there'd been a constant murmur of Calum anxiety, now there is nothing.

Solas yawns, opens her petal mouth and roots around. She doesn't really remind her mum of Calum. It's been too many years, and besides, Solas is entirely her own unique self. Already it is obvious from her serious eyes and economical cries that she is quite intelligent.

Milk fills Alison's breasts till they're absurdly hot and hard. She's not aware she's crying till the tears fall on her daughter's face. She cries a lot these days, as if her tear ducts are incontinent. Not gut-wrenching, more pressure-relieving. She cries as she pays attention to all the little necessary things a baby demands: burping, feeding, changing, rocking. And she minds none of this. It is all real and even the nappy rash is welcomed and dealt with.

Solas has not entirely returned Alison to the world, but she is making her mother's eventual return inevitable. A baby has the power to break up heavy chunks of time into a million lighter less thought-filled pieces, simply by needing constant care. With every sad dream interrupted by infant cries, Ali moves closer to the world. Calum's death leached

225

the colour out of everything, and Solas is pumping it back in.

Teddy stretches his arm behind Alison. Whispers, 'Go on, hen. Feed the poor wean.'

And she feeds Solas all the way home.

Neal Walks All the Way Home

Another Saturday night, and they're watching telly. *Inspector Morse*. Her legs stretch over his lap, and he absentmindedly strokes her ankle. He wonders if her ankles are an erogenous zone, and if so, if they are a major erogenous zone or only a minor one. He mildly enjoys stroking them – maybe she only mildly enjoys it too. Maybe at their age, only minor zones are left. Where have the major ones gone? He manages to follow the film closely while having these very familiar thoughts. Then Neal lifts her legs off and stands up.

'Fancy a cheese toastie?'

'No, no thanks.'

'Oh aye, forgot. Bread. Gluten.'

'And the dairy. Cheese is dairy.' She doesn't take her eyes off the screen.

'Sorry. Fancy a . . . an oatcake and . . . peanut butter?'

'Aye, thanks. Sounds delicious.' She turns and gave him an extra big smile.

In the kitchen, he turns on the grill, grates the cheese, butters the bread, hums to himself. Makes a cup of tea while the cheese is melting. His thoughts wander where they will, down the usual paths. He returns to the sitting room, still humming, and is startled momentarily by the sight of a nice-looking woman wearing pink lipstick sitting on his sofa. A woman that is neither his wife nor Alison.

'Where's my oatcake, then?' she asks. 'And is that a cup of tea? Lovely.'

So, Suzie slips his mind easily, but isn't that a good sign? He's already taking her for granted; it's wonderful to be at that stage again. So relaxing. He's going through the motions, but from the outside it looks exactly, but exactly like the real thing.

A week later, Neal invites the woman who'd originally taught him to live like that, his learner-wife, out for lunch.

'Alright,' Sally says on the phone. 'Where?'

'That new café in the courtyard behind the Tesco car park?'

'What's it called?'

'No idea.'

'I know,' she says in her precise tone. 'Courtyard Café.'

'Makes sense,' he concedes.

'Yes. Lovely pancakes. Coffee . . . not strong enough for me.'

'No. Do a nice pot of tea, though.'

On and on, the sort of small talk they always talked. Eerily like it's just been a few hours since their last conversation. He's not seen Sally for almost two months, and the first sight of her pierces him. Her familiarity is physically painful. Her double chin is adorable.

After she orders pea soup for them both without even asking him, in her usual way, she tells him she has a boyfriend. Which explains the glow he now notices. In fact, she is looking damned pretty. Far prettier and nicer than pink Suzie. Not Suzie's fault she's just an inferior Sally replacement, but. The words he's been rehearsing suddenly sit up and gasp. A boyfriend? What the hell!

'What? Who?'

'James Black. From Jamestown, remember?'

'You and James Black?' Neal giggles now, he can't help it. There's not an ounce of humour in his heart, this is a nervous reaction.

'What are you sniggering about?'

'Not laughing, really. Sorry. Bit shocked, to tell you the truth. God, Sally, he's like, like, I don't know. You never even used to like him.' Jealousy, an emotion he's never experienced before, is rising like a bilious storm in his gut.

'Have you lost weight, Neal? You look great.' True. All that sex has burned calories. He looks more toned, more alert, altogether more attractive now.

'Don't change the subject, Sally. You used to laugh at James. You said his breath always stank. Hali whatever. His breath pongs!'

'Things change. How are you, anyway? Has Alison returned?'

'What? No!' How dare she bring that distraction into the conversation.

'Well, are you seeing anyone?'

'No.' Suzie and Saturday nights, what are they? Less than nothing right now.

'Oh. Well, really glad you wanted to meet. I was thinking we should start sorting out things, Neal.'

Nothing about this lunch is going according to plan, and his soup gets cold.

'What do you mean? Sort what things out?'

'Neal! Honestly! We have to sell the house, for one thing. It's my house really, and I need that money now. Unless you want to buy it and stay there.'

'I don't want to sell. I'm sorry. I do not want to sell.' This is making him feel about four years old. He knows he's sounding ridiculous but cannot stop himself. There are tears in his voice. 'Why should I move?' he says petulantly.

In this moment, she actually likes Neal far more than she's liked him for a while. He feels like someone she could be friends with. For a moment, she actually prefers Neal to James! Neal makes her laugh, without even trying. His face is funny, especially now. It reveals so much male vanity and male naivety, all mixed up. This is not a face that could break any woman's heart, that's for sure.

'So, are you serious about James? He what . . . buys some mouthwash, so you ju-ju-jump into bed with him?' His face is red.

'Hey, you started this,' she begins gently.

'Ah!' This ah is dangerously low. 'I was waiting for that. I get it now. No matter what happens to you for the rest of your, your, your *righteous little life*, you'll blame me. For a one-night stand.'

Neal pauses here, shaking. He has so little practice saying mean things, it takes him far from himself, depletes him. What was he going to say to her? Those rehearsed words. It's all going horribly wrong. He takes a breath and says in a single exhalation, 'I wanted to say something to you today, Sally.'

'Go on.' Expressionless.

'I wanted to apologise. And to explain. I don't think I ever properly explained.'

'Go on.' Still dead.

'Alright. About Alison. And Golspie. I didn't want to do that. It wasn't my plan at all. The whole thing. And I am so sorry.'

Sally doesn't say anything, just stares, still the unreadable eyes.

The waitress clears their table and asks, 'Are you wanting some dessert? We have a lovely chocolate gateau today.'

'No thanks,' says Neal.

'Yes. I'll have the pancakes and maple syrup please,' says Sally.

How can Sally eat at a time like this? His gorge rises just hearing the word syrup.

'I believe you, Neal, about it not being intentional. I do! You're not a bastard philanderer, and I'm not angry at you anymore. Truly.' Her voice is suddenly genuinely warm, so much like her old self, he wants to hug her right now, hold her and squeeze tight, like they used to.

'I want you to come home, Sally. Come back!' he says, his voice quivering like a girl's, pressing his thin lips together at the end to hold back an outpouring.

'Ah, Neal.'

'Please. Please, Sal.'

Her face scrunches up, as if she's eaten something that doesn't taste like she expected it to. Surprise, but not necessarily dismay. Doesn't open her mouth to say anything. Just scrunches.

'I love you,' he whispers. 'I love you, Sally, and I miss you.'

'Ah, Neal. I love you too. I really do! You're bit annoying sometimes and you screwed up big time. But you're a good man, really.'

'Come home, Sally.'

'Sorry. It's too late. I can't come back now, Neal.'

'Why not?' Hating the whine in his voice.

'James is in love with me,' she says helplessly. 'I couldn't do that to him.'

'Go on. Do it anyway. He'll get over it.'

Sally rubs her eyes, waits as the waitress places her dessert in front of her, then says, in her old taking-charge voice, 'Neal, listen. You know what I've been thinking?' She raises her fork, holds it over the pancakes. Pauses, then shakes her head as if she's decided not to say those words after all. Laughs briefly and says, 'I am so bossy. I'm a terrible bossy-boots all the time.'

It's true, Neal thinks. Sally always makes the rules. She begins to eat her pancakes with gusto, and he suddenly remembers the first time he saw Sally. Her unlined, yet strangely grown-up expression when he introduced himself as the reporter. The way she'd smiled quietly, even while talking, assessing him. He remembers the way she'd given his hand a secret squeeze as they parted. Said *See you soon*, though as yet no date had been made. As if a deal had just been brokered, with a satisfactory conclusion. *That's what I've been missing, more than anything else*, he suddenly realises. *Sally's certainty.*

'But I kind of liked you being the boss. Be my boss again, Sally.'

She begins to laugh.

'Please.'

'Sorry. Really, Neal, I am so very sorry. The problem is, I'm the boss of James now, and you know me. Loyal as stink.' She reaches for his hands with both of hers, and he tries not to mind that her hands are sticky with maple syrup. It's one of the things he cannot stand, normally.

'The thing is, it's too late now. But we can be friends.'

After an eighty-seven-second stare-down, during which Sally mouths *Sorry*, Neal concedes. Withdraws his hands. Puts on his jacket. Walks away and keeps walking. With every step, and there are many – he leaves his car behind

232

and walks all the way home – he thinks he understands more.

Oh! His romantic life is the victim of massive bad timing, and he's doomed to love who he has lost. Oh! He's developed a flair for melodrama and feels stupid after the first mile. His feet are killing him. When he gets home, he'll need to call a taxi to take him back to his car. Even his dramatic gestures end pathetically and expensively. Then as if to underline his foolishness, it begins to rain in cruel icy bursts, and his feet are quickly soaked.

Prodigal Sister

Raining so loudly, Chrissie doesn't hear the doorbell and Alison opens the door and shouts, 'Hello!'

'Jesus! I can't believe it! Fuck me, for fuck's sake, Alison Ross,' Chrissie says, gaping in her doorway at her little sister with a baby under her arm. 'Oh my God, *thank you God,* oh dear, oh dear,' she says over and over, as she passes the obscenity stage of surprise. 'And who in the world is this? Give her to me, what a weight, what a perfect wee face, how old is she?'

'Just over three months.'

'Bless. What's her name?'

'Solas.'

'Solas? What are you like, Ali? What kind of name's that for a bonnie wee girl like this? She's yours, I take it? Looks very like you, actually. Aside from the ginger hair, of course. Your eyes.'

'Aye, she's mine.'

'Wow, you work quick girl. And who with? Have you got a fellow, then?'

'No, not as such. A friend who helps me out. A man called Teddy. In fact, it was his idea that I come up for a wee visit.'

All this time, Chrissie pulling Alison into her over-heated house, pulling off her coat, her gloves, pressing her into an armchair, bringing her a cup of tea, touching her hair, patting her shoulders. Making a fuss of the baby.

'Is this the only bag you've got, then? Not much to show for all this time away, then.'

'I'm just here for a visit, Chrissie.' But the bag contains a brown body-shaped container.

'Could have phoned, Ali. I've been so worried. All this time. You don't know. I thought, for a while, you were dead somewhere.'

'I sort of was. Sorry.'

'So did Neal. He even went to Glasgow to look for you.'

'Neal?'

'Aye. He'll be dead chuffed to hear you're okay.'

'Don't tell him just yet, will you? Not ready.'

'Okay. But why, Ali? Why did you just bugger off like that?'

'I don't know. I just couldn't. I . . . I just couldn't stay, Chrissie. It was so hard to even talk.'

'Hard to talk to me? Surely.'

'To anyone. Anyone who . . . knew me. I didn't have a plan, but . . . I couldn't be here anymore. I can't explain it.'

'Alright, darling. But are you okay now? You seem . . . well, different.'

'Well. I am, I guess.'

'Of course you are. Ignore me, that was a stupid thing to say. Being here again, it must feel like you're . . . I don't know. Re-entering an orbit or something. Bits of you scraping off on re-entry, falling to earth. Like that satellite a while ago.'

'I'm fine, Chrissie. Honest. Not the same, obviously, but I'm okay. Is the pot empty? Could do with another cuppa.'

The next afternoon, Alison and Solas are in the play park, even though it's freezing and will probably begin to rain in a minute. Solas is warm enough, tucked under her mother's jumper, sucking away. They're waiting here till Chrissie finishes the shopping.

Alison feels like she's floating. Her tired heart is beating quickly. There is so much to take in, so many forgotten cues to memories. The yeasty smell of the distillery, the sound of the gulls. Even the graffiti on the see-saw, the way the middle swing is still cock-eyed. She holds Solas closer. Tells her silently, *It won't be long, love. Won't be long till you're begging to be pushed higher and higher on a swing somewhere. You'll probably scream as if you're scared to death, then moan when I stop pushing.*

Chrissie is in Gateways supermarket. Wants to prepare a big celebratory meal. In the cereal aisle she passes the old minister.

'Hello, Henry,' she says.

'Hello there, Chrissie. You're looking very well!'

And while Chrissie explains that Alison has returned, and Henry pauses to listen, God slips away from her. She notices Him going, adjacent to the shelf of Coco Pops, and she misses Him for a minute. Then Him becomes him. She'll need to think about it later, say her goodbyes properly, but basically God's job is done now. Her sister has returned. She tells Henry about Solas, how sweet she looks, but he doesn't seem to be listening anymore.

In fact, he suddenly looks sedated and kind of stupid. Drunk? No, no. Henry is feeling himself inflate with ... what is this familiar feeling? Hey there, it's You again. I missed You! Standing in this most ludicrous of all

236

supermarket aisles, grace courses through his veins and muscles, reaches his brain and effervesces like champagne. Deliciously obliterating. He experiences such relief, he's swooning by the time he reaches the queue. Atheism had begun to exhaust him. Utterly exhaust him. There's simply too much in his heart to compress into a single lifetime. He needs eternity to expend it all, and he has no use at all for rationality. Not really.

Chrissie, in the queue ahead of him, is laying six boxes of chocolate éclairs on the conveyor belt, as well as four bottles of fizzy wine and six huge steaks. Her old heathen self is planning a welcome home party for herself as much as Alison.

In Henry's basket, there is broccoli, porridge oats, bread and milk. He'd meant to buy some double cream and strawberries, but now he's thinking Lent. Not for another month or so, but why not start practising now? He looks forward to depriving himself again, that sweet ache of unfulfilled desire.

'Ali! Will you stop that, you'll give some poor geezer heart failure, exposing yourself like that,' Chrissie scolds, walking into the park.

Alison is wrapping Solas up again, and buttoning her own coat because it's begun to rain in thin icy needles. Her sister wants them to come home, into the warm. Drink tea, watch telly. So they do.

Christmas was over two weeks ago, but the tree is still up. It's a fake tree, so needles aren't a problem, and besides Solas stops crying when she sees the twinkling lights. Chrissie explains how she'd waited months, then when the Council needed the house back, she'd rented a storage unit and packed up Alison's house. Not everything of course, quite a lot of stuff went into black bin bags for Blythswood. And she'd kept some of Calum's things. His good running shoes and the prize he'd been given in P7 for sports. A few other small things like that.

While she peels potatoes, chops onions, the house gradually fills with her daughters, and their daughters, including the new baby. Another girl. Since they moved into their own houses, it's such a pleasure to see them. She'd thought they'd never leave. They swarm round Alison and Solas. Hugs, kisses, squeals, tears, more hugs.

'You look fabulous, Ali!'

'No, no. You look fabulous!'

'And look at your wee girl, too adorable. Can I hold her?'

'Here, take her.'

After a while, Alison sees the framed photograph on the mantle above the fire. Herself and Calum on Mangurstadh beach. Stares at it. Everyone follows her eyes, and after a second of awkwardness, offers Ali another cup of tea, or a glass of wine perhaps?

'We miss him too. Like mad,' says one niece.

'Every minute,' says the other.

Alison opens her mouth to say Calum's absence is carved in her bones, but doesn't. It sounds melodramatic. Pretentious even. She nods her agreement, and they all lament the fact the family is just three generations of women now. No matter that they are years into the post-feminist era, they agree it feels a bit rudderless without a man. Ridiculous, but there you go.

'So bloody brilliant to have you home,' says Chrissie again the next morning over coffee. Behind her are mountains of dirty dishes from last night. Pans sliding into the sink, food-crusted cutlery everywhere. Bottles lined up by the bin.

'Great to be home,' says Alison, and it's true. But it's also surreal, and this is not her house. Janet and Teddy are in her thoughts often. Even that daffodil on tartan wallpaper seems more real than Alness, though it seems a good sign that Solas slept through the night for the first time last night.

Later she takes a walk to the shops while Chrissie watches Solas. When she sees Finn and William walking separately down the street, they remind her so sharply of her son, she almost can't speak to them. They notice her, and also notice each other. Their faces turn pink and their walk slows till they are both in front of her.

'Alison!'

'How are you, William?'

'Alright. Freezing, like. But.'

'And you, Finn?'

'Oh, fine. Great to see you. It's been a long time. How are you?'

'Okay, it's good to . . .'

Then her throat constricts and her words stop. Eyes filling, she smiles and nods to release them. They start to turn away, when suddenly she reaches for their hands, one in each of hers, so they form a chain, and she squeezes their hands tight.

'Take care of yourselves, boys. I mean it. Good luck with . . . everything.'

Then she drops their hands and rushes away. After a minute, Finn says to William, 'Heard she's got another kid now.'

'Aye. A wee girl.'

'Calum would have loved that. A sister.'

'So he would.'

Pause.

'Heard you got married, Finn. That was sudden like, eh?'

'Aye. Well.'

'Congrats, man!'

'Ta. Heard you've joined the army.'

'Aye. Well.'

Then Finn and William, Calum's pals from playschool, from Coul Park Primary, from Alness Academy, from that desperately confusing post-funeral rain-soaked morning, look like they might hug. But they don't. They hurl hands towards each other, and smile. Pump each other's hand for a second or two. A hard pumping, but nothing mere acquaintances mightn't do. Then each turns and walks away in an opposite direction. Shoulders squared, steps quick. William hops on a bus. Finn disappears round a corner, then his mobile phone beeps with three rising notes.

Take care of yrsel man.

Finn smiles and texts back: *U 2.*

The Sign

Saturday morning, Neal takes the sign and hammer and wanders about his own front garden. Wonders where would be the best place to announce an era has finally ended. Where should his marriage be buried? Under the cherry tree, which will be hideously cheerful in a few months? Down by the pavement, where folk can get a good look?

It is all very strange. This time last year Neal had a good job, a good marriage and a nice house without a For Sale sign stabbed into the front lawn. He stands holding the rough wooden sign in one hand, the hammer in the other, and it begins to rain silently. Straight up and down rain, soft and soaking. This helps somehow, and by the time his face is wet and his shoes damp, he's driven the For Sale stake into the ground, halfway between the tree and the road. He returns to the house, quickly changes his clothes and goes out again. He gets into his car and drives to the newspaper office. He's not going to work because he doesn't exactly have a job anymore. He has a weekly slot, and that's all. Last month, the editor took him to lunch at The Mallard and explained the situation:

'Sales down, Neal, and the paper's shrinking. Happening everywhere! But we'd like you to carry on with the Years Ago Today column please. If you want, I mean. Not much money in it, I'm afraid, but we could offer you a stipend.'

Neal had slumped over the table a bit, his face pink. 'Oh, you don't have to let me keep the history column. Honestly.'

'Hey, you think I feel sorry for you?'

'Aye.'

'What, sorry for a sad bastard who actually enjoys reading ancient newspapers? Fucking right I feel sorry for you. Want to keep doing 150 Years Ago Today or not?'

'There wasn't a paper 150 years ago.'

'Crap, Neal. Who but you would know that? Who would care?'

He's been given a goodbye and good luck party, and since then he's tried to avoid the office during work hours. Goes in on the weekend when it's empty because it feels rude to re-appear when they've all said goodbye so sweetly. They've given him a hundred pound book voucher, of which he still has twenty-five pound. He ekes out this treat on mid-week forays into Inverness. Thin's Book Shop, then Leakey's for a bowl of soup. The job hunt has been humiliating of course. A history degree is not, it turns out, much use, and all the other papers are cutting back. Plus, it's common knowledge that Neal has become less punctual, less reliable.

Time has taken on a whole new shape. There's lots of the stuff, but once corralled into segments, it slips by as painlessly as when he worked full time. Many of his daily tasks, like getting dressed and eating breakfast, have simply expanded into the larger time frame, and some days he actually feels like he is rushing from one task to another.

242

He arrives at the empty office, unlocks the door and makes a cup of strong coffee. Switches on his old computer, which is someone else's now. Automatically, he avoids looking at this other person's personal detritus, like the framed wedding photo, the lipstick-stained I Love NY mug, the discarded tissues. Neal is intruding, and he is a very tactful man.

But after a minute his old bubble begins to descend and he is happy as a clam. Look at him: There he is, humming away, calmly tapping in details from a time not that long ago, but already almost completely gone from most memories.

26th April 1976: TWENTY-ONE YEARS AGO TODAY

- Rooms to rent, Alness. HW and colour TV. Mrs MacKenzie 884087
- Heat wave; Black Isle farmers panic about crops and hold emergency meeting with minister in Inverness.
- Black Rock Rovers FC dance, Diamond Jubilee Hall, Evanton 9:30.
- The Tools play at the Royal Hotel, 8:00 Friday night. 50p entrance.
- Found: Yellow offshore jacket and helmet, left in National Hotel, Dingwall. Claim at reception.
- Staff wanted: Welders, engineers, fitters, catering and cleaning staff. Apply labour exchange, Kishorn.
- Dingwall Academy – Spring concert with a performance by local choral group, with guest singer Isobel McDonald.
- Daffodil Tea at Foulis Castle, Evanton, to be held Saturday between 2 and 5. Teas, cakes, stalls, and jumble. All proceeds to the Red Cross.

- Sixty-two 2 and 3 bedroom houses now available in Westford Estate, Alness. For information contact Highland Council Housing office.

And then he types in the very ad that led to this current situation:

- Farm cottage to rent in Alness. Suit Nigg workers. £40 a month. Contact Mr Ross 885498.

He's not been aware of it, but this is what he's been looking for all along – evidence of his own past, preserved somewhere, aside from his own grey brain cells. The twenty-three-year-old virgin Neal had read this same paper, and wondered if it was too late to ring Mr Ross. Sat in the National drinking a Carlsberg Special, and hoped no one had beaten him to it. This led to that, and that led to this.

By the time he finishes his coffee, Neal is tranquil. He looks older than his age, but that's just his contented slouch, his receding hairline, this air of calm resignation. Things are alright. He's signing on while he looks for another job. He has enough to get by, if he's careful. A perfectly nice woman with a cheerful disposition has invited him to live with her, meantime. For a second or two, he can't recall her name – but he doesn't panic. Attributes this blankness to his middle age, to all the other thoughts filling his head. Anyway, what's a name? A name is nothing. Suzie! That's it. Another S woman in his life. Sex with S women, that seems to be his lot. S for safe. S for civilised, phonetically.

Later, he drives back home, stopping on the way to buy milk, bread, Fruit and Fibre. The For Sale sign is still on the lawn, looking like it means business. The house already looks shifty, ready to belong to someone else.

Alison borrows her niece's car, which used to be her own car. She straps Solas into the borrowed car-seat. Solas is fat in her winter outfit, bulked into a stiff little package. She stares at Alison.

'What're you staring at?' her mother mock-growls, a silly voice, and Solas smiles, showing no teeth. Every time Solas smiles, Alison smiles back and it's like a door in her chest opening to a warm uplifting rush of air. Smiling is still so new for them both.

Halfway down the High Street, a man waves her down, and she stops her car. 'Ali! Hey! Wow, brilliant to see you, Ali. Missed you, babe.'

'Jimmy. Good to see you too.'

'Ian.'

'Sorry.'

'No worries. Christ, it's been a while. Totally get it. Fancy a drink later? You staying with your sister, yeah?'

'Aye.'

'Grand. See you later, then. About eight, yeah? Cool.'

'Okay.'

Alison considers driving through Evanton, avoiding the crash place, but at the last minute doesn't. Heads south on the A9. Says hello to the ragged remnants of Zara's memorial. Her heart leaps out. It doesn't even tell her it's leaping. Crows perch on the wire above the embankment, the sun glinting off their feathers. They all face the same way, but one.

At the Ardullie roundabout, she continues south into Dingwall, then west to Strathpeffer. She's never been to Neal's house, but she has the address scribbled down on a piece of paper which slides around the dashboard. Strathpeffer is not a big place. She'll just drive around, and if she doesn't find it, well, she'll just go back home. She doesn't feel strongly motivated; this is a journey with mixed feelings. Solas whinges a bit, then falls asleep as The Cat's Back looms up, a dark swell of treeless hill, like a wave. Her mouth puckers in suck dreams.

Oh dear. Neal's house is easy to find, and Alison is in front of it before she knows it. Now what? She looks at it – *very nice, very prim*, she thinks. A traditional Victorian stone house with a For Sale sign in front. *I'll get Chrissie to put him off*, she thinks. *Jimmy, Ian, whoever*. What on earth had she ever seen in that man? Or any of them?

Then she thinks: *Closed curtains. Good, no one is home.* But she can't leave just yet. She sits and thinks of things she hasn't thought about in a long time. Some of these things she has never properly thought about before. Well, it's Neal's house, why shouldn't she have Neal thoughts so near it? Loch Achilty, and countless other times float through the car. A blurry sensation comes over her. And she silently says, *Check it out, Calum. Nice house, eh?*

Then she turns the key in the ignition. Begins to reverse. Turns around, then hears a pounding on her window. Puts it in neutral, pulls the handbrake on.

'Neal! What are you doing here?' she says stupidly. Then she rolls down her window and says it again.

'Me? Alison, I live here. This is my house.' He stares at the woman he's been searching for. None of the expected responses are forthcoming. No joy. No relief. Some surprise that they seem to be arguing. And a numbness. He feels peculiar. Faint.

'Oh. Is it? Sorry, I knew that.'

'Alison? It's really you. I saw you from the kitchen window.'

'Yeah. I was just about to . . .'

'I like your hair short like that. And the colour too. Nice.'

'Ta. Easier. Keeping it. My own colour.'

Pause, while she runs her fingers nervously through her hair. It spikes up above her forehead, giving her an exposed startled look.

'I thought your house. Looked empty. I was about to leave.'

'I saw you. I can't believe it. You look great. When did you get back?'

'Oh. Not long ago. A while ago.'

'Chrissie just stopped ringing. I never thought.'

'Been trying to lay low.'

'Sure. You okay now?'

'Better. Thanks. Chrissie told me you'd been asking. After me. And looking for me.' She can't stop speaking in staccato.

'Aye. Well, I was worried, Alison.'

'Yes, I know.'

Pause.

'Aye,' says Neal, his numbness evaporating. His head straightens up, then he tilts it in another direction, this time towards her. Every word Alison says, every movement, her breath even, these are all sharp arrows to his heart, which now lives on the outside of his shirt. He tilts his head to divert their aim, or ease their entrance. He can't tell. It's like entering a different element, just being this near her.

'Chrissie said you and, and, and . . .' She gestures to his house, to the For Sale sign.

'Me and Sally?'

'Yes. Chrissie said you and your wife spilt up. Sorry.'

'Yeah. Me too.' He flaps his hands around a bit then lets them settle.

She has to make herself breathe deeply now. Where's this going? Why has she come? A shudder rolls visibly through Alison's body, and Neal suddenly knows he'll never live with Suzie. He says, 'You're cold. Come in for a warm drink. A cup of tea.'

Silence. Alison looks straight ahead. Her head does not tilt, but the world does.

Neal stares at her profile a minute then reaches in and turns off her ignition. Very unlike him to be so masterful, and they are both a little stunned. He opens her door. After a minute, puts a hand on her arm to ease her up out of her seat. Her head suddenly feels too heavy, and she's horrified to find it moving towards Neal's shoulder. It's seeking the shelter of that spot between his shoulder and neck. There it goes, coorying in like a kitten.

'Alison,' he says with relief, which is finally pouring in, the immense simple relief of her. But she is not relieved, and her muscles tense.

'Neal, what happened? Golspie. It was a one-off. You know that, right?' She is talking into his shoulder.

'Aye. I know,' he says calmly, though his heart has just broken like the most delicate china cup on a concrete floor. To smithereens. Only splinters left.

'I was a little crazy that night. I used you, Neal,' she whispers, tears running now.

A small cloud of unrequited *I love you* starts to drifts from Neal's chest, over Neal's shoulder, over his neighbourhood rooftops, not unlike the chill wind that rushed over Evanton when Calum died (only not chill). It has no other place to go. And yes, it must go somewhere. Love is a substance, a measurable entity with specific attributes. It emits electricity, fills hearts, defies gravity.

'I'm so sorry, Neal.'

'Shush. I know. It's alright.'

They continue standing, holding on to each other in silence, while nearby, various residents experience inexplicable happiness. (When Calum died, a woman in nearby Evanton slumped inside, dropped some salad cream into her shopping basket, even though it wasn't a brand she liked. Remember?) Now, the woman next door to Neal's house begins to dance in her kitchen for no reason at all.

'Still friends, then?' she whispers.

'Of course. Friends.'

But they don't let go. Alison cannot let go. In fact, she is paralysed. As if falling in love is an anaesthetic before some life-saving surgery. And because Alison has never fallen in love with a nice man before, she thinks she's ill. Needs to hold on to keep upright. If she saw a flying saucer, she couldn't be more shocked.

'Hey, hey,' Neal says soothingly.

All year long, she's been noticing things she never noticed before. And now she notices that Neal's voice is like a sensuous blanket around her shoulders. Everything suddenly feels simpler. Lots of things simply slide away. There they go! Her mental shopping list for dinner, Solas's nappy rash, the pile of un-opened bills, that permanent panic, the edginess she'd given up trying to shake.

Four minutes pass. Outwardly, they look the same, but Alison is melting into Neal now, and that cloud of *I Love You* is being sucked back into Neal's heart. *Whoosh!* It is intelligent, very, and returns the second it senses an echo. Then it pours from his heart into Alison's, filling it like a warm liquid. (And the dancing kitchen woman, well, she is still dancing anyway because all she needed was a kick-start.)

Neal wants to talk about this shift, to kiss Alison, to dance and shout it from the rooftops. But Alison still cannot move, so he can't either. So there they stand, while clouds disperse, reform, shuttle across the sky, and the sparrow nearby has time to build half a nest in the cherry tree.

Then, just as Neal decides enough is enough, and if no one else is going to take charge of this moment it must be him, Solas wakes with a small girly yawn and squeals.

'What's that noise?' asks Neal.

Road Trip

So cold, Neal has to scrape yesterday's inhalations off the inside of the car window. Heating on full blast, he heads south. Glances at Fyrish Hill, edging over Evanton in a protective curve. That is where Calum loved to run, and that is where his ashes were finally spilled one misty Sunday morning. Just the three of them, and a flask of whisky-laced coffee. Neal is taking time off work, is on his way to Skegness to visit his father and Myrtle at last. In the back, Solas is strapped in her car seat, already nodding off.

He glances at the A9 memorial to Calum. If he didn't know exactly where to look, he wouldn't notice anything. Hard to tell, this time of year, what the true potential of things is. He doesn't sense Calum here or anywhere. For Neal, there is no afterlife. The world is grown from what has been, but the dead themselves are simply gone. Just the way Calum's car, that old Vauxhall, is no longer recognisably a car. The salvageable bits have joined other cars, and the rest is rusting into the earth. All still there, every bit, tossed back into the mix.

Alison has kissed Neal and Solas a sleepy coffee-smelling goodbye, then headed back to bed. Well, she half-kissed

Neal. Marginally still in her sulk, and her heart hadn't been in it. He knows her well enough for that particular nuance. Neal looks in his rear-view mirror at Solas. Her hair is still baby fine, and on the red side of blond. Like spun gold gone fiery. Her daddy, who knows without a doubt that he really is her daddy, turns off the music. This wakes her, and she says very clearly, 'Daddy, did you remember my purple teddy with ribbons on? Did you? Did you?'

Yes, Solas is two and a half now. A bit bossy and quite a good talker for her age. In fact, hardly ever shuts up.

'Yes,' says Neal. 'Course I did, darling. Mummy put it in the car last night so we wouldn't forget.'

'Clever Mummy. I love Mummy.'

Perfect Mummy! Stupid Daddy!

Alison had shouted at him last night, tired and red-faced. Called him paranoid because he'd locked the door again even though he knew she never remembered to take her keys, and why did he never put the new loo roll on, just leave the empty one on? He'd called her senile for always forgetting her keys, and why couldn't she put the CDs back on the shelf in alphabetical order? Was she having a go at him, or was she just thick? They'd not spoken again, but then sometime after midnight, their bodies had drawn together, so that by the time they awoke, the tension had almost dissipated.

Thinking back on it, Neal wonders if they are normal. To be so angry with each other sometimes, and come back again and again to this careless tenderness. Sally had never shouted such unfair, emotionally charged accusations, and neither had he. Politeness had reigned in his first marriage, had promised to reign again with Suzie, and now he's on an unruly rollercoaster. He has no choice. Getting what you want is always tricky.

Moving in with Alison had been like moving to a favourite summer holiday resort, but in the middle of winter and not just for a fortnight. Alison is not who he thought she was. Sometimes he finds himself saying: *before we met*, and he means *before that kiss*. These days she talks less than she used to, is more prone to detached silences. And her laughter is different. That old raucousness is gone, and when she occasionally giggles, the sound surprises even herself, and her eyebrows lift. A giddy laughter which initially alarmed Neal but now disarms him. It is too rare. Where she used to skim the surface with her quick movements and confidence, now she is slower, more tentative. There is a solemnity to her quietness, even when she is sulking about something stupid, which makes it difficult for Neal to remain angry. Sure, she still swears, but with much less gusto. She is both warmer and more ferocious, kinder and more critical than he'd thought possible in a single human being. Not solid and steady at all, and Neal has to be a different person. A more definite person, more alert, active. Sally had never needed him, and Alison does. Right now, he's worrying that she'll forget to turn the immersion off, or that dentist appointment Monday, or she'll have discovered that mess in the closet he promised to tidy up before he left. Oh, they argue so much! Is it too much? But the worrying itself consumes time and in any case, alters nothing.

He thinks back to that day of the first kiss. How he'd thought to himself: *This is the end of the story. Us, together, forever.* And in a way, it was. But then another story had started up, almost immediately. And this story is deeper, more complicated, bleaker, more maddening and more wonderful than any story he could have imagined. He feels like his life is hurtling forward into the future, almost out of

253

his control, and some days it trails unsavoury tendrils from his past. Of missing Sally, of regrets and uncertainties. It is not as he thought it would be, this ongoing story. *It is this, instead.* Alison with her silences, him with this frightening responsibility, and between them, strawberry-blond Solas, fan of purple teddies. Some days he has to hang on to his life for dear life. Knuckles white, teeth clenched. And as far as he can see, there's no ending in sight.

Like the road unfolding before him. God, it feels good to get a break. Driving south feels like driving downhill to Neal. As if they are literally falling down the globe, and he relaxes into it.

Solas falls asleep again as they slide by Inverness, Carrbridge, Aviemore, Kingussie. All those towns clustered along the A9 like un-matching pearls on a tarmac necklace. He hasn't gone anywhere in years, and travelling feels new. Ahead the Cairngorms are just visible, still snow-peaked and mysterious. And beyond that, all the places he has never seen, and all those people he has not met yet. Even Skegness and his father's Myrtle acquire an exotic sheen. The whole shebang, just waiting. Neal's heart expands and lifts just thinking about all the unknowns. As if the world is a huge unopened Christmas present, and it is Christmas Eve right now. Why has he never considered the world this way? Always yesterday, never tomorrow.

Within seconds a small puff of excitement enters the car, like a discreet fart. Both occupants breathe a little quicker, each heart beats a little stronger. Solas dreams of chasing wild waves at Rosemarkie beach, though Rosemarkie has the calmest bay imaginable. She twitches her feet with excitement.

And Neal instantly wishes Alison was with him. It's no good, feeling this way alone. He wants her here, next to him in the car, sulks and all. Alison, and the absence of Calum that accompanies her everywhere. A family of four. That's what he keeps forgetting; that's what he must remember.

Alison's dreams are curiously impersonal, as if she is stuck in someone else's dream world. They have that nightmarish quality of an over-long, very bad movie in a cinema which is too crowded and quiet to simply get up and leave. She wakes for the second time, feeling un-rested. Rises and showers. Considers the child-free, husband-free week ahead. Film later today with Chrissie. Gut the house. Maybe visit Kate in Gairloch tomorrow? Phone Teddy, thank him for that birthday present. Better yet, email him on the computer they finally bought last weekend. Saves time, all this emailing and texting. Teddy's such a blether, on the phone. And ring Neal, apologise properly for last night. But he is so irritating sometimes!

It helps that they moved to Evanton after they got married. It's between Strathpeffer and Alness, geographically and socially. Like Goldilocks finally settling into Baby Bear's bed, Evanton is just the right place for them. A sweet two-bed-roomed mid-terraced house on Hermitage Street, built in 1860. Roses in the garden, a tiny fireplace in the living room. The only problems are minor, for instance there's very poor mobile phone reception. Evantonians are always outside their houses, waving their phones in the air. And the buses are less frequent than in Alness. But in Evanton, Solas is not so obviously stepping in the footsteps of her brother. Not the same playschool, the same bedroom, the same corner shop and bus shelter and post office.

It was the right move, but living with someone, well, Alison is still not used to it, and maybe it will always be this way. Maybe not being used to it will eventually be something she gets used to. Aside from Calum, Neal is the only man she's ever lived with, and though there is an air of familiarity about some of his little habits – he always had a thing about alphabetical order – it is still hard some days. She has her own way of doing things, and he seems to forget that she managed just fine before him. He always wants to do things for her, to help her. They are both messy, but in quite different ways. He likes organising things into logical heaps of clutter, and she prefers shoving mess into drawers and cupboards willy-nilly. Clearing the decks. She loses the remote controls, doesn't know how to use them; he finds them, uses them slowly but effectively. There they sit right now, neatly on the table. A population explosion of remote controls, and proof of his recent presence. His possessions are blending in with hers now, but it still annoys her when he leaves stuff on the kitchen table for days on end, and acts hurt when she finally removes it.

Then she has to remind herself how grateful she is, how lonely she'd be without him. How only he can make Solas chuckle so hard she pees herself. And oh yes, how wonderful, how delicious his kisses still are. And how she cries less now. A lot less. All these good things about Neal, so her irritation – that spiky, energetic, righteous bully – retreats back under her ribs, ashamed. She loves this man, body and soul. It's a wave, warm and salty, that rises and falls, rises and falls and rises again. Each time it rises, it saves her.

She combs her hair, and today she doesn't consciously notice Calum's Fyrish Hill race photo on the wall by the mirror. She gets in her car and drives to Inverness. She has driven past the A9 shrine to her son often. Almost every day, on her way to work, to the childminders, to Tesco. She sees it so often it no longer has the power to hurt. In fact

256

today, she kind of likes it. Proof that her gawky unemployed son had stolen more than just her own heart.

These days, for her, the state of possessing a beating heart or not is the only difference between people that really matters. The dead, Calum among them, are just as present as the living, but they are unchanging, whereas everyone else is still jigging about the place. Getting older, crankier, messier, happier or not.

No, Alison has not found God, nor has she sought out mediums or been visited by angels. But increasingly, it feels like Calum is still somewhere. It's just that no one knows anything at all about that other place. How does she know it's there? *Because it must be.* Inconceivable, life amounting to nothing in the end. All those to do lists and bills paid and lessons learned and weeds pulled and cars washed and pledges of love and appointments kept and French learned and ovens cleaned and teeth filled and birthdays remembered and gifts wrapped and guitars practised and hangovers cured and clothes mended and New Year's resolutions kept and saying please and thank you and I'm sorry and kissing to make up and secret midnight prayers and holiday photographs and giddy laughter and salty tears and waves of salty warm love rising and falling and rising again – how could nothing come of all that? All that . . . *trying*, gone to waste.

As for proof, well, if you ask Alison, she'll talk about the internet, about mobile phones, about radios and television. About electricity. She'll argue that if voices, movies, written words can travel invisibly through the air yet still be bound by the laws of physical matter, still travel through a bedroom window but not to the downstairs hallway because the wall is too thick, if they can reconstitute the same instant they are sent in one of a trillion possible destinations, from a hill top in Caithness to a kitchen in San Francisco, then is it so very unlikely Calum has some kind of existence still? She will not rule out that possibility. The air is full of things she cannot see or touch. Maybe the dead are like mobile phones just out of reception. Weak signal, and mostly no signal at all. Maybe being dead is like . . . living in Evanton.

Everywhere Alison looks, but especially in open places like here on the A9 with the light-filled firth to her left, she visualises them all in their separate place. Somewhere like the Black Isle, with filigree roads linking quiet hearts to ones that beat. Here we are and there they are. And she wonders, *If the dead are aware somehow of the life they cannot re-enter, are they jealous? Are they pressed up against some transparent barrier, blinded with light and full of yearning?* She hopes that if he is capable of knowing anything, Calum knows that he is loved still.

Alison talks to Calum about these theories sometimes. Some days he argues with her. Says the traffic jam would be hellish if everyone who ever existed was still loitering.

That's sad, Mum. Crazy talk.

She replies, *Glass houses, my boy.*

She also tells him things like:

I'm never dyeing my hair again, what do you think?

Solas slept well last night for a change. You'd think, at her age!

And hey, by the way, the shoes you loved aren't being made anymore because another style is popular now.

And when she moans about Neal, he doesn't sympathise.

But he's well good for you, Mum. You suit each other. Couple of old hippies, you two. I'm well chuffed.

Today she re-tells Calum the story of his own birth. The way he glared at her, red and angry at one minute old. The way the midwives cooed, said he was a wee charmer. How from that minute forward, she'd felt a better person.

But under all the chatter, and through every silence too, what she is really saying is: I miss you, I miss you, *I miss you son*. Then she overtakes a car after Tore, because if she's not quick, she'll miss the matinee with Chrissie. Her mobile phone rings, and though she's promised herself a million times to stop talking on her mobile while driving, she glances to see who it's from. Well, he can wait. It took him long enough to finally buy a mobile phone, then almost as long to learn how to use it. Maybe one day he'll learn how to text. She wonders if he's forgotten something. At least he's remembered his mobile. He's always accusing her of being forgetful, but the times that man leaves his mobile at home! Then suddenly she thinks *Solas*. And picks up the phone, pulling over to the slow lane.

'Is everything okay? Solas okay? Where are you?'

'A lay-by near Dunkeld. Solas is sound asleep. Listen, you should have come with us, Ali.'

'What?'

'It's not too late. Get the next train to Glasgow and we'll meet you there. We can visit Teddy.'

'I thought you wanted some time on your own with your dad?'

'Aye, aye, and I thought you needed some time off Solas. But come.'

'I'm halfway to Inverness right now. Going to meet Chrissie at the cinema.'

'We can do anything we like! Have you ever been to Wales? We could go there first. Or the Lake District. The London Eye! Paris on the Eurotunnel! Get on a train, Ali. Chrissie will understand.'

'You're off your head. I've nothing with me. Not even a proper jacket. And I'm flat broke.'

But he can hear her smile, even while she's arguing, and he says, 'Great. See you there, Ali. I love you. We love you.'

He shifts up gears and there it is: The A9 rolls out before him like a ribbon of possibilities. Like a personal invitation to adventure for them all. Ah! His speedometer reaches fifty-five, sixty, sixty-five, and a black Corsa overtakes him, cuts in front so sharply Neal has to brake, as does the car behind him. Heart pounding, he watches as the black car with its young male driver edges out again. The road ahead is a gradual downhill curve away from them so no one can see what is coming.

Black car jerks back into Neal's lane, and one second later a northbound Tesco lorry thunders past, buffeting his car.

Neal glances at it in his rear-view mirror, imagining the almost-crash. Then black car pulls out again with a roar and within seconds is out of sight.

A9

Every day, almost a thousand vehicles travel north and south on this stretch of the A9, following the coast and the green North Sea. A route for escape or return. For nuns and thugs, buyers and vendors, tourists and locals, ambulances and fish lorries, combine harvesters and Land Rovers, Yamaha motorcycles and skinny-wheeled road bikes. Some people find they talk easier, listen more carefully, while driving. Some like to be in motion for its own sake, feel their lives suspended temporarily. Some find resonance with the rhythm of the road, a particular musical beat, a lullaby. Some people like to drive when they're angry because going fast feels good. But mostly the A9 is a place to combine necessary transport with daydreaming. It's been over three years since the accident. So far 1,095,255 cars have passed Calum's memorial, and hardly anyone notices it anymore.

Zara last tended the shrine half a year ago. Winter again, it's hardly visible now. The single pine is green. Everything else she planted is black and dead looking. But it won't look dead for long. The bulbs lurking under three inches of decaying leaves and soil have already begun sending up green shoots, and the birch leaves are furled fists of yellow and green. Get tae fuck, Winter, they all say in their Weegie-Alness accent.

Zara and her young man pass the memorial on their way to Orkney for a holiday. He is in love and she is not, and ever since Calum she's been terrified of this very situation. If she dumps him, she may regret it forever. If she surrenders, she may end up marrying him. He's a gardener, and her parents already like him. It's possible she'll fall in love with him in a few years or decades, right? Not being in love no longer seems a good enough reason to say goodbye.

She nods to the memorial. Says, *Hey, Calum*, silently.
Hey, Calum.

She imagines Calum shifting up a gear again, squinting in the winter light, on his way to the scrappy to see if they have any exhaust spares. Hears his phone ring and hopes it's herself, saying sorry. He's speeding. Is a bit sleepy, a bit careless, a bit reckless on the road because he's a young man and young men never believe they will die. Reaches for the phone, tells himself it's her. This makes him happy, and he's very beautiful just now. Less than three inches of the rubber on his tyres are touching the A9, and as he stretches that little bit more to reach his phone, his right foot presses down marginally more on the accelerator, and even less of the tyres are holding on to the cold road.

Calum is fifty-four seconds from dying and wondering if his favourite blue shirt is clean enough to wear tonight. And when he shouts *Mum!* this time, Zara wonders if it's not because he needs saving. It's too late for that. Maybe it's simply that he doesn't want to die alone.

She frowns a little. Sighs. Takes a quick look at her boyfriend, and his intentness touches her. She thinks he is too serious sometimes, but very intelligent, very thoughtful.

'Hey, what do you think happens after we die?' she asks, and he glances at her, startled.

'Seriously?'

'Seriously.'

'I have no idea, Zara.'

'Me neither.'

'But I'm working on the assumption this is it. For better or worse. What you see is what you get.'

'Me too,' she says softly after a minute.

She puts her hand on his thigh, leaves it there because that's where it wants to stay. Then suddenly, from her side window she sees a whole sky-full of geese. Coming back, going away? Zara can't tell. A few geese leading, more geese following in the traditional V shape, and quite a few just straggling in the general vicinity, looking like they're not too sure what's happening but they don't want to miss the action. As she watches, the leading geese start veering away from each other, and some of the geese from one V decide to join the other V, and vice versa. It looks like none of them quite understand their roles. Amateur attempts at being geese. Even their racket sounds more like a rowdy rehearsal than a performance. Are they arguing about asking for directions, or geese hierarchies, or more essentially, the point of migration? All of this pleases Zara, though she couldn't say why.

She suggests they stop for coffee at Tomich, even though they've just started. Tells him about the scones with ginger, apricots and cinnamon. No hurry, is there? They could just sit a while, maybe. Drink strong coffee and watch the cars whoosh past on the A9. Look at the map of Orkney they bought yesterday, talk about little things that worry them. His expiring MOT, her lost library books, his father's ulcer. The way, one way or another, most things come right in the end.